MURDER at
Mountain Creek

Phyllis
God bless you +
yours. Be one
Nancy Boff
10/6/2015

MURDER at
Mountain Creek

Nancy Bone Goff

TATE PUBLISHING
AND ENTERPRISES, LLC

Published by Tate Publishing & Enterprises, LLC
127 E. Trade Center Terrace | Mustang, Oklahoma 73064 USA
1.888.361.9473 | www.tatepublishing.com

Tate Publishing is committed to excellence in the publishing industry. The company reflects the philosophy established by the founders, based on Psalm 68:11,
"The Lord gave the word and great was the company of those who published it."

Book design copyright © 2012 by Tate Publishing, LLC. All rights reserved.
Cover design by Kenna Davis
Interior design by Sarah Kirchen

Published in the United States of America

ISBN: 978-1-62024-112-7
1. Fiction / Mystery & Detective / General
2. Fiction / Family Life
12.08.13

This book is dedicated to my husband, Gary,
for encouraging me to continue to write.
Thank you, Gary. I love you.

Acknowledgments

Special thanks to my daughter, Linda, for giving me advice about developing my characters more thoroughly. I would also like to thank my friend and fellow author, K. T. Archer, for taking time out of her busy life and writing schedule to write the forward for my book. Thanks to my book club friend, Beth Scott, for her help with editing. Thanks also to all the people at Tate Publishing for helping me publish not only *Murder at Mountain Creek* but also *The Adventures of Slump Thacker* and *One-Arm Boy in a Two-Arm World*.

Foreword

I t is my belief that everything happens for a reason and nothing will happen before its time. As a newbie author in the summer of 2010, there was a particular independent bookseller in Montgomery, Alabama, I hoped would carry my debut novel and allow me to do a signing. Prior to its release, I spoke to the owner on several occasions without any luck. Three weeks after the release, I received an e-mail stating they'd host a signing for only an hour, and it was going to be with another author. Success! Finally my persistence had paid off. But in retrospect, it was never about that bookseller. It was about the introduction that would be made on that faithful July day. Had the bookseller agreed to my earlier pleas, then my path might not have crossed with author Nancy Bone Goff. Everything happens for a reason, and nothing will happen before its time.

One hour provided us more than enough time to get to know each other, talk about our writing, and share our work. Upon leaving the signing that day, we traded books then began e-mailing about signings open to local authors and festivals.

We had read each other's work and had shared it with our own readers. In writing, when you don't have an agent or a publicist and you find yourself on the *New York Times* best-sellers list or sitting down with an anchor on the *Today Show*, you depend on the help of fellow authors, and I'm eternally grateful for the help Mrs. Goff has given me.

I was so honored when she asked me to read an advance copy of her newest story, *Murder at Mountain Creek*, and write this Foreword. Mrs. Goff's stories always transports me through time, and this one proved no different. The setting will reveal you have been taken back to the early 1950s. As you turn the pages, you'll be transfixed by the realism of the characters and their trials and tribulations, and you'll be captivated by the story as it unfolds. This whodunit story may leave you wondering if what is obvious is truly real or just a delusion of the imagination. Mrs. Goff has articulated the details so well, you may feel uneasy as the reality of these two families play out. I may have to ask Mrs. Goff where she did her research because I found myself believing the only way she could've captured the detailed scenery so well is if she had been there herself.

As I stated in the opening, everything happens for a reason, and nothing will happen before its time. Nothing truer could be said about *Murder at Mountain Creek*. Once you start, there truly is no good place to put it down.

—K. T. Archer
Author of Editor's and Reader's Choice,
The Silver Spoon and *Kismet*
www.ktarcher.com

Part One

A rusty keyhole provided a restricted view of the comings and goings in the adjoining room. An ear pressed against the door gave little insight into what was being said. The voices she heard through the door were real—unlike the voices she heard at night when darkness took over her thoughts, depriving her of much needed sleep. Peering through the keyhole, she watched with bated breath as her new neighbors prepared to move into their new residence.

It was a pretty spring day in the Mountain Creek community, with temperatures in the low seventies. Sudie carried an armload of clothes into the house. She, her husband, Dawson, and their eighteen-month-old daughter, Beth, would be sharing the three-room house with Dawson's Uncle John and Aunt Stella. Dawson and his father, Lon, were putting together the iron bedstead Dawson's mama had given them. Sudie opened the two bottom drawers of the chest and carefully divided her clothes from those belonging to Beth. Dawson was cussing at one of the wooden slats, which appeared to be too wide to fit the bed. Lon watched as his son tried to force the slat into place.

"Why not just lay it in there at an angle?" asked Lon. "That's how we done it."

Dawson stopped, looked at his father, and replied, "Do ya think ya could'a told me that five minutes ago? I been trying to make this thing fit crossways. Now ya tell me it ain't the way it's supposed to fit."

Before answering his son, Lon walked to the front door, opened the screen, and spit a streak of amber across the narrow porch onto the ground. Their blue tick hound, Mack, happened to be walking by at the same time. His quick reflexes as he jumped aside were the only thing that kept him from being dotted with tobacco juice. Lon smiled, wiped his mouth on his shirtsleeve, and walked back into the house.

"I thought ya might figure it out for yourself, son."

Before Dawson could respond, Beth came toddling into the room with a daffodil in her hand. She smiled and held the beautiful yellow flower up for all to see.

"Ouwer."

Sudie smiled at her little blonde-haired, blue-eyed girl.

"I see the flower," Sudie said, correcting her pronunciation. "Flower. That is a daffodil."

"Dadil," said Beth.

Dawson laughed.

"You're getting there, sweetie," he said. "It won't be long, and you'll be talking up a storm."

Dawson's mama, Cora, called out from the kitchen. "She's gonna be a smart one, all right. Takes after her Grandma Hubert."

As Sudie was arranging the clothes, Dawson looked her way. She was a rather small woman standing barely five feet two inches tall. Her once pale blonde hair had darkened to a dirty dishwater blonde. Dawson's mama said it was from Sudie's pregnancies. She said most women's hair got darker once they started having babies. Whether that was true or not, Dawson didn't know. What he did know was her beautiful sky-blue eyes were still as blue and lovely as ever.

Sudie only recently had found out she was once again pregnant. She and Dawson were very excited but worried too. Her first pregnancy had ended prematurely. It was a baby boy. He was stillborn. They were both devastated. A year later, Beth was born. She became their pride and joy.

Dawson was a big man with broad shoulders and a narrow waist. He had dark, wavy hair and dark brown eyes. His jawline was stern and sharp, much like his personality. Sudie fell in love with his good looks the first time she laid eyes on him. Despite a dominant personality, he was also quite charming, in a masculine sort of way. When he and Sudie were dating, he picked wildflowers from alongside the road and gave them to her as a token of his adoration. Only later did Sudie learn about his darker side. He could be intimidating at times and expected complete complacency from his loved ones.

The three-room, wooden slat house had two rooms adjacent to one another. Each room had a door that opened onto the front porch. There was also a door between the two rooms, but it stayed closed for privacy's sake. The room on the right was occupied by Lon's twin brother, John, and his wife, Stella. A long, narrow kitchen across the back of the house was to be shared between the two families. There was also a double fireplace along one wall. One opened out into their room, the other in John and Stella's room. The two fireplaces shared the same chimney.

John and Stella had agreed to let Dawson and Sudie share the house and rent. Both Dawson and Lon worked at the same sawmill and each earned ten dollars a week. Dawson wanted to save up enough money to buy a house. Sharing rent seemed to be a good way to put back a little in savings each week. Sudie was not particularly thrilled about the living arrangements, but what Dawson said went. She did not necessarily have a problem with John; her main objection was living next door to Stella.

Stella was extremely simple minded. She had long black hair, high cheekbones, and dark skin. Although she had no children of her own, the neighborhood children loved her, and she loved them. She would take them on picnics down by the creek. She would bake teacakes and share them with the children. She would play games with them like hide-and-seek, Red Rover, and Mother May I. The children were her only real friends. They understood her childlike ways and her simple mind.

John was a short, stocky man. He had straight, dark-brown hair that he parted down the middle and slicked back with an ample amount of hair cream. His deep-set, dark-green eyes showed signs of worry and disappointment. His skin looked like wrinkled leather from years of working in the sun. Although he was only forty-two, he looked like he was sixty. His identical twin brother, Lon, was married to Dawson's mother, Cora. As he stood back watching the comings and goings of his soon-to-be, extremely close neighbors, he wondered how Stella and Sudie would get along. He tried hard to overlook his wife's unusual behavior, hiding it as best he could from his family. However, with Dawson and Sudie living in the same house, the secret of his wife's darker side would surely be revealed.

Cora was also short. She stood barely five feet tall but weighed well over one hundred and fifty pounds. She had pale blue eyes and close-cropped, dark brown hair, with a hint of gray showing through around the temples. She was a jolly person. When she laughed, her belly jiggled up and down like a bowl of Jell-O. She took care of three children while their mothers and fathers worked. She was very strict, but the children loved her very much. Her life consisted of caring for those around her with little time for herself.

It took most of the morning to get settled into their new house. Once they were finished, Sudie looked around the room. In one corner was the bed where she and Dawson would sleep. It was the same bed Dawson had slept in before he and Sudie married. The thin, cotton-filled mattress sagged slightly in the middle. Several tattered homemade quilts covered the bed, and two feather pillows stained with sweat lay at the head of the bed.

In another corner was a somewhat small chest of drawers, that held various articles of folded clothing. Next to it was the chifforobe where Sudie kept their hanging clothes. On one door of the chifforobe was a mirror. Along the wall beneath the window was a red-and-green floral-covered couch, that Sudie's mama had given them when she and Dawson first married. It was used when she purchased it and was clearly showing its years of wear.

Between the couch and their bed was a small wooden table. On the table was a kerosene lamp and a small figurine of a beautiful dancing ballerina, that Dawson had given Sudie on their first anniversary. The ballerina wore a flowing, powder-blue, knee-length ballet costume. Her dark brown hair was pulled back in a bun at the nape of her neck. Her delicate features and slim body were frozen in time as she performed a dazzling pirouette. It was Sudie's most prized possession.

Next to the table was a small cot where Beth would sleep.

It had a small pillow and a ragged patchwork quilt covering the only cushion on the cot, a heavy dark-green army blanket. Sudie seemed pleased with the layout of the room.

Cora took it upon herself to cook dinner for the two families. The night before, Lon had caught several nice catfish on his trotline. She skinned then fried the catfish in an iron skillet full of grease. Once the fish were done, she cooked a batch of hush puppies to go with the fish. When the food was done, she called everyone to come eat.

Sudie came to the kitchen first.

"I surely do thank ya for cooking our dinner, Mama Cora. It smells so good. I love fish and hush puppies."

Cora hugged her daughter-in-law.

"You're plumb welcome, honey. I knew everybody would be hungry. Get ya a plate and go to eating."

"I'll wait for Dawson and the other menfolks to get their food first," said Sudie. "Dawson likes it that way."

Cora put a fish and a hush puppy on her plate and sat down at the small wooden kitchen table.

"Lon likes it that way too, but he ain't in here, is he? If ya wait on men to get to the table, ya might be waiting half the afternoon. They talk 'bout women gossiping. Shoot! Men do as much or more gossiping than most women I know."

Sudie laughed at Cora and reached for a piece of fish. At that moment, Stella opened the door to their room and peeped in.

"The men ain't gonna like y'all eating first," she commented. "In my family, the men always eat first. Then the women eat. The children eat last."

Sudie began pulling small pieces of fish off the bones and placing them on a small plate.

Sudie looked at Stella defiantly.

"I'm making this plate for Beth. As long as I got a say, my child will eat whether me and Dawson eats or not."

"Ya might get a beating," sassed Stella.

"Yeah, I reckon I might at that," said Sudie. "But at least I'll know my child won't go hungry."

Cora looked at both of them like they were crazy.

"Dawson ain't gonna beat Sudie for fixing Beth a plate. If he was to try, I'd break me off a switch as long as my arm and wear his butt out. He may be grown, but he ain't too big for his mama to whoop."

Dawson, Lon, and John walked through the kitchen door. Dawson was carrying Beth on his shoulders.

"Who ya fixing to put a whooping on, Mama?" he asked.

Cora laughed. Her belly shook up and down.

"You. If ya don't behave yourself."

Stella spoke next.

"I told Sudie ya was gonna beat her for fixing Beth a plate 'fore the menfolks got their food."

Dawson put his arm around Sudie's slender shoulders and joked, "I don't beat her but once a day, and she's done got her beating for today."

Sudie gently poked him in the ribs with her finger. He jumped to the side. Beth laughed out loud. Then everyone else began laughing too—everyone except Stella. She went back into her room and closed the door without getting anything to eat.

When everyone had their fill, John fixed Stella a plate from the leftovers and carried it in to her. When she finished eating, she opened the door just wide enough to push the plate through, laid the plate on the floor, then shut the door with a bang.

Sudie looked at Mama Cora with a puzzled look on her face.

"I don't quite understand that woman. Is she crazy or something?"

Mama Cora put her finger to her lips in an effort to let Sudie know she shouldn't speak so loudly.

"Shhh. She might hear ya."

Sudie got up from the table and lifted Beth out of her high chair.

"I can't help it, Mama Cora. She gives me the willies. I ain't sure this here living next to her is gonna work out so good."

Dawson reached for Beth and placed her on his shoulders.

"She'll be fine, Sudie. She just needs to get to know ya."

Sudie picked up the kettle full of hot water from off the stove and poured it into two separate dishpans. To one of the pans, she added a bar of lye soap. Mama Cora scraped the fish bones into the slop bucket and placed the dirty dishes into the water with the soap. Steam rose up from the water and quickly dissipated into the air. As Sudie began washing the dishes, Mama Cora leaned in close to her.

"I wouldn't worry too much 'bout Stella. She's a good old gal, once ya get to know her. She's just a bit peculiar. I don't think she means no harm to nobody."

Sudie dipped the first clean plate into the other dishpan then handed it to Mama Cora.

"Well, I think she's plumb strange if ya ask me."

Dawson interceded. "Listen, Sudie," he said rather sternly, "we've got to get along with these folks if we're gonna live in the same house with them. I suggest ya make an effort to like Stella. She's our aunt, and she deserves our respect."

Sudie whirled around to face Dawson.

"She's your aunt, not mine. I may have to live here with her, but I ain't got to like it."

Before he realized what he was doing, Dawson slapped Sudie squarely across the face. In that exact moment, when his large rough hand connected with Sudie's delicate soft skin, he immediately regretted his actions. However, it was too late to take it back. Sudie grabbed the side of her face with her wet hand and looked at Dawson with both fear and contempt. Their eyes met. Tears began flowing down her cheek. She threw the dishrag into the water, stomped her feet, and ran from the kitchen and out the back door. The back door slammed shut so hard, it rattled the window next to it.

Mama Cora popped Dawson on the arm with her drying rag.

"Dawson Hubert, ya should be ashamed of yourself," she scolded.

Beth began to cry. Dawson took her off his shoulders and handed her to Mama Cora.

"She needs to learn respect, Mama," he replied.

Mama Cora bounced Beth up and down in her arms, trying to comfort her.

"Now I know that ain't how I raised ya, son. Lon ain't never hit me but once. When he did it, I cracked him over the head with a frying pan. He learned right quick I wasn't gonna put up with that kind of foolishness. I know ya got a temper, son, but if ya intend on staying with Sudie, ya best learn to control it, 'fore she leaves ya and takes this young 'un with her."

Dawson bowed his wide shoulders back defiantly.

"Ain't nobody gonna take my baby girl away from me, Mama. If Sudie can't learn to respect me, then she can go on her way. Beth stays with me, and that's that."

Mama Cora shook her head and swept past her son, headed for the front porch. When she opened the front door, Sudie was sitting in the swing at the other end of the porch. Mama Cora could see the red mark on the side of Sudie's face. She walked over to the swing and sat down beside her daughter-in-law. Beth reached out to her mother. Sudie took Beth into her arms and held her tightly. Mama Cora put her arm around Sudie's shoulders; they both cried.

Later that afternoon, Mama Cora and Lon went home. Dawson went about his chores as if nothing had happened.

Sudie avoided him as much as possible and only spoke to him if he asked her a question. Beth played in the yard while Sudie planted a row of daffodils along the front of the house. When night came, they ate supper without saying a word to each other. When it got dark, they went to bed.

When Beth was asleep, Dawson reached for Sudie. At first she pulled away. His grip on her tightened. She knew there was no way to avoid letting him have his way with her. She lay there with her head to the side, not wanting to look at him, pretending to be somewhere else. When it was over, he rolled over on his side and quickly fell asleep. Sudie lay there in the dark, touching her stomach, thinking about the tiny life growing inside her.

The next morning, Dawson heard John in the kitchen making coffee. He arose from the bed and pulled on his overalls. Sudie was sleeping. He started to awaken her but decided to let her sleep. Instead, he went into the kitchen.

"Morning, John," he said, quietly.

"Morning, Dawson," John replied. "Coffee's ready if ya want some."

"Yeah, I smelled it soon as I woke up."

He took a cup from the cupboard and filled it to the rim with the steaming liquid.

John poured some bacon grease into the iron skillet and placed it on the stove.

"Ya want some eggs, Dawson?" he asked.

Dawson sat down at the table.

"Sounds good to me. Ya want me to wake Sudie so she can cook them for us?"

John shook his head.

"Boy, ya got a lot to learn about women, if you're aiming on keeping one for any length of time. After what ya done yesterday, best ya let her sleep."

Dawson reached for his shoes. "Ya mean to tell me ya don't never have to put Stella straight when she gets disrespectful?"

John laughed.

"Ya got to be kidding me, son. If I was to ever hit my Stella, why she'd knock me in the head with a baseball bat. Ya don't never want to make my Stella mad. No sir. And I'll tell ya something else too, boy. Your little gal ain't gonna put up with it neither. She may not be one to hit ya back, but she'll shore enough leave ya if she takes a notion."

When the eggs were done, John put half on Dawson's plate and the other half on his. The idea of Sudie's leaving put Dawson to thinking that perhaps he should try to control his temper better. After all, Sudie was basically a good woman. She took good care of Beth. She cooked his meals and cleaned his clothes. Maybe he should apologize to her. Yes, he would do that very thing as soon as he got home from work. He picked up his fork and began to eat. *As soon as I get home,* he thought.

However, when he returned home that night, all Sudie's and Beth's clothes were gone from the chifforobe. He found a handwritten note lying on the nightstand next to their bed. It read:

Dear Dawson,

Me and the baby are going to Mama's house to stay. I'm tired of all this arguing. All we do lately is argue. You need to do something about your violent temper. When you slapped me yesterday in front of everybody, that was the straw that broke the camel's back. Right now I don't know if I'll be back or not. So don't come looking for me.

Sudie

He didn't even take the time to wash his face and hands. He walked to the nearest neighbor's house, borrowed a truck, and headed for his mother-in-law's house some ten miles away. All the way there, he tried to get control of his anger. He knew he had a temper, and Sudie seemed to know just which buttons she needed to push to get him angry. He had planned on apologizing but not anymore. *Still, this time,* he thought to himself, *I'm not going to let her rile me. I'm gonna stay calm and not raise my voice.* Upon arriving, all Dawson's good intentions flew right out the window. He was angry and upset that Sudie had taken his baby girl. He immediately got out of the truck, ran onto the porch, and tried opening the screen door. It was latched.

"Sudie!" he called loudly. "Ya better open this door before I bust it down."

The wooden door opened to reveal Sudie's daddy, Samson Newton. Samson was a short, light-skinned, stocky man with broad shoulders. When he saw Dawson and the angry look on his face, he looked worried as he ran his hand through his thinning gray hair.

"She don't want to talk to ya now, Dawson. Best ya just get on home."

Dawson's anger grew. "I ain't going nowhere, Mr. Newton. I come to get my baby girl. If Sudie wants to stay, that's fine. But Beth is coming home with me. Ain't nobody gonna take my baby girl away from me. Ya best tell her that."

Mr. Newton could see how angry Dawson was. He feared Dawson might actually start a fistfight with him. "I'll go see if I can talk to her. Ya wait out there on the porch."

"Don't make me wait too long, Mr. Newton. My patience is wearing thin."

Dawson paced up and down the length of the porch. A pot of what appeared to be dead purple violets was sitting on the handrail at the end of the porch. The third time he approached the dried, withered flowers, he angrily shoved them onto the ground. The red clay pot broke into several pieces. The dirt and flowers lay strewn across the yard. Just as he was about to call out to Sudie again, the wooden door opened. Sudie peered at him through the latched screen door.

"What are ya doing here, Dawson? I told ya not to come looking for me."

Dawson crossed his arms across his wide muscular chest.

"I came to get my baby girl, Sudie. If you're of a mind to stay here, that's fine by me, but Beth's coming home with me."

Sudie shook her head. "Ya fool. Ya can't take care of a little baby. Who's gonna see after Beth? What are ya gonna do with her while you're working?"

"Ya don't worry yourself none about that. Mama'll look after her."

Sudie stepped back, reached for the edge of the wooden door, and began closing it. "Well, ya can't take her, Dawson."

Quickly, Dawson grabbed the handle on the screen door, giving it a powerful jerk. The latch easily pulled loose from the door frame. To keep her from closing him out, he immediately reached inside and placed his hand on the door, stopping it from closing.

"I told ya I ain't leaving here without my baby!" he shouted, angrier than ever.

Pushing through the open door, he crossed the room to where Beth lay sleeping on a pallet on the floor. He looked down at her. She looked so peaceful, like an angel. Carefully, he removed her from her sleeping place and turned to leave. Mr. Newton blocked his path.

"Now, Dawson, I know ya love that baby, but ya can't just take her away from her mama," he reasoned.

Dawson held fast to his endeavor.

"I can and I am, Mr. Newton. Best ya get out of my way. I don't want to have to hurt ya."

Sudie's daddy knew he was no match for his son-in-law. Shaking his head, he stepped aside, allowing him to pass. Sudie stood in the hallway crying.

"Please don't take her, Dawson," she begged.

Dawson walked past her and pushed open the screen. "You're welcome to come too, Sudie. After all, ya are my wife. I'm sorry I slapped ya yesterday, but ya was being disrespectful. I'm the man of the house, and ya need to understand, what I say goes."

With that, he exited the house, got in the cab of the truck, and drove away, leaving his wife behind. As the truck pulled out of the driveway, Sudie stood at the edge of the porch crying. A few days later, Sudie decided to go home. The incident was never spoken of again.

As the months passed, Sudie immersed herself in preparing for the new baby. She crocheted a baby blanket from some yarn Mama Cora purchased at the Salvation Army store in Montgomery. To her surprise, Stella even offered to teach her how to sew. Together they made a sleeping gown from a flour sack and some diapers from an old bed sheet. Sudie found Stella to be hauntingly strange. One day she was as friendly as could be. The next day she would stay locked in her room the entire day. She never knew how to take her. Yet the children in the community, including Beth, seemed to like her.

The closer time got to the arrival of Sudie's baby, the stranger Stella became. Sudie could feel her staring at her through a crack in the door. She would watch Sudie intensely as she went about her daily chores. Sometimes, she would act as normal as the next person. At other times, she would stare blankly, without talking, for hours on end.

The first time Stella had one of her spells, as John called it, it frightened Sudie and scared little Beth so badly, it took her several days before she would go near Stella again. It was actually one of Stella's good days. Sudie and Stella were in the kitchen canning a bushel of green beans. Beth played nearby with a small corn shuck doll Mama Cora made and gave to her for her birthday. Sudie was telling Stella a story about her mother finding her hiding in the salt box and the terrible whipping she'd gotten when suddenly, without warning, Stella collapsed onto the floor. Her eyes rolled back in her head; her body began jerking uncontrollably. Fortunately, John was just outside the kitchen door. Sudie screamed for him to come quickly. Beth ran to her mother crying. When he saw what was happening, he knelt down beside his wife, reached into Stella's apron pocket, and took out a spoon, placing it in her mouth.

"This is what ya have to do when she has one of these spells," he said to Sudie.

Sudie held Beth tightly in her arms.

"What's wrong with her, John?"

The spell subsided almost as quickly as it began. Stella's body was no longer jerking and bouncing around on the floor. She lay there, appearing to be exhausted. Her eyes were closed and her breathing shallow.

"Is she dead, Uncle Johnny?"

John stood up and placed his hand on Sudie's shoulder.

"No, she ain't dead. She has these kinda spells every once in a while. The doctors call it epilepsy. If she ever has one and I ain't here, just stick that spoon in her mouth. It's supposed to keep her from biting her tongue."

A few minutes later, Stella opened her eyes and sat up. She looked dazed and confused. John helped her get up from the floor then escorted her to their bed. She immediately fell asleep. When John got back to the kitchen, Sudie was sitting at the table with Beth still in her arms. Both were crying.

"I'm sorry ya had to see that, but I reckon it was good it happened while I was here. She'll be fine after she sleeps for a while. She's always give out after one of them spells. The important thing is to try and keep her from hurting herself. That's about all anyone can do."

Sudie wiped Beth's tears away with the corner of her apron.

"It'll be all right, sweetie," she said to her little girl.

John patted Beth on the back.

"That's right, little Beth. Aunt Stella will be just fine. She just needs to rest for a while."

Sudie looked at the clock. The processing time for the beans was finished. It was time to take the pot, full of quart jars, filled with beans off the stove to let them cool.

"Uncle Johnny, will ya take the beans off the stove for me? I don't think I need to be picking up something that heavy."

John picked up two dish towels to protect his hands from the steaming hot pot.

"Sure I will, honey," he answered as he lifted the pot from off the stove and set it on the table. "I know canning is a lot of work, but these beans will surely be good this winter."

"I sure hope so," said Sudie.

Beth had stopped crying and was wiggling to get down. Sudie put her on the floor. As she turned toward John and Stella's bedroom, Sudie caught a glimpse of Stella. A chill ran up Sudie's spine. Stella appeared to be staring at her with a strange, almost frightening look in her eyes. Sudie took Beth by the hand and headed for the back door.

"Let's get some fresh air," she said to Beth.

That summer proved to be long and hot. A fire at the sawmill resulted in many hours and long days of work for Dawson and John in order for the mill to keep up with all the back orders for lumber. It also meant Sudie had to spend many long hours alone with Stella. Most of the time, Sudie dealt with the situation as best she could. Other times, things got heated between the two women, especially when it came to Beth.

Late one afternoon in early August, Sudie was sitting on the front porch reading a week-old newspaper her mother had given her. Beth was playing in the yard. Stella came out the door with a basket hanging across her arm. Without a word to Sudie, she walked down the steps and over to where Beth was playing in the dirt. She reached down and took Beth's hand, pulling her to her feet.

"Come on, Beth," she said as she started leading Beth toward the woods. "Let's go have a nice picnic down by the creek."

Sudie jumped to her feet and called after them, "Stella! Where do ya think you're going with Beth?"

Stella acted as though she didn't hear Sudie. Instead, she continued walking toward the woods. Again Sudie called out to her.

"Stella! Stop!"

Stella was nearing the edge of the woods. Sudie threw the newspaper on the porch and ran down the steps as quickly as she could. Across the yard she ran, catching hold of Beth's arm just as they were about to enter the woods. Stella turned on her like a wild, fighting rooster. Sudie felt as though Stella's eyes tore into her flesh like knives through butter. Stella's nose flared, and her voice became deep.

"Get your hands off my baby girl!" Stella yelled angrily.

Sudie grabbed Beth up and held her tightly in her arms.

"Your baby? Beth is my baby, Stella. Ya can't just take her off like that without asking me. What's wrong with ya? Have ya lost what little sense ya had?"

If Stella's eyes had been a gun, Sudie would have been dead.

"I'm taking her on a picnic," Stella said as she reached to take Beth from Sudie's arms.

Beth turned and started toward the house.

"Oh no you're not. Ya ain't taking her nowhere."

Sudie felt the wind from the basket as it flew past her head and hit the edge of the porch. She expected food to fall from it, but when it hit the ground, Sudie realized it was empty. She quickened her pace. As she started up the steps, she glanced back over her shoulder. Stella had a stick in her hand and was coming toward her. Sudie rushed up the steps and into the house, closing and locking the door behind her. She went to the door leading into the kitchen. It didn't have a lock on it, only a small latch. She closed the door, secured the latch, and then sat Beth on the floor. She could hear Stella at the front door. She was turning the knob, trying her best to get in. The knob stopped turning, and she heard Stella walking across the front porch. She heard the door on their side of the house open and slam shut. With all her strength, she pushed the heavy dresser in front of the door and leaned against it as best she could.

Stella came to the bedroom door and tried to open it too.

"Please, God," Sudie prayed, "don't let her get in here."

Stella began pushing on the door, trying her best to get it open.

"Let me in!" she yelled. "I just want to take Beth on a picnic. I want my baby girl."

Sudie continued leaning against the dresser.

"Go away, Stella!" she yelled back. "Beth is not your child. She's mine. Mine and Dawson's. And he's gonna be real mad when I tell him about what you're doing."

When Stella realized she couldn't get in, she stopped pushing on the door and called out to Sudie.

"Dawson is gonna whoop your butt good for taking my baby girl from me. Ya just wait till he gets home. Cause I'm gonna tell him too. I'm gonna tell how ya wouldn't let me take

Beth on a picnic. He's gonna whoop ya good. Ya hear me in there? He's gonna whoop ya but good."

Sudie was relieved when she heard Stella walk back to her side of the house.

"Thank ya, God," she said as she slowly slid down the front of the dresser and onto the floor. Beth came and got in her lap. Sudie cried.

It was past dark when John and Dawson got home that evening. Sudie and Beth were still in the bedroom with the doors locked and the dresser still sitting in front of the kitchen door. Sudie and Beth had fallen asleep on the floor in front of the dresser. Dawson knocked loudly several times before Sudie heard him and came to unlock the door. As soon as he walked inside, Sudie fell into his arms, crying.

He took her by the shoulders and pushed her an arm's length away.

"What in the world is wrong with ya, Sudie? Has somebody hurt ya? Why in heaven's name are ya crying so?"

Sudie could barely speak. After a few minutes, she finally told him what had happened.

"Are ya sure she didn't ask ya earlier about the picnic and ya just forgot?

Sudie assured him Stella did not ask.

"I'll go talk to her," he promised.

Dawson moved the dresser from in front of the door. Stella and John were standing in the kitchen. Stella was stirring a pot of butter beans on the stove. She turned around and spoke to Dawson like nothing out of the ordinary had happened. When he asked her about the incident, she told him she didn't know what he was talking about.

"I've been in my room all afternoon," she assured him. "The only time I came out of my room was when I put these beans on to cook for our supper. I seen Sudie wasn't gonna cook nothing. I knew y'all would be hungry when ya got home, so

I fixed these here beans. They got a ham hock in them. Smell good, don't they?"

Dawson didn't know who to believe. *Surely Sudie wouldn't make up a story like that*, he thought to himself. Then on the other hand, he knew she didn't like Stella. *Could the story be a ploy to get him to agree to move from their home?* He went back into their room where Sudie was sitting nervously on the couch.

"What did she say, Dawson?"

"She said she didn't know what I was talking about. Ya don't reckon ya dreamed all that, do ya?"

Sudie jumped to her feet. "No, Dawson!" she yelled angrily. "I did not dream all that! I told ya what happened. Don't tell me you're gonna believe her over me."

Dawson shook his head. "I don't know who to believe, Sudie."

Sudie stood there staring at him with tears welling up in her eyes. "Fine. Believe her then. But if ya come home one day and she's done killed me and run off with Beth, maybe then you'll believe me."

It was early autumn. The leaves had begun to turn. The days were getting shorter. The baby in Sudie's womb was growing bigger. Dawson teased Sudie, saying she looked like she'd swallowed a basketball. Each day that passed brought on more movement. What was once the flutter of a butterfly's wings was now a push and occasionally a slight kick. Excitement and anticipation grew with each passing day.

Mama Cora invited her daughter-in-law and granddaughter to spend the day at her house. She wanted to talk to Sudie about the baby shower she was planning for her. When they arrived, Beth went outside with Grandpa Lon. They liked playing hide-and-seek together. Sudie could hear Beth laughing when Grandpa Lon found her and would take off running with him right behind her. Mama Cora was washing the breakfast dishes. Sudie poured herself a glass of freshly churned buttermilk.

"Can I ask ya something, Mama Cora?" Sudie asked.

"Why, shore ya can, Sudie. Ya can ask me anything ya like."

"Don't ya find Stella to be a might strange? I surely do."

Mama Cora looked up from her dishpan.

"Why, Sudie? Did she do something to ya? She didn't try to hurt Beth, did she?"

"No. She just gets strange acting sometimes. I know she watches me through the keyhole in the door between our rooms. I tried putting a piece of cotton in the hole, but Beth keeps taking it out. Some days Stella is nice as can be. Other times, she scares me. It's like she's two different people."

"I know what you're talking about. I been knowing her for years—long before John married her. I tried to tell him how she was, but he didn't listen."

"Have ya ever seen her have one of them fits she gets?"

"Oh yeah. When she was younger, she used to have them all the time. Sometimes two and three a day. She's got better now. I remember one time, back when we was in school, she had one of them fits. She bounced round so hard, she broke her arm. After that happened, the teacher wouldn't let her come back to school no more. Everybody was kinda scared of her. I just felt sorry for her."

"She's real nice to Beth and the other young 'uns."

'Yeah, she loves children."

"How come she ain't never had a baby?"

"Nobody rightly knows, Sudie. She wanted lots a children. She used to talk about it all the time. She used to say she was gonna have a yard full of children. As far as I know, she ain't never even been pregnant. After ten years or so of talking about it, she just quit saying anything about it anymore."

Sudie took a big swallow of milk. A thin line of white formed across her upper lip. She wiped it off with the back of her hand.

"Her not having babies might be a blessing."

"Ya might be right about that, Sudie," agreed Mama Cora.

"I know I'll be glad when we can save up enough money to get us a place of our own."

Mama Cora put the last clean dish on the rack to dry and dried her hands on the towel hanging next to the back door.

"I know ya will. I'll be glad too. Everybody needs a place of their own, especially young folks."

"All I know is Stella is a strange woman."

The screen door slammed shut. Beth came running into the kitchen giggling. Grandpa Lon followed close behind. She grabbed her grandma's leg. Mama Cora laughed and grabbed her up. Beth put her arms tightly around her grandma's neck. Grandpa Lon ran up to Cora and began tickling Beth. Beth wiggled and tried climbing onto her grandma's shoulder.

Grandma Cora jokingly slapped at Grandpa Lon.

"Get away from my baby!" she yelled. "Don't ya mess with my baby."

Lon was laughing too.

"I'm gonna get ya, little gal," he joked. "I'm gonna get ya."

Sudie laughed. She liked watching Dawson's parents playing and laughing with her daughter. They were good grandparents. To be sure, she and Dawson had their differences but he was a good father. She couldn't ask for a better father to her precious little girl. She knew how badly Dawson wanted a boy, but she also knew how much he loved his daughter. Regardless of whether the baby turned out to be a boy or a girl, there was no doubt in Sudie's mind that it would be loved.

Soon the green of summer was replaced with the reds,

yellows, oranges, and browns of autumn. The hot days of summer had melted into the more pleasant days of fall. With temperatures in the low seventies, everyone seemed to feel better. Sudie continued to keep her distance from Stella. As often as possible, she stayed at either her mama's house or Mama Cora's house during the day.

Thanksgiving Day was drawing nigh. It was Mama Cora's year to have the gathering at her house. Mama Cora sent word to Sudie to invite her family too. Sudie reluctantly invited them, despite Dawson's objection. When Thanksgiving Day arrived, everyone gathered at Mama Cora's house for dinner. There was Cora's mother, Lula, and Lon's mother, Bell. Both great-grandfathers had already passed away. Several aunts and uncles on Dawson's side of the family were there also.

On Sudie's side of the family was her mama, Althea; her daddy, Samson; her older sister, Massey; and her younger brother, Ed. With the exception of Ed, none of them cared for Dawson. They wanted Sudie to leave him, but she refused. Massey's husband, Clayton, hated Dawson so much that he refused to come to the dinner or allow his son, Pete, to come. Instead, they went to his mama and daddy's house in Vida.

The trouble between Dawson and Clayton started several years back, when the two of them had a falling-out over a mule Dawson sold to Clayton. When the mule died a week after Clayton purchased it, Clayton accused Dawson of selling him a mule he knew was sick and demanded his money back. When Dawson refused to return his money, Clayton punched Dawson in the nose. A terrible fight ensued. It took several onlookers to break up the fight. When all was said and done, Clayton came out with his two front teeth missing, and Dawson had a bloody nose. They had not spoken to each other since the incident.

Mama Cora was an excellent cook. Lon killed several hens and dressed them out, and Mama Cora made chicken and cornbread dressing. There were also black-eyed peas, green beans, pan-fried corn, sliced tomatoes, collards, rutabagas, sweet potato pies, and a chocolate cake.

When they gathered around the table, Dawson's Uncle Will gave thanks for the food.

"Lord, we thank ya for this bountiful meal. We ask ya to bless it and the hands who prepared it. We give ya thanks for all our blessings. We ask ya to bestow a special blessing on Delta and Sudie, so the babies they carry inside them will be born healthy and will prosper. Go with us this coming year that we may see another good harvest. In Jesus's name, I pray. Amen."

"Amen," everyone said in unison.

The men filled their plates first. Next the women helped the children fill their plates. The women filled their plates last. The tension between Sudie and Dawson's family was obvious. Dawson's side of the family sat together around the table inside, while Sudie's family went outside and sat around a makeshift table Lon had set up in the yard. Although the food was delicious, the ill feelings between the two families made for a not-so-pleasant day. Sudie decided it would be best not to invite her family to another Hubert gathering.

When it was time to leave, Samson offered to take Dawson, Sudie, and Beth home in his car. Dawson declined the invitation. They would walk. On their way home from the dinner, Sudie and Dawson had words. Sudie began the discussion, which soon turned into a full-fledged argument.

"I can't believe how rude your family was to my family," she said as soon as they were out of hearing distance.

Dawson was carrying Beth on his shoulders. He stopped dead in his tracks.

"My family rude!" he said loudly. "Your family is the ones who went outside to eat."

Sudie put her hands on her hips, which were quickly

disappearing as the baby grew larger. "Well I think the reason they did that was quite obvious. Your daddy sat that table up out there for a purpose. I think it was so they wouldn't have to eat at the same table with my folks."

Dawson shook his head and continued on without replying to her accusation.

"It's your fault, ya know."

Dawson stopped again. It seemed to him, everything that happened lately ended up being his fault. Cora had assured him it was Sudie's pregnancy that caused her to act that way. Still, he couldn't let the matter pass without objection. "My fault!" How do ya figure it's my fault?"

"If ya would'a given Clayton back his money for that mule ya sold him, there wouldn't be no ill feelings."

"Sudie!" he shouted. "Ya didn't see the shape that mule was in. Clayton beat that poor mule with a two-by-four. I seen it laying there beside the stall. It had blood on it. Poor old Ben was bleeding out his nose, his ears, and his mouth. Now I don't know why he beat him, but I wasn't about to give that S.O.B. back his money after he beat poor Ben to death. Ben was a good mule. Believe me, I wish I hadn't sold him to Clayton in the first place."

"Well, I still think ya should'a give him his money back. If for no other reason than to keep peace in the family."

Dawson put Beth on the road so she could walk.

"It would'a made no never mind. Your folks ain't never liked me or my family. If it'd been up to them, we wouldn't be married now."

Sudie mumbled under her breath.

"What was that ya said, Sudie!" Dawson yelled.

Sudie yelled back, "I said I'd probably be better off!"

Sudie knew exactly how to push Dawson's buttons. Unfortunately for her, that day she had pushed one too many buttons. Without thinking, Dawson slapped Sudie across the face. Immediately, she grabbed her face and began to cry. Beth began to cry too. Dawson knew he'd made a mistake by slapping her but she needed to learn respect. He picked Beth up and walked away, leaving Sudie standing in the middle of the road crying.

The day before Christmas, Dawson went into the woods behind their house and cut down a big cedar tree. He also cut a slab of wood into two equal-sized pieces and made a stand for the tree. It was perfectly shaped and was so tall, it practically touched the fifteen-foot-high ceiling in their room. When he brought it inside, Beth's eyes got as big as saucers.

"Twee, Mama!" she squealed. "Twee!"

Sudie's belly was getting so big, she could barely bend over to pick Beth up.

"I see the tree!" Sudie exclaimed. "Big tree."

Dawson stood back, admiring the tree.

"Isn't she a beauty?" He smiled proudly.

Sudie did not seem to be as impressed. "Dawson, why did ya get such a big tree? It takes up half the room. Where are we gonna get decorations for such a big tree?"

Still smiling, Dawson replied, "We'll make them."

"Make them out of what, Dawson?" she scolded. "Our imagination?"

Dawson's demeanor changed rapidly. His jaw tightened. His eyebrows lowered, almost meeting in the middle of his forehead.

"Do ya have to ruin Christmas, Sudie? I know we ain't got much to give Beth for Christmas, but we've got a tree. It's a beautiful tree. It'll be even more beautiful when we get it decorated."

He took Beth from Sudie and held her in the air. "We like the big tree. Don't we, Beth?"

Beth giggled. "Eg twee."

That night after supper, they began to decorate the tree. They had a few shiny red balls and some crocheted snow-flakes Mama Cora had given them. Althea had also given them a small box of decorations. In the box were some tin can lids. Each one had a hole punched in the top by which to hang them. There were also three small angels someone had carved from a piece of wood and a tiny porcelain doll made in Japan. Once all the ornaments were on the tree, it still looked extremely bare.

"Now what?" Sudie asked, looking disappointed.

Before Dawson could respond to Sudie's question, Stella and John walked into the room from the kitchen. Stella was carrying a bowl of popcorn and her sewing basket. She was smiling.

"I have something that might help," she offered.

Dawson beamed. "Perfect," he said, taking the bowl of popcorn from her hand. "We can make strings of popcorn to hang on the tree. I completely forgot 'bout using popcorn."

John was carrying a box. "I picked some holly off that tree down the road." He held it up. "I got some mistletoe too. And some big pinecones."

He set the box on the floor next to the warm fire burning in the fireplace.

Everyone pulled a chair close to the fire to join him. Stella and Sudie began working on a strand of popcorn. John tied strips of colorful material from Stella's sewing box around sprigs of holly and mistletoe. Dawson tied string onto the pinecones then tied them on the tree. As they were working, Sudie began singing a Christmas carol.

"Oh Christmas tree, oh Christmas tree, how lovely are thy branches."

The others joined in. They sang and made decorations for the tree until nearly midnight. When they were finished, the tree was the most beautiful tree any of them had ever seen. Dawson put his arm around Sudie's shoulder.

"Ya see, Sudie. I told ya it was a beautiful tree."

He turned around to see what Beth thought about the tree. To everyone's surprise, she had laid down on her cot and fallen asleep. As Dawson, Sudie, John, and Stella stood admiring their work, they all began to sing.

"Silent night, holy night. All is calm, all is bright."

When the song was finished, they bid each other a "Merry Christmas." John and Stella went to their room. Dawson and Sudie put on their nightclothes. Before getting into bed, Dawson wrapped the hot iron that had been heating beside the fireplace, in a towel and placed it at the foot of their bed. Sudie crawled into bed and put her cold feet on the towel. Before going to bed himself, Dawson took a package from atop the chifforobe and placed it under the tree for Beth. He also put an orange, an apple, a few nuts, and a peppermint stick in her stocking, which hung from the mantle. When he was finished, he blew out the light in the kerosene lamp beside their bed and crawled into the bed beside Sudie. He so wanted to make things better for his family. He knew how unhappy Sudie was living here with John and Stella. He wished Sudie understood why he felt it was their only option if they wanted to one day buy a place of their own. It was hard just making enough money to support the family he had already. With a new baby on the way, it was going to get even harder. Still, he could hardly wait for him to be born. Then again, what if it was a girl? To be sure, he would be somewhat disappointed. He wanted a boy really badly. However, if it turned out to be another girl, he would love her too. Just before going off to sleep, he looked at the tree one last time. *It sure is a beautiful tree, all right*, he thought to himself.

The next morning Dawson and Sudie were awakened by Beth jumping up and down on their bed. She was giggling and shaking them, trying desperately to awaken them so they could see the pretty dolly Santa had left her under the tree.

Just after the first of the year, the bad feelings between Sudie and Stella intensified. The bigger Sudie's belly got, the more withdrawn and strange acting Stella became. One day after the men left for work, Stella did something Sudie had never seen her do before.

During the winter months, the chickens did not produce eggs as well as they did the rest of the year, which was not uncommon for chickens. Sudie was ironing some clothes when she heard a terrible commotion in the henhouse. Her first thought was a fox had gotten inside the henhouse. Beth was asleep. Sudie got her broom and went out to see what was going on. By the time she got to the henhouse, the squawking had stopped. When she opened the henhouse door, she got an unexpected surprise. Stella had killed every chicken in the henhouse. Sudie was shocked. Stella looked at her and smiled with satisfaction. She was holding an axe in her hand. She was covered in blood. Every chicken was dead, their heads chopped clean off.

"I guess I showed these chickens who's boss. I bet they'll start laying now," bragged Stella.

Sudie looked at Stella like she'd lost her mind. "Ya showed them all right, Stella. Now what are we gonna do for eggs? Dead chickens shore don't lay no eggs."

"I knew ya would say that!" Stella yelled. "That's how come I didn't tell ya bout what I was gonna do."

Sudie was at a loss for what to do next. She hated to see the chickens go to waste.

"I reckon we'll just have to clean them, cook some of them, and can the others," she told Stella. "Get them out of here and go to plucking. I'll put some water on to boil."

Sudie went to the house and put a pot filled with water on the stove. *We're gonna need plenty of water if we're gonna have to clean all those chickens at one time,* she thought to herself. *Whatever possessed Stella to do such a thing is beyond me.* When the water began to boil, she carried the pan out back to where Dawson always cleaned the chickens.

Dawson used the shabbily built wooden table, that was connected to the side of the corncrib, for cleaning fish, chickens, and wild game. When Sudie rounded the corner of the crib, neither Stella nor the chickens were anywhere to be seen. She looked in the henhouse. The hens were gone. She looked in the smokehouse, no chickens. She looked in the barn. No chickens there either.

She called out to Stella, "Stellaaa. Stella, where are ya?"

No answer.

Where in blue blazes can she be? thought Sudie.

A bone-chilling wind had begun to blow. Sudie shivered as she carried the pan of hot water back into the house. Beth was awake. She was sitting between the big bed and her cot, playing with something. Sudie couldn't make out what it was she was playing with, so she sat the wash pan on the table and went into the adjoining room.

"What ya got there, Beth?"

Beth held up her toy, but it was not a toy. It was Sudie's prized ballerina. Sudie stayed as calm as she possibly could so as not to alarm Beth and cause her to drop it. She reached out her hand.

"Can Mama see the pretty doll?"

Beth smiled and handed her the delicate porcelain ballerina. Sudie was relieved and inspected it for chips and cracks. It was fine. Sudie decided the pretty ballerina was much too tempting to leave sitting around where Beth could reach it. Instead of setting it back on the table beside the bed, she set it on the mantle. In its place, she handed Beth the new doll she'd gotten for Christmas. Just as she was about to go back into the kitchen, she heard the front door rattle. She stopped and waited to see if there was someone at the door. Complete silence. She decided it must have been the wind rattling the door.

At around five o'clock that evening, the sun had already disappeared behind the far distant tree line. Sudie had not seen or heard Stella all afternoon. She fried the squirrels Dawson had killed the afternoon before and was just taking a pan of biscuits from the oven when the front door opened. She peeped around the corner. It was Dawson. Beth ran to him with open arms. He picked her up, kissed her, and asked her where her mama was. Beth pointed toward the kitchen. Dawson threw his hat on the bed and headed in that direction.

"You're just in time," said Sudie. "The biscuits are done. I cooked them squirrels and made gravy on them like ya like."

Instead of looking pleased, Dawson looked puzzled. "Sudie, would ya mind telling me why there's a dead chicken hanging on the front door?"

Sudie almost dropped the pan of biscuits. "What! A dead chicken?" She paused. "Well, I'll give ya three guesses, and the first two don't count."

"Ya don't mean Stella put it there."

"Well, who else would have done such a thing?"

"But why?"

"That's a good question. And while you're asking her about the dead chicken on the door, ask her where all the other dead chickens are."

"What other dead chickens are ya talking about, Sudie?"

"Every chicken in the henhouse is dead as a doorknob. She killed them. Cut their heads off. I told her we'd have to clean them, but when I got back out there with the boiling water, she and the chickens were nowhere to be seen. In fact, I ain't seen her since."

Dawson kissed Beth on the cheek then sat her in her high-chair. He didn't know what to say. He poured some hot water into the basin, grabbed the bar of lye soap, and proceeded to wash his hands. When he was done, he dried his hands and face on the towel that hung from a nail on the wall.

Sudie put the plate of fried squirrels on the table alongside the bowl of gravy and pan of biscuits. Dawson sat down at the table. Sudie knocked on John and Stella's door.

"Supper's ready."

Immediately, John opened the door. "Smells good in here," he said.

Sudie set out four plates. "Where's Stella?" she asked.

"She says she ain't feeling none too well," answered John.

"I don't expect she does," Sudie said sarcastically. "The old gal had quite a busy day. I expect killing all our chickens got her good and wore out."

John dropped his fork onto his plate. It bounced off his plate and landed on the floor.

"What did ya say? What do ya mean? Are ya saying Stella killed the chickens?" he asked.

"Shore did," answered Sudie.

John shook his head in disbelief. "That doesn't seem reasonable. Why would Stella kill all the chickens?"

"I reckon that's something you'll have to talk to her about," said Sudie. "After I found out she'd killed them, I tried to get her to help me clean them. I went inside to get some boiling water. When I came out, she and the chickens had disappeared."

"Disappeared?"

"Yes, John. Disappeared. Now Dawson tells me one of the chickens is hanging on our front door."

"What!" John replied as he pushed his chair back from the table and rose to his feet. "I reckon I best get to the bottom of this right now."

John opened the door and went into his room, closing the door behind him. Sudie and Dawson sat quietly, eating their supper and trying to overhear what John was saying to Stella. They heard him ask about the chickens. They heard no answer from Stella. They heard him pacing back and forth across the floor. He asked her about the dead chicken hanging on the front door. No answer. They heard him ask her why. Still no answer. A few minutes passed with only silence filling the room. Suddenly, they heard a loud crash.

John yelled out, "What the heck!"

Sudie started to get up, but Dawson touched her on the arm and motioned for her to sit back down. Less than a minute passed when John opened their door again. All the color had drained from his face. He was as white as a sheet. He walked into the kitchen and closed the door behind him. He looked as though he was about to faint. Dawson helped him to his chair.

"What happened, John?" Dawson asked. "Are ya all right?"

There was a long moment of silence before John was able to speak. He looked Dawson squarely in the face. "She just tried to kill me, Dawson. She has a knife. If I hadn't seen her shadow on the wall, holding the knife over her head, I'd be a dead man now."

"What was that noise we heard?" asked Sudie

"I knocked over a chair when I was trying to get out'a her way."

"Did she tell ya why she killed all the chickens?" asked Dawson.

"No. She just kept looking at me with a crazed look in her eyes. What am I gonna do, Dawson? I'm afraid she's gone completely mad."

To everyone's surprise, the door to John and Stella's room opened. Stella was standing in the doorway. She had a smile on her face.

"Did I hear somebody say supper's ready?" she asked as calm, cool, and collected as anyone could be.

Part
Two

Stella Hubert shuffled nervously around the dark, damp room. Although John had placed several large logs in the stone fireplace before he left for work, the room felt colder than usual. Her thin cotton nightgown and the un-insulated wood slat house did little to protect her from the below-freezing February temperatures outside. She had not slept well the night before, and her nerves were on edge. The voices had kept her awake. Where the voices came from remained a mystery to Stella. At first they only came to her at night while she lay awake and unable to sleep. Now they were beginning to haunt her in the daylight hours as well. She looked for the voices all the time, but she could never find them. Sometimes they told her to do things she didn't want to do.

As the voices got louder, Stella began pacing wildly around

the room, mumbling to herself in low, undetectable tones. Her dark skin showed signs of perspiration popping out on her forehead. Her long raven-black hair swayed back and forth across her face like a bed sheet draped across a clothesline on a windy day. As she passed her dresser, she grabbed her boar-bristle brush and began brushing at her hair with short, quick strokes.

Earlier that morning, she heard Dawson and Sudie talking about her. The thin wall between her room and their room left little room for privacy. She heard Sudie call her crazy. Anger festered inside Stella. She hated Sudie. How dare Sudie call her crazy? She slammed the brush against the wall. The loud noise echoed around the room, becoming louder and louder as it bounced around the floor like a fish out of water. Stella covered her ears with her hands. She felt as though her head was going to explode.

Finally the clanging of the brush stopped. Then came the voices again. *Who does Sudie think she is? She is evil. She is the reason you can't have a baby of your own. She doesn't deserve the baby she's carrying in her womb. It should have been you having a baby, not Sudie. She deserves to die.*

Stella began pacing again. She could hear Sudie in the other room, opening drawers and talking to little Beth. She knelt down next to the keyhole and peered into the room. She could see Beth in her highchair eating what appeared to be a biscuit. With her ear pressed against the door, she could clearly make out what Sudie was saying.

"It's gonna be a wonderful day, Beth, honey. Mama Cora is giving me a shower today for the new baby. Eat your breakfast quickly so I can get ya dressed. I've laid out your pretty pink dress ya like so well."

Stella knew the pink dress of which Sudie was speaking. She herself had given it to Beth. Stella was a good seamstress. She made the dress from a piece of pink satin she purchased at the Salvation Army store. Beth looked so pretty in pink. She was a beautiful child. Her blonde hair hung in ringlets around her small, round face. Her blue eyes sparkled like twinkling stars in a dark, moonless sky. Deep down inside, Stella wished Beth was her child. Dawson and Sudie certainly didn't deserve a lovely child such as Beth. Nor did they deserve the child Sudie was carrying now.

It isn't fair, the voices told her. *Sudie killed the first baby she carried. It died in her womb. It was all Sudie's fault the baby died. She and Dawson argued all the time. That is why it died.*

Stella stood up much too quickly. Her head felt dizzy, as though she was about to faint. The room began to whirl around her. Suddenly everything went blank.

Sudie rose early that cold twenty-first day of February in 1951. The house was cold and damp. She wanted to stay under the warm covers, but she knew she needed to get the fire going in the wood-burning cook stove. She wanted to get the biscuits in the oven so Dawson could eat breakfast before leaving for the sawmill.

In the spring and summer months, John and Dawson walked to work. It was only a short distance through the woods to the sawmill. However, in the cold winter months, Dawson's boss, Jack Hill picked them up in his car. The narrow dirt road that ran in front of their rental house was long and winding. Riding to work in Jack's car was much better than walking through the woods in the cold.

While Sudie added wood to the still smoldering ashes, she heard her husband beginning to stir. When Dawson heard the fire begin to crackle, he sat up on the side of their bed, pulled on his pants, and tucked in his gray flannel shirt. Moving quickly, Dawson headed for the warmth of the kitchen.

He pulled a straight-backed cane-bottom chair as close to the stove as he could get it, and then reached for his socks and brown brogan boots.

"Morning, Sudie," he muttered. "Shore is cold this morning."

"Morning," Sudie replied. "This baby is kicking like a bull yearling in a china shop. I shore don't remember Beth kicking like this."

"Maybe it's a boy," Dawson said with a whisper of hope in his voice.

He leaned forward and placed his hands close to the stove to warm them. Dawson watched Sudie as she went about preparing the biscuits. He knew she must be feeling miserable. Her belly was huge. From the size of her stomach, Mama Cora had determined she was going to have a big baby. He could hardly wait for him or her to get here.

Dawson finished lacing up his boots. By then the stove was hot, just right for cooking the biscuits. Sudie opened the heavy cast-iron door, slid the biscuits in the oven, and then poured Dawson a cup of strong black coffee. As she was placing the coffeepot back on the stove, she suddenly flinched and grabbed at her side.

"Oh, God!" She gasped.

Dawson reached out to her. "What's the matter, Sudie?"

Clutching her hand to her back, she replied, "I'm all right. I just had a pain hit me in my side. I think this baby is gonna be a big one. I shore will be glad when it gets here."

When the biscuits were done, Dawson took the dish towel from Sudie's hand, removed the biscuit pan from the oven, and placed it on the table. Although the fire in the oven was blazing hot, it did little to cut through the exceedingly cold chill that filled the long, narrow kitchen.

Dawson hung the dish towel on the nail next to the stove

and sat back down. "Don't ya think ya best wake Beth so she can eat too?"

Sudie peeked around the corner of the kitchen door, which lead into the main room. Beneath a folded quilt lay their beautiful daughter. The early morning sun breaking through the window at the head of her bed cast a soft golden glow on her curly blonde hair. As Sudie looked at her sleeping child's face, she thought to herself, *This must surely be what the angels in heaven look like.*

Sudie reached for the bucket of sorghum syrup on the shelf. She placed the bucket on the table in front of Dawson. From the icebox, she took out a bowl of freshly churned cow's butter and placed it on the table too.

"I think I'll let her sleep," she said. "She's warm under the covers. I'll feed her later. I've got a lot to do before Mama and Daddy pick us up this afternoon to take us to the shower."

Dawson's mother and two of his aunts, Edith and Josie, were giving Sudie a baby shower at three that afternoon. It was only a short distance to the house where Mama Cora lived, but Mr. and Mrs. Newton felt it was best to drive their daughter to the shower. It was less than a month away until their grandchild was due. Her mother feared for both the baby and Sudie. Every night she prayed the baby would be healthy. She didn't think her daughter or Dawson could get through another baby being born dead.

Dawson broke open two of the largest biscuits and put them on his plate. He dipped out a large helping of butter and spread it over the steaming hot biscuits. The butter melted quickly as he poured a generous portion of syrup on top.

"Yep. Me and Uncle John will be out working hard today while ya and Stella'll be partying," he teased.

With the very mention of Stella's name, Sudie's entire attitude changed. "Well I don't know why Stella has to go with me to the shower," she bellowed. "I don't even want her there. It's bad enough having to live in the same house with her."

"Now, Sudie, Stella is my aunt, so keep your voice down. She's right in the next room, ya know. She might hear ya."

"I don't care if she does hear me, the old biddy. I tell ya, Dawson, that woman is crazy as a betsy bug. I don't care what nobody says. I know in my soul it was her that hung that dead chicken on our front door. She's crazy, Dawson. I'm here to tell ya she's crazy."

"I know she's a bit peculiar, Sudie, but she loves Beth and the other young 'uns around here. She's always taking them to the creek for picnics and walks in the woods. The children all seem to like her. She can't be all that bad."

Sudie got up from the table, took the coffeepot from off the stove, and poured more coffee into Dawson's half-empty cup.

"Your mama told me she threatened to kill her two weeks ago, right in her own house. Mama Cora said she was getting onto one of the kids about something they was doing that they shouldn't. They kept on doing it, so Mama Cora told them she was gonna whoop them if they didn't stop. That was when Stella told her she would kill her with a butcher knife if she dared hit one of them. It really scared Mama Cora. She said Stella had a wild look in her eyes when she said it."

All Dawson wanted to do at that point was to ease Sudie's mind. "I'm sure Mama was exaggerating a bit. I don't think Stella is really capable of actually killing anybody."

"She had another one of them fits yesterday. I heard her in there flopping round on the floor. I looked through the key-hole, and sure enough, she was flailing round like a chicken with its head cut off. I went over there to see if I could help. I found the spoon she keeps in her pocket, so I stuck it in her mouth like Uncle John showed me to do. I kinda tried to hold her down to keep her from hurting herself. It wasn't easy with this big belly sticking out. She finally calmed down and came to her senses, what sense she's got anyhow. When she realized where she was, she went to cussing and raising a fuss. Told me to get my fat butt off her. Here I was down on my hands and knees trying to help her, and she was cussing at me. I tell ya, Dawson, the woman is crazy."

The door to John and Stella's room opened and interrupted their conversation. Dawson was relieved when he saw it was his Uncle John. He knew Stella wasn't quite right in the head, but she was his aunt by marriage. And it was good of her and Uncle John to let his family live in one side of the house. It wasn't much, but it was a place to live until they could do better.

John looked at Sudie with a rather strange look on his face. It was obvious he had heard what Sudie was saying about his wife.

"The boss is here to pick us up," he said to Dawson.

Dawson stood up and pulled on his heavy work coat. "I'm coming, Uncle John. Let me get my hat, and I'll be right out."

Dawson quickly kissed Sudie on the cheek then grabbed his tan felt hat that hung on a nail just inside the door.

"It's gonna be cold today, Sudie. Y'all bundle up when ya get out."

"We will," Sudie answered. "We should be back by the time ya get home for supper."

John closed the door to his and Stella's room. Stella was pacing back and forth in front of the fireplace. He knew she had heard Sudie call her crazy, so he tried to console her.

"Don't pay no never mind to what Sudie said, Stella. She's pregnant. Pregnant womenfolk get a little persnickety. She don't mean nothing by what she said."

Stella did not answer back but continued to pace back and forth. John put on his hat and left without saying good-bye.

Dawson hurried out the door and across the yard. Ice

crunched under the weight of his body as he made his way toward the waiting vehicle. As he was approaching the car, he felt in his jacket pocket and realized he'd forgotten his wallet.

"Sorry, fellers," he called to them, "I forgot my wallet. I'll be right back."

By the time Dawson got back to the house, Sudie was waiting just inside the door, ready to hand it to him. She opened the screen door just wide enough to get the wallet through then threw up her hand and waved hello to the others waiting in the car.

Dawson returned to the car. He crawled into the backseat next to John. Sudie watched as the car drove away then shut the door behind her. As she made her way over to the chifforobe, she secretly wished they owned a car and a house of their own. She hated living a room away from Stella. There were times when she knew Stella was watching her through the keyhole. Recently, every time she was cooking in the kitchen, Stella would sit just inside the door to her room and peer around the corner at her. She didn't like the way she looked at little Beth, either. It was as though she thought Beth was her baby—like the time she tried to take Beth on a picnic without asking permission.

When Sudie reached the chifforobe, she opened the door and took out her favorite blue print dress. Laying it on the bed, she ran her fingers around the dainty lace collar. Next, she reached for Beth's pink satin dress. She always looked so pretty in pink. The dress was the one thing Stella had given Beth that Sudie was pleased with. It was stitched by hand and very well made.

From the bottom drawer of the chest, she took out a clean pair of socks for Beth. As she turned to place them on the bed, she was startled at the sight of Beth standing close behind her. Sudie smiled then scooped up the tiny girl into her arms and carried her into the kitchen where it was warmer.

"We have to get some breakfast in ya, little sleepy head. We've got a big day ahead of us. Your grandpa and grandma are coming by later to take us to Mama Cora's house. We're gonna see Aunt Ruth, Aunt Emma, Aunt Carrie, Aunt Adell, Aunt Annie, Aunt Edith, Aunt Josie, and Aunt Delta. They're gonna give us some new things for the baby. Won't that be fun?"

Beth clapped her hands together excitedly. "See Mama Cora."

Sudie slipped on Beth's shoes and socks and placed her in her highchair.

"That's right. Ya love Mama Cora, don't ya?"

"'Love Mama Cora,'" Beth repeated.

Sudie took a biscuit from the warmer and put her finger inside it, making a hole. She then poured the hole full of syrup and handed it to Beth to eat while she washed up the morning dishes. A short time later, someone knocked at the back door. Sudie dried her hands on her apron and looked at Beth.

"I wonder who that could be."

Beth had dripped some syrup from her biscuit onto the highchair tray. She was having too much fun running her fingers through the sticky liquid to be concerned about who had come calling.

Sudie opened the back door. There on the steps stood a middle-aged man with shoulder-length salt-and-pepper hair. It was hard to see his eyes, for his hat was pulled low across his face. His unshaven face and dirty fingernails made him look as though he hadn't seen a drop of bathwater in several days, perhaps even weeks. His cheeks were hollow and his pants baggy. His gray coat was tattered and worn along the sleeves and around the edges. The tops of his shoes were being held to the thin soles with a piece of twine. When he smiled, half his teeth were missing, and the other half were yellowed and starting to rot.

"Can I help ya?" Sudie asked.

The stranger removed his hat revealing a head of hair that was in bad need of a good washing and a combing.

"Howdy, miss," he began. "I was wondering if I might do some work round your place in exchange for a hot meal."

The railroad track was just over the hill from their place, so it was not unusual to have strangers come by asking for work or for a handout. Hobos frequented that area. The Great Depression had hit everybody hard. Times had gotten a bit better, but work was still hard to find. Most of them were just folks down on their luck. However, there were those who would take what they wanted, sometimes with force if need be. Sudie looked up at the latch on the screen to make sure it was secure.

"I'm sorry, mister, but we ain't got no work what needs to be done. I can give ya a few biscuits I got left over from breakfast."

"That'd be mighty nice of ya," he answered. "I ain't eat in nigh onto three days now. Do ya mind if I come in? It shore is mighty cold out here this morning."

Sudie hesitated about letting him in her house, but she felt sorry for him. She unlatched the screen door and pushed it open. "I reckon ya can come in for a little while. My mama and daddy are coming to take me and my daughter to a baby shower for my new baby what's coming soon. What's your name, mister?"

"My name is Silas," he answered as he closed the wooden door behind him and locked it.

"Well, Silas, have a seat here at the table. Would ya want a hot cup of coffee?"

Silas sat down at the table. "That would be fine, miss. And who is this pretty little girl?"

Sudie took a cup and saucer from the shelf, filled it with the steaming hot coffee, and handed it to Silas.

"Her name is Beth. She's my daughter."

"She shore is a pretty little thing."

Sudie smiled and looked at Beth. "Can ya say thank ya, Beth?"

Beth pinched her thumb and index finger around her nose. "Man stink."

Sudie blushed, embarrassed by her child's comment. "I'm so sorry. She didn't mean nothing. She's just a little girl."

Silas's face twisted into a gruesome frown. From beneath his coat, he took out what appeared to be a sawed-off shotgun and laid it on the table in front of him.

"Ya need to teach that little gal some respect," he muttered.

Sudie felt threatened by the gun and the rapid change in his demeanor. "I think ya need to leave now, Silas. I'll fix ya a bag of biscuits to go. Mama and Daddy will be here in a few minutes, and we still need to get ready."

Stella could hear a man's voice coming from the adjoining room. It wasn't like the voices she was accustomed to hearing. She thought about opening the kitchen door to see who it was, but she had no desire to see Sudie right now. Instead, she waited just inside her room, close to the door. She longed to hear what the strange voice was saying. However, the other voices were getting too loud. She wished she could make them be quiet so she could hear what the man in the other room was saying. Still they persisted: *Look in the corner, Stella. The gun is in the corner. You can stop the voices with the gun. The voices are coming from behind the door. Use the gun, Stella. Stop the voices.*

A few short minutes passed or perhaps longer. Sometimes it was hard for Stella to keep up with how much time had actually passed. At times she found herself somewhere without knowing how she got there or how long she'd been there.

This was one of those times. She looked around. The fire had burned down to ashes. The sun was well above the treetops.

She thought she remembered hearing a gunshot. It must have been someone hunting in the woods behind her house. Maybe John decided to come home and go hunting. Maybe he would kill some squirrels for their supper. Squirrels and dumpling stew would sure be good on a cold day. She looked down at her clothes. They were covered in something red and sticky. She should change them. She didn't want to go to Sudie's shower with dirty clothes.

Around two thirty that afternoon, Samson and Althea Newton arrived at Sudie's house. Althea was a broad-faced, dark-skinned woman with short, light brown hair. She was not a pretty woman and neither was her demeanor, but it was easy to see where Sudie got her sky-blue eyes. They were exactly the same color as her mother's eyes. When Samson drove the car into the yard, Althea noticed Stella sitting on the porch in a rocking chair. She was sitting there alone, violently rocking back and forth, staring blankly into space. Her eyes had a wild look about them, much like a shark's eyes, blank and uncaring. Although it was the middle of the afternoon, the temperatures were still below freezing, yet Stella sat there with nothing on but a thin cotton dress and a light sweater.

Althea rolled down the window and called out to her. "Are y'all ready to go to the shower, Stella?"

Stella did not respond. Althea rolled the window up and turned to Samson. "That is one strange woman."

Samson opened his door and got out. "Ya stay here, and I'll get Sudie and the baby. Ain't no need of both of us getting out in this cold."

Samson tipped his hat to Stella as he approached the front

steps. She still made no response. He walked up the steps and onto the porch. A loose board creaked loudly under his feet. He knocked on the screen door, but no one answered. He could hear Beth inside the house. She was crying loudly. He pulled back the screen door and knocked again, this time on the wooden door. Still no answer. He tried the doorknob. It was unlocked. He opened it and stepped inside.

Just inside the door, Samson suddenly fell to his knees in disbelief. His beautiful daughter's mutilated body was halfway in and halfway out of the fireplace. It looked as though someone had tried to toss her into the burned-out ashes. Her mangled body was covered in blood. He was terrified. His heart felt as if it would pound right out of his chest. He could hardly believe his eyes. The air inside the room turned heavy. It was hard for him to breathe. The taste of iron filled his mouth.

Beth was covered in blood and ashes. Unable to stand up and walk in the slick pool of blood, she crawled to her grandfather. Her nightgown, heavy with blood, slid along the floor, leaving a trail of red behind her. She was crying uncontrollably. Samson took her in his arms, cradling her close to his chest.

"What happened here, baby girl? Who could have done this?"

Terror turned to hatred as his mind raced, bewildered by who was responsible for such a despicable slaughter. Slowly, he got to his feet, staggering backward as he rose. His mind could barely wrap itself around what he was seeing. He began backing out the door and down the steps, with little Beth still clinging tightly around his neck. He felt as though his legs were made of jelly as he made his way across the yard to the car. When he got to the car, he opened the passenger door. He had to practically pry Beth loose from her hold around his neck. When she finally let go, he handed her to her grandmother.

"We have to get help, Althea."

Althea looked at her grandbaby. She was covered in blood.

Althea looked for where the blood was coming from. As her husband started around the front of the car, she called to him, "What's happened? Why is Beth covered in blood?"

Samson did not answer until he opened his door and slid in under the steering wheel. Pausing for a moment, he took a deep breath. Althea looked at him. All the color had drained from his face.

"My God, Samson, ya look like you've seen a ghost. What's going on? Where's Sudie? For God's sake, man, tell me what has happened!"

Samson turned and looked his wife straight in the eyes. "She's dead, Althea. Our girl is dead. We have to get help. We have to get to a phone and call the sheriff. We'll take Beth to Sara Nell's house. This baby don't need to be in the middle of all this. She's already terrified."

Althea grabbed Samson's arm.

"Are ya sure she's dead, Samson? Maybe she's still alive. I have to go see for myself."

Althea reached to open her door. Quickly Samson reached across and closed it back.

"No, Althea. Ya can't go in that house. There's no doubt in my mind. She's dead. Our girl is dead. Somebody murdered her, and I think we both know who it was."

No one in the immediate area had a phone. Samson would have to go to the nearest pay phone, which was located some five miles down Highway 31 at the gas station in Verbena. When they arrived at Sara Nell's house, Althea took Beth inside while Samson went for help.

When Sara Nell saw Beth, she was at a loss for words. As the two bewildered women stripped Beth of her bloody clothes, Althea told Sara Nell what Samson had found.

"Sudie is dead, Sara Nell. We went to pick her up to take her to the baby shower at Cora's house. I stayed in the car while Samson went inside to get her. She was dead! Poor little Beth was crying hysterically and soaked in blood."

Sara Nell was shocked. Her tall thin body began to tremble as she put some water on the stove to heat so they could give Beth a bath. While they were waiting for the water to heat, Sara Nell wrapped Beth in a blanket. Althea sat down close to the fire and began rocking her.

"Does Dawson know yet?" Sara Nell asked.

Althea stopped rocking and looked squarely at her friend. "Samson and I figure he's the one who killed her. Ya know how mean he is and what a temper he has."

Sara Nell shook her head. "Ya can't mean that, Althea. I know Dawson has a temper, but he would never hurt Sudie. At least not when she was carrying his baby."

"I wouldn't have thought so either, but she's dead. That I do know."

For the first time, Althea began to cry. Sara Nell laid her hand on her shoulder.

"It'll be all right, Althea. Sudie's in God's hands now."

Althea's tears turned to anger. "And I hope Dawson Hubert rots in hell."

Suddenly, Sara Nell thought about Stella. "Where was Stella while all this killing was going on?"

Althea stared into the fire. "When we got there, she was sitting on the front porch. She had the strangest look in her eyes. I know she must have been cold. She didn't have nothing on but a thin sweater. She was just sitting there rocking. I asked her if she was ready to go to the shower, but she didn't say a word. She just kept on a rocking."

Sara Nell pondered her comments for a moment. "Ya don't reckon she had something to do with Sudie's murder, do ya?

She don't seem to be the smartest chicken in the henhouse. A might unusual, if ya ask me."

Althea had already convinced herself of Dawson's guilt. Another possible suspect had not crossed her mind. "If anything, Stella might'a witnessed Dawson killing my young 'un, but it ain't likely she done the deed. Dawson is the one what done it. I'd bet my life on it."

As soon as the water was warm, Sara Nell poured it into a dishpan, set the dishpan on the floor near the fireplace, and reached for Beth. Althea reluctantly handed her over to Sara Nell then leaned back in her chair and began to weep again. Sara Nell lathered up a washcloth with soap and began to bathe Beth. The blood in her hair had begun to dry. Sara Nell poured warm water over Beth's head. The water ran red as it trickled down her soft white skin.

Sheriff John Thornton and several of his deputies arrived on the scene around three fifteen. Sheriff Thornton was a short, stocky man with deep-set eyes and one eyebrow that ran the width of his forehead. Most of his responsibilities centered around breaking up domestic arguments, arresting folks for public intoxication, serving warrants, and investigating the whereabouts of local moonshiners. This was the first murder investigation Sheriff Thornton had been involved in since he took office.

Word of the murder spread quickly; the yard was soon filled with bystanders. After a brief discussion with Samson Newton, the sheriff and his deputies went inside to view the crime scene. Upon entering the house, they were shocked at what they saw. The scene was so gruesome, one of the younger deputies turned sick to his stomach and hurried out the door. He went immediately to the edge of the porch and vomited.

Even the sheriff felt a bit queasy. It was the most heinous crime any of them had ever seen.

It was determined that the fatal shot was fired from the kitchen area by someone either sitting in a chair or crouched down on the floor. The gun blast entered the victim's left side just under the ribcage and exited out her right shoulder and neck area. A huge pool of blood just inside the front door revealed the place where the body had fallen as well as the place where the mutilation had taken place. Bloody footprints were everywhere—those of the murderer and those of a small child; the larger of which led out the back door and to the well.

There were signs of blood on the well curbing. It appeared the murderer had either washed his or her hands or washed the object used to mutilate the victim. Deputy Coy Rucker, a five-year veteran on the force, was sent to investigate the area around the house. Rucker stood more than six feet tall with dark, curly hair and a handlebar mustache. While checking in the shed, he found what appeared to be the axe used to chop open Sudie's abdomen. Although it had clearly been washed, the blood was still apparent on the wooden handle and along the edge where the blade and the handle connected. Rucker's further investigation of the area produced a bloody piece of stove wood, which had been placed back on the stack of wood near the back door. The stick of wood appeared to have been used to further bash in the head of the victim. The evidence showed the murder was clearly a sign of passion and hatred.

Deputy Ralph Meed, the young man who had turned sick, was instructed to question any possible witnesses. Meed still felt sick to his stomach and was more than happy to leave the crime scene. He began his investigation by attempting to question Stella. At first she was unresponsive and unemotional. She continued staring blankly and rocking violently in her chair, as though she was completely unaware of what was going on around her. Cora arrived shortly thereafter. When she saw the shape Stella was in, she encouraged her to go inside and lie down.

"Stella," she said to her, "you're as cold as a well-digger's butt. What do ya mean sitting out there on the porch with nothing on but this little thin sweater? You're gonna be sick."

The bed remained unmade from that morning. The fire had burned down to cold ashes. Cora pulled back the covers and made Stella lie down on her bed then covered her with several quilts. Cora feared she had been severely traumatized by the sight of the horrible crime. How much she knew about what took place was still left to be discovered.

"Now ya just lay here and get warm, Stella," Cora told her. "I'm going outside to see if I can find out anything. I'll bring in some firewood and build ya a fire too."

When questioning the neighbors, Deputy Meed discovered Stella had gone up the road to the Faulkner's house earlier that morning. Lucy Faulkner was the nearest neighbor. She was in ill health and was hesitant about talking to Meed. After several minutes, she eventually reported Stella had told her someone killed a woman down at her house and threw a baby in the well. She said she asked Stella who the woman was, but Stella had told her she didn't know. Mrs. Faulkner said she knew Stella was a bit touched in the head, so she simply disregarded her ranting. She said when Stella saw she wasn't going to help her, she left.

When Deputy Meed reported the conversation with Mrs. Faulkner to Sheriff Thornton, he asked Samson Newton about the possibility of a baby being involved. Samson had been so disturbed about his daughter's death that he had completely forgotten about the baby she was carrying.

"Yes, Sheriff," he answered, "my daughter was pregnant. That is why we came here today. We were driving her to a baby shower this afternoon. Cora Hubert and two of her sisters were giving it for her."

The sheriff scratched his head. "Exactly how far along in her pregnancy was she?"

Samson's eyes filled with tears. "At least eight months."

Sheriff Thornton patted Samson on the shoulder. "I know this is tough, Samson. I'm sorry about all this. Rest assured, me and my deputies will find out who did this, and they will pay."

Samson dropped his head. "Thank ya, Sheriff, but I know who done it. It was Dawson Hubert. Ain't no need to look no further. He done it shore as I'm standing here."

Dawson's uncle, Will Deason, was a constable in Autauga County. He also dug wells for folks in the area. Sheriff Thornton sent word for Will to come to the scene. Since Stella told Mrs. Faulkner someone had thrown a baby down the well, he wanted Will to go down into the well to look for the baby's remains.

Will was a tall, thin man. He always wore a khaki hat that covered his nearly bald head. He was an honest, simple man, uneducated but wise when it came to common sense. He was also well respected in the community. He and his wife, Delta, and their new baby girl, Debra, arrived around five o'clock that evening.

Delta was Cora's youngest sister. She was shocked when she heard the news about Sudie's death. When she arrived, she went inside with the baby and joined her sister. Cora was sitting by Stella's bedside. Delta and Cora hugged. She could tell Cora had been crying. Stella was barely visible, hidden by the heavy quilts on her bed.

"Ya don't reckon Stella done this?" Delta whispered to her sister.

Cora looked surprised. "Why would ya say that, Delta?"

"Well, didn't ya say she threatened to kill ya here awhile back?"

"Yeah, she did."

"Ya know she didn't like Sudie. I wouldn't put it past her myself."

Stella pulled the covers back just far enough to see who else was in the room. Her eyes stared blankly at Delta and the baby she carried in her arms. When Delta turned in her direction, Stella quickly hid herself beneath the covers again.

As the sun began to set, the temperature began dropping quickly. A cold northern wind whipped around the corner of the house. People gathered around the well as Will was lowered down into the darkness. He carried with him a coal oil lantern and a burlap bag. Sheriff Thornton called down to him. "Do ya see anything, Will?"

"Not yet, Sheriff."

"Maybe the body is on the bottom."

Will hated having to get in the cold water, but it was the only way he could be sure if a baby's body had indeed been thrown into the well. He knew the water was no more than several feet deep because he had dug the well himself less than a year ago. Still holding onto the rope, he called up to them.

"Lower me down slowly."

The men at the top began to lower the rope. As soon as the icy water soaked through Will's clothes, the coldness took his breath, and he began to shiver. He knew he would have to find the body as quickly as possible before he succumbed to hypothermia. He removed his legs from around the rope and stood up. He then used his feet to feel around on the bottom. He searched the well for several minutes when suddenly he came across something, something that felt like it shouldn't be there.

"I may have found something," he called up to the others.

Will reached down into the water and took a hold of the

object. His mind raced as he brought it to the surface. He had never retrieved a baby from inside a well before. He had removed wild animals, rats, and even an occasional snake but never a body. As the object broke the surface, to his relief he could see it was not a baby.

Again he called out to the men at the top of the well. "It's a chicken. Someone has thrown a chicken in the well. There's no baby down here."

It was obvious the chicken had been immersed in the water for several days. The stench almost took his breath away. Will quickly put the chicken in the bag, held it closed, wrapped his legs around the rope, and instructed the men to haul him up. He was shivering violently by the time he reached the curbing. Will handed the burlap bag to one of the onlookers. Everyone turned their heads as the awful smell floated through the air. Will's feet and hands were numb. One of the men helped him get over the edge of the curbing. Someone in the crowd handed him a blanket to wrap around him.

The sheriff patted Will on the back. "Thank ya, Will. Ya better get somewhere and change into some dry clothes a'fore ya catch pneumonia."

When Delta realized Will was on his way out of the well, she left Debra with Cora and went outside to help him get to their car. Will was shivering and his teeth were clattering. When they got to the car, Delta helped him take off his wet clothes and put on dry ones. As he was changing, he looked at Delta.

"I thank the good Lord there weren't no baby down there. At first I thought for sure that chicken was the baby. I was shore glad it wasn't. If it had been, I think I would'a been sick."

A short time after Will was pulled from the well, headlights were seen coming down the dirt road toward the house. The sheriff suspected it was Dawson and John returning home from work. The sheriff knew about Dawson and

Sudie's on-again, off-again relationship. He had been called out on at least two occasions in which domestic problems were reported. Although Dawson and John usually left for work early in the morning, the sheriff was still anxious to question both of them, especially Dawson.

Dawson's boss was the first to notice the array of cars in the yard, including that of the sheriff's.

"Wonder what's going on at your house, John. You don't reckon your wife has killed somebody," he joked.

John didn't answer.

Not knowing why, Dawson suddenly got a sick feeling in the pit of his stomach, as though he instinctively knew something was terribly wrong. Before the car came to a complete stop, Dawson was out of the car and running toward the house. He was abruptly stopped at the front steps and held back by deputies.

"What's going on!" he yelled frantically. "Where's my wife and daughter?"

The sheriff walked around the side of the house, followed by several onlookers. Sheriff Thornton broke the news.

"Your wife has been murdered, Dawson. Ya wouldn't happen to know anything 'bout that, would ya?"

Dawson dropped to his knees. "Would I know anything about it?" he asked, looking shocked, his eyes filling with tears. "What about Beth? Where is my baby girl? Is she … ?"

"Your daughter is fine, Dawson. She is with her grandma Newton," the sheriff answered.

As the deputies helped Dawson to his feet, he asked, "How? Who did this?"

"We don't know at present. I thought ya might help us with that," replied Sheriff Thornton.

"Me!" Dawson yelled. "How could I know who did this? I've been at work since early this morning."

"Perhaps there was an argument this morning before ya

left for work," suggested the sheriff. "Was she planning on leaving ya again, so ya decided to kill her instead?"

Dawson clinched his teeth. The muscle in his jaw tightened. He could hardly believe what the sheriff was implying. The thought of Sudie being dead was inconceivable. A knot formed in the pit of his stomach. He felt as though he was going to pass out.

"No!" he yelled. "There was no argument. When I left for work this morning, she was alive. She was excited about going to her baby shower this afternoon."

The sheriff turned his attention to John and his boss from the sawmill. "Did either of y'all see Sudie this morning?"

Dawson's boss, Jack Hill, stepped forward.

"I saw her. She was standing at the door when Dawson went back to get his wallet. She waved to me out the screen door."

"Are ya sure it was Mrs. Hubert?"

"I'm sure," Mr. Hill replied.

"So, Dawson, ya say ya was at the sawmill all day. Are ya sure ya didn't leave at any time?"

Dawson shook his head. "No, Sheriff, I was there all day."

At that point the sheriff saw the coroner pull into the yard, so he went to meet him. As soon as he and the coroner finished talking, Jack walked up behind him.

"Excuse me, Sheriff, but I think there is something you need to know."

Sheriff Thornton turned to Jack. "And just what is it ya think I need to know, Jack?"

"Well, sheriff, I heard you ask Dawson if he left work at any time today," Hill told him.

"Yeah."

"Well, he did leave for a short time around noon. 'Course, he wasn't gone more than thirty minutes. When he came back, he was breathing real hard, like he'd been running. I asked him where he'd been. He said he got hungry, so he hitched a ride down to the store in Marbury. He said the feller he rode with wasn't coming back this way, so he had to run to get back to work on time."

where he'd been. He said he got hungry, so he hitched a ride down to the store in Marbury. He said the feller he rode with wasn't coming back this way, so he had to run to get back to work on time."

"I see. Well that puts a whole new light on the subject. I think I might need to talk further with Dawson. His leaving and lying 'bout it makes him a prime suspect."

"Now, Sheriff, don't get the wrong idea," cautioned Jack. "I don't think for one minute Dawson Hubert killed his wife. He was looking forward to the new baby. I can't see why he would have any reason to kill her."

"Sometimes folks don't need a reason, Jack. Sometimes they just kill 'cause they want to."

As the night grew darker and colder, the coroner placed Sudie's remains in a body bag and carried her to the morgue.

In her room, Stella remained quiet and still beneath the covers of her bed, listening to the voices inside her head. The voices were still there, haunting her every thought. *Why hadn't the voices stopped?* she wondered. The voices told her she could make them stop. She had done what they told her to do, yet they were still there. Her eyes darted rapidly back and forth, scanning the room. *Where could the voices be coming from now?*

Once Will changed into some dry clothes, he went back to talk to Sheriff Thornton, who then told Will about what they had found. He showed him the axe and the stick of stove wood. Will surveyed the crime scene for himself.

"Ya say ya believe she was shot first, Sheriff?" he asked.

"It would appear so. We believe the shot came from the kitchen area. These bloody footprints here lead outside to the well."

Will noticed there were several rows of footprints leading outside and then returning in the opposite direction. It seemed as though the killer visited the crime scene several times. They went to the shed, back into the house, then over to the well. There were also footprints going from inside the house to the pile of stove wood, where the deputy found the bloody stick believed to have been used to crush Sudie's skull.

"Has anybody found the gun?" Will asked.

"Not yet. We're still looking for it. We recovered several lead pellets, which were embedded in the dresser near the place where she fell. That tells me the killer used a shotgun to shoot her. Ya would think that would have been enough to have killed her without having to beat her head in with a piece of stove wood or chop her up with an axe."

Will rubbed his chin with his rough, calloused hand.

The sheriff could see Will was in deep thought. "What do ya think happened, Will?"

"I figure the gunshot didn't kill her so the killer decided he needed something to finish her off. One set of prints lead to the woodpile where he found the stick of stove wood. Why he felt it necessary to chop the baby out of her is what I don't understand."

Sheriff Thornton wondered that himself. "What ya reckon he done with the baby?"

"Since we didn't find the baby in the well, I suggest ya get together a search party to comb the woods. Unless he took the baby with him, which I doubt, the woods would be the logical place to dispose of the body."

"That's a good idea. I'll tell the men to be here at first light. No need to try to look for it now. Hopefully the wild animals won't get to the body before we do."

"Has anybody tried to talk to Stella? She must have seen or heard something."

"I think Stella is in shock. One of my deputies tried to talk to her, but all she did was just stare off into space."

"I could try and talk to her if ya want me to. She knows me. Maybe she can give us a clue as to what happened."

"That's fine with me, Will. She and little Beth are the only possible witnesses. And I don't think Beth will be able to tell us anything."

Will knocked on Stella's door. John came to the door.

"What can I do for ya, Will?" he asked.

"I'd like to talk to, Stella."

John looked toward the bed. Stella's eyes were closed.

"I think she must be sleeping, Will. Can it wait till the morning? She seems to be pretty upset. I don't think I need to wake her."

"Okay, John, but I will need to talk to her if she happens to wake up."

John began shutting the door. "Maybe in the morning, Will."

Just before John closed the door completely, Will noticed there was a shotgun leaned up against the wall in the corner of the room. He would have to remember to take a look at it the first chance he got.

Will and Delta spent the night at Cora's house, but Will got very little sleep. His mind kept going back to the shotgun he'd seen in John and Stella's room. Stella was so simpleminded, it was hard for him to imagine her killing Sudie. However, over the last few months, he had noticed a change in Stella. Thinking back, he realized the change started about the same time Sudie found out she was pregnant again.

John had told him about one night awhile back when Stella tried to stab him with a butcher knife. When Will asked him why, he said he didn't know why.

Cora had also told him about the incident when Stella threatened to kill her with a butcher knife if she spanked one of the children. Still, Will just couldn't comprehend Stella murdering Sudie in such a gruesome and hideous manner. However, he was certainly anxious to have the opportunity to talk to her.

When Sheriff Thornton got home that night around eleven, his wife told him Samson and Althea Newton had called several times insisting on talking to him. His wife told him they said to call as soon as he got in, no matter how late.

The sheriff sat down in the chair next to the phone and picked up the receiver. The operator answered.

"Number please."

"Nora, this is Sheriff Thornton. Connect me to Samson Newton in Prattville."

"Hold please while I connect you, sheriff."

Samson answered the phone.

"Hello."

"Mr. Newton, this is Sheriff Thornton. Edie told me ya called wanting to talk to me. I hope I didn't wake ya."

"Ya didn't wake us, Sheriff. I don't know if I'll ever be able to sleep again."

"I know what ya mean. I shore am sorry 'bout your daughter."

"Listen here sheriff, have ya arrested Dawson yet!"

"No, Samson. The investigation is ongoing. I don't have enough evidence to arrest anybody at this point."

"Evidence! Ya don't need to look no further than Dawson Hubert. Them Huberts are mean folks. I would bet my last dollar he did it."

"Well, Samson, last dollar or not, as I said before, I don't have enough evidence to arrest Dawson or anybody else for that matter. When Stella gets in her right mind, she'll be the first person I'll want to talk to about Sudie's murder. After all, she did go down to the Faulkner's house to try and get help. Surely she saw something or someone."

Samson's anger welled up inside him again.

"Maybe if they had listened to Stella, my little gal wouldn't be lying on a slab down at the morgue."

Sheriff Thornton thought the same thing, but he didn't want Samson blaming half the county for Sudie's unfortunate demise.

"Now, Samson, ya can't go blaming the Faulkners for not believing Stella. Everybody knows she's a might touched in the head."

"I know that, Sheriff, but I just can't hardly stand the thoughts of my little gal and my unborn grand baby being dead. Ya reckon Dawson killed her just to get the baby? Ya reckon the baby might still be alive and he's got it hid somewhere?"

The sheriff could tell there was no need to talk to Samson about any other suspect other than Dawson.

"I've called on several of the locals to put together a search party. They'll start searching first thing in the morning. That's about all we can do for the time being. You and Mrs. Newton try and get some rest. There ain't nothing else can be done tonight."

Samson bid the sheriff good-bye and went back to his bed. His wife had drifted off to sleep so he lay down beside her as quietly as he could so as not to wake her. He closed his eyes, but all he could see was his daughter's bloody, mangled body lying in a pool of blood. He wondered if he would ever get that vision out of his head.

By morning light, a group of volunteers assembled outside the Huberts' house. Sheriff Thornton began giving them instructions on where and how to look for the body of the missing baby.

"Men, I want y'all to comb these woods with a fine-tooth comb. Look under every bush, in every ravine, and in every pile of debris. If that baby's body is in these woods, I want one of y'all to find it. Understood?"

The men shook their heads. Ollie Brown led the way with his bloodhound, Red, the best tracking dog in Autauga County. He was a big dog, even for a bloodhound. His ears were so long, they dragged the ground as he sniffed out a possible trail. Before heading out, Ollie turned to the man next to him.

"If Red can't find that baby, can't nobody find that baby."

The others muttered low in agreement then began their search.

Dawson spent the night at his mother's house with Beth. Althea had put up quite a fuss when he and his mama came to get Beth at Sara Nell's house. At first she refused to give her to him. Walter, Sara Nell's son, was a lawyer. He explained to Althea that she had no right to keep Beth from her father. Reluctantly, she agreed to let him take her.

Dawson still could not believe what had taken place. As he watched his young daughter sleeping, he wondered to himself what she had seen. If she could only tell them who it was who had done this terrible thing. He wondered too if she would be permanently affected by what she had witnessed. His mama assured him she most likely would not remember the incident because she was so young. Still, he wondered. All night, thoughts ran through his head: *Who had the opportunity? Who had the motive? Why so brutal? Who could hate someone that much to have killed her in such a horrific manner?* All questions, no answers.

By the time the sun rose the next morning, he was on his way back to the house he'd shared with his Uncle John and Aunt Stella. Hopefully his aunt would be up to talking today. Maybe she could shed some light on who had murdered his wife. When he arrived back at the house, the search party was already in the woods. He could hear Red barking as he searched the ground for a trail. Smoke billowed from the chimney. When he approached the porch, Deputy Meed stopped him at the top of the steps.

"Ya can't come in here, Dawson. This is a crime scene."

Dawson looked at the deputy with anger in his eyes. "I know it's a crime scene, ya fool. It was my wife who was killed here yesterday. But I need to get my child some clothes. I won't touch anything except my baby girl's things."

The deputy put his hand on Dawson's chest. "Sorry, Dawson. Sheriff's orders. No one is to come in or out of this house until the scene has been cleared."

"What about my uncle and aunt? Did the sheriff run them off too?"

"No, they're still here. They're just not allowed to go in the room where the murder took place."

"Fine," Dawson said. "I want to talk to Aunt Stella. Am I allowed to talk to my aunt, or is that part of the sheriff's orders too?"

The deputy scratched his head. "Well, Dawson, I ain't rightly sure 'bout that. I think I best ask the sheriff before I let ya go talking to our only witness. I wouldn't want ya compromising our investigation."

Dawson stormed off the front steps and headed for the back of the house. As he rounded the corner, he saw Sheriff Thornton standing near the back door.

"Sheriff," he called, "I need to get some clothes for my daughter. Your deputy told me I can't go inside. How am I supposed to take care of my baby girl without her clothes?"

The sheriff saw how irritated Dawson was. As a show of authority, he rested his right hand on the handle of his gun, that hung at his side.

"Now look a here, Dawson. We ain't trying to keep ya from getting your daughter some clothes, but that don't mean ya can get them yourself. I'll have one of my deputies get them for ya. Ya just tell him where they are, and he'll get them packed up."

Dawson shook his head. A part of him wanted to see where Sudie had been murdered. Another part of him just wanted to crawl in a hole and hide from the reality of it all. However, as headstrong as he was, it seemed senseless to argue with the sheriff. "They're in the dresser drawer, second one from the top."

The sheriff pointed to one of the deputies standing nearby.

"Get his daughter's clothes for him," he ordered.

Dawson was about to ask the sheriff a question when the back door opened and John stepped outside.

"Morning, Sheriff. Morning, Dawson."

"Morning," replied Dawson.

"Morning," said the sheriff. "How is Stella this morning? Do ya reckon we could ask her some questions about what happened here?"

John dropped his eyes toward the ground. "To tell ya the truth, Sheriff, I ain't sure but she's the one what done it."

For a moment, Sheriff Thornton was at a loss for words. "What makes ya say that, Mr. Hubert?"

"Well ya see, sir, she's been acting a might peculiar as of

late," answered John. "It's for shore she ain't been right in the head."

The sheriff reared his shoulders back and sorta grinned. "Well now, Mr. Hubert, everybody knows Miss Stella ain't always played with a full deck. But do ya really think she's capable of murder? I mean we're talking about a downright hideous, vicious murder."

John did not back down. "I know, she's my wife, and if ya had told me a few weeks back she was capable of such a thing, I would have called ya a downright liar. But she pulled a knife on me a few weeks ago. I believe to my soul if I hadn't seen her shadow and moved, I'd be a dead man now. You'd be investigating my murder."

The sheriff rubbed his clean-shaven chin with his hand. "A knife, ya say."

Dawson never considered his Aunt Stella as a suspect. However, Sudie had mentioned how crazy she thought Stella was. If only he'd listened to Sudie, maybe she would still be alive. If only he'd moved away from there when Sudie tried to tell him how crazy Stella was. Guilt rose inside him like flood waters in a creek. He also remembered her telling him about Stella threatening his mama.

"Come to think of it, Sheriff," he said, "yesterday morning, Sudie told me about Aunt Stella threatening to kill my mama with a knife if she spanked one of the children she babysits for."

The sheriff raised his eyebrows. "I see. Well maybe we do need to talk to Mrs. Hubert. Perhaps she knows more about this crime than we previously thought."

John looked troubled. "That's just it, Sheriff. She ain't talking. She ain't said not one word to me or anybody else for that matter. She just lays there looking into space like her mind is blank. I try to talk to her, but she don't say nary a word."

The sheriff turned to Deputy Turner.

"Has Will Deason got here yet?"

"Yes, sir." He drove up just a few minutes ago," answered the deputy. "Do you want me to get him for you?'"

"Yes, son. Get him for me."

John shook his head in agreement. "If she talks to anyone, it'll be Will. She's always liked Will. She says he's the only one who's ever treated her with respect."

"Uncle Will's a good man," agreed Dawson.

Nearly all night, Will had thought about the shotgun he had seen in the corner of Stella and John's room. *Was Stella really capable of murdering Sudie? Did she really have the kind of demons in her, which would cause her to do something so despicable?* He tried to put those kind of thoughts out of his head, at least until he could get a better look at that gun. He hoped Stella would feel more like talking today. As he was about to exit his car, he heard someone call out his name. Looking over his shoulder, he saw it was one of Sheriff Thornton's deputies. The deputy made his way over to where Will was now standing.

"What can I do for ya, Deputy?"

"The sheriff wants to see you, Mr. Deason."

"Just call me Will, son. Everybody else does."

"Yes sir, Mr. Will," replied the deputy. "My name is George Turner."

Will extended his hand, and the two men shook hands.

"Glad to meet ya, George. Ya say the sheriff wants to see me?"

"Yes, sir. I think he wants you to try and talk to Mrs. Hubert."

"I see. Well best we be getting on with it then."

The two men walked around the side of the house. As they were passing the window, Will looked up to see Stella peeking through the heavy, dark curtains. When she realized he was looking her way, she quickly closed the curtain shut. *Talking to Stella may not be so easy,* he thought to himself. *She's acting mighty peculiar.*

As Will and George were coming around the back corner of the house, Sheriff Thornton threw up his hand.

"Morning, Will."

"Morning, Sheriff, Dawson, John."

The four of them shook hands.

"Will, I'm glad you're here," said Sheriff Thornton. "We need to talk with Mrs. Hubert. John thinks she might talk better with you than with any of the rest of us."

Will rubbed his rough, calloused hands together to try and warm them.

"Well, I'll be glad to see what I can do. I can't guarantee anything, but I'll give it a try."

He turned to John. "How long have y'all had that shotgun I saw standing in the corner, John?"

"I got it a couple of weeks ago. Why?"

"I didn't know ya was a hunter," Will answered.

"Hunter?" John said, shaking his head. "Not me. I got it cause Stella said she was hearing people rambling around outside. I never heard nobody, but I figured if it'd make her feel safer, it wouldn't hurt."

"I'd shore like to get a good look at that gun, John," said Will.

John headed up the back steps, trying to avoid stepping directly onto the dried, bloody footprints.

"I'll get it for ya."

Soon, John returned with the 12-gauge double-barrel shotgun. Will took the gun and checked for shells. When he opened the barrel, he discovered one of the shells had been fired. The other was still intact.

"Someone fired this gun recently," Will said.

Alarmed, John looked at Will. "Ya don't reckon Stella is the one what shot Sudie, do ya?"

"There's no real way to know until I can talk to her, John. Ya reckon she's up to talking today?"

"Your guess is as good as mine, Will. I can't begin to figure that woman lately. Just go on in and see."

Will handed the gun to Sheriff Thornton.

"Now's as good a time as any," he said as he opened the screen and started inside.

Dawson put his hand on Will's arm. "Can I go in with ya, Uncle Will?" he asked.

The sheriff answered for Will. "I don't think that is such a good idea, Dawson. Best ya stay out here with us. I don't want ya influencing anything she might say."

That was not what Dawson wanted to hear. His jaw tightened. Before he could say anything, Will intervened.

"The sheriff is probably right, Dawson. We need to find out if she knows anything. I'm not sure she would open up with ya in the room. Heck, she might not talk to me either. There's only one way to find out and that is to try."

Dawson nodded his head and let go of Will's arm.

The kitchen floor was still dotted with bloody footprints. There were a few hard, stale biscuits in the warmer above the stove. A pot of cold coffee from the morning before sat on the stove top. Will looked into the room where Sudie's body was found. It was hard to imagine what Sudie had gone through. Had she suffered long? Was she still alive when the baby was being cut from her womb? Will hoped for her sake the gunshot had killed her instantly. He thought about Beth and that poor baby witnessing it all. *She must have been scared half to death.* He walked over to the door to Stella's room and knocked.

"Stella," he called, "it's Will Deason. Can I come in? I want to talk to ya."

A minute or so passed, and he knocked again.

"Please, Stella. If ya don't talk to me, you're gonna have to talk to the sheriff. Wouldn't ya rather talk to me?"

Finally he heard steps coming toward the door. Slowly the door opened. Stella was still in her nightgown. Her eyes darted from one side of the room to the other.

"Are ya alone?" she whispered.

"Yes, Stella, I'm alone. Can I come in?"

Stella pulled the door open and Will stepped inside.

"How ya doing, Stella?"

Stella began pacing back and forth across the floor.

"Fine. I'm fine," she answered in a low, deep tone. "We have to be careful, Will."

Will took a seat in the rocker next to the fire. "Careful? Why do we need to be careful, Stella?"

"They're listening, Will."

"Who's listening, Stella?"

"I don't know who they are. They won't come out so's I can see them. But I can hear them. I can hear them talking. They tell me things."

"What kinda things?"

"Things ... I tried to make 'em stop. They told me they'd stop ... but they didn't stop."

"Stop what, Stella?"

"Stop talking. They told me they'd stop talking if...." She paused.

"If what, Stella?"

"If I done what they told me to do."

"And what did they tell ya to do, Stella?"

Stella began to get more agitated. Her footsteps quickened.

"I can't tell ya. It's a secret."

"Ya can tell me, Stella. I'm good at keeping secrets."

Stella stopped dead in her tracks and turned toward Will. Her eyes blazed with anger.

"I told ya I can't tell ya! I told Sudie my secret, and ya see what happened to her. They killed her. I don't want 'em to kill ya too."

"Who killed her, Stella? Who killed Sudie?"

"I told ya, I can't tell ya!" she yelled. "Now get out! Get out!"

Will rose to his feet. "Calm down, Stella. Everything is gonna be all right. There's nothing to be worried about. Nobody is gonna hurt me. But ya need to tell me who did this to Sudie."

Stella's anger grew. Suddenly she picked up a glass kerosene lantern that was sitting on the table beside her bed, and threw it at Will. He dodged the lamp, and it hit the wall behind him. The glass scattered and kerosene spilled across the floor, barely missing the fireplace. The men outside heard the loud bang and rushed in. By the time they got inside, Stella was in a full-fledged rage. She was throwing everything she could find. Finally she began pulling the sheets off the bed.

"We have to find them, Will. We have to find the voices. We have to stop them before they kill the baby too."

The men looked at one another.

"Where is the baby, Stella?" asked Sheriff Thornton.

Stella had completely stripped the bed of sheets and blankets. She turned toward the sheriff, but her eyes were transfixed on something in the corner of the room.

"I hid it so the voices wouldn't find it. They told me to put the baby in the well. I couldn't do that. I told them I couldn't do that. But they said I had to do it if I wanted the voices to go away. I told them the baby would drown if I put it in the well. They didn't care. But I didn't want to hurt the baby, so I hid it from them. But they know. They know everything. Ya can't fool the voices. That's why they're still here."

Everything Stella was saying didn't make sense. Sheriff Thornton drilled her further.

"Did ya see who killed Sudie, Stella?"

Stella's eyes began to dart back and forth from one side of the room to the other. Once again she began pacing back and forth. As she passed the window she would stop, pull back the curtain, and look outside, as if she were looking for someone.

Dawson stood in the doorway watching Stella with increasing alarm. She was talking crazier than he had ever heard her before. Was this what Sudie meant when she called her crazy as a betsy bug? How could he have been so blind?

Stella looked directly at Dawson. "Where is Sudie? Did they get her? I tried to warn her. She didn't believe me. I knew they would get her. She didn't deserve another baby. It was my baby. Mine! I couldn't let her keep my baby from me. I need to tell her. I'm not crazy. Sudie says I'm crazy. She can't say that anymore. I told her not to say that. I don't like it when people say I'm crazy. I'm not crazy. It's the voices that are crazy."

Will stepped in front of Stella, placed his hands, one on each of her shoulders, and stopped her. "Look at me, Stella."

Stella looked up, her eyes blank, like those of a killer shark. Her body felt stiff, as though rigor mortis was about to set in. Will held her shoulders tightly between his strong hands.

"Stella, do ya know who killed Sudie and took her baby?" he asked assertively.

In lieu of replying, Stella's body went limp. Her knees buckled. Her eyes rolled back in her head. Had Will not been holding her, she would have collapsed onto the floor. Instead, Will eased her over to the bed and laid her across it. John lifted her legs and placed them on the bed also. She was out cold.

The men stood beside her bed, looking down at her. She looked so peaceful. Yet, it was plain to see her mind was troubled. The sheriff was the first to speak.

"What do ya think, Will?"

Will looked at him, shook his head, and then motioned him over to the other side of the room next to where Dawson was standing. Dawson looked like a man who had lost all hope. Will laid his hand on his shoulder then looked at the sheriff.

"I don't rightly know what to think, Sheriff. We know John's shotgun has been fired at least once very recently. To say the least, it would appear Stella's mind is out of sorts. I'm no doctor, but I'd say she's gone plumb loony. Did she kill Sudie and take her baby? Maybe. Did she see someone else kill Sudie and take the baby? Maybe. Regardless, I'd say she needs to be in a hospital. Somewhere there are folks who can figure stuff like this out."

John looked at Will. "Now, Will, ya know I ain't got no money for no hospital. Them places cost money."

The sheriff ignored John's comment. "I'd say you're right, Will," Sheriff Thornton replied. "Maybe Benton Hospital in Tuscaloosa."

John piped in again. "But, Sheriff, I ain't got money for no mental institution."

Sheriff Thornton looked at John. "There are ways to get her in there so the state will pay for it. However, in order to do so, we'll have to arrest her for Sudie's murder."

John dropped his head. "Well, Sheriff, to tell ya the truth, chances are, she did it. She didn't like Sudie none too well. And she did overhear Sudie call her crazy the morning before she was killed. I just don't know what she did with the baby. I can believe it about her killing Sudie but not the baby. She loves babies."

Will spoke up. "She may have killed the baby not meaning to. The way Sudie was hacked up, it would be a miracle for the baby to have survived."

"Then what did she do with the baby's body?" asked Deputy Rucker.

Sheriff Thornton looked at his deputy. "Well, truth is, unless the search party happens to run across it in the woods, we may never know what happened to the baby. If it was alive and she hid it in the woods, it would surely have frozen to death last night. Wild animals could have eaten it. Who knows?"

"What are ya gonna do, Sheriff?" asked Dawson, speaking for the first time since he entered the house.

"I'm gonna arrest Stella Hubert for the murder of Sudie Hubert. Once the doctors have a chance to talk to her, we'll go from there. I think it's for the best."

The sheriff pulled his handcuffs off his belt. Will touched him on the arm.

"Do ya really think handcuffs are necessary, Sheriff? She might not understand what's going on. Let me take her out to the car. I'll ride with her in the backseat. I think she'll take it better than being cuffed."

The sheriff nodded his approval. Will went over to the bed. Stella had come to and was actually quite calm. He reached down and took her by the arm.

"What's say we go for a ride, Stella?" he asked, smiling.

Stella looked up at him and smiled back. "I would like that, Will."

Will helped her off the bed. John handed her a robe then helped her put on her shoes. She put it on over her nightgown. As Will was escorting her out to his car, Dawson got his first good look at the room he had once shared with his beloved wife. The smell of dried blood seeped into his nostrils, making him feel sick to his stomach. He quickly looked away and hurried toward the door. He'd seen and been a part of killing and dressing out hogs. He'd cleaned and gutted rabbits and squirrels all his life. Yet the sight of Sudie's blood pooled up on the floor and spattered on the walls was too much for even a tough guy like Dawson.

After putting Stella in the front seat beside him, Will turned to the sheriff.

"I decided I'd take her there in my car. She'll feel more comfortable that way. Ya can follow behind."

The sheriff agreed to let Will drive her to jail rather than putting her in the patrol car. Anything to make the transition easier was fine with him. How she was going to take being locked up in a jail cell remained to be seen. From what he'd heard and seen, she could become quite violent when angered and the voices she kept talking about bothered him too. Although he hated to see a woman go to the electric chair, if she were the guilty one, then certainly she would deserve whatever punishment she got. After all, this was the worst, most gruesome murder case he had ever encountered.

While Will was putting Stella in his car, two men from the search party came walking up from out of the woods behind the house. Their britches were wet from the knees down from the crisp morning dew. One of the men was Joe Clayton, the other Mack Cummings. Joe's brown, tattered hat was pulled low across his face. A brown scarf was tied around his head, and the ends were tucked inside his gray overcoat. Mack was wearing a heavy, black sweater. A briar limb was stuck to the back of it. It was easy to see the two men were cold and tired. Someone had built a roaring fire in a fifty-gallon barrel. The two men headed straight for it. The sheriff decided to talk to them before leaving for the county jail in Clanton, some twenty miles away. As soon as they were in hearing distance, he called to them.

"Joe."

Joe looked up.

"Has anybody found anything?"

Joe rubbed his gloved hands over the fire.

"Not a thing, Sheriff," he replied. "We thought Old Red was on the trail one time, but when he reached the railroad tracks, he lost it."

"There's a thermos of hot coffee on the back steps if y'all want some," called Will.

The two men threw up their hands to let Will know they had heard him. However, at that moment, all they could think about was getting warm by the fire.

Will walked around to the driver's side of the car, opened the door, and slid inside. The steering wheel was as cold as an icicle. Will took the keys from his coat pocket and put them into the ignition. He pulled out the choke, pressed down on the clutch, and turned the key. The car hesitated for a few seconds before cranking. The motor revved up as Will pushed down on the gas pedal. He looked at Stella seated beside him. She looked very calm, even quite pleasant. *If only she knew what was about to take place,* he thought to himself.

Stella looked over at Will and smiled. "Where are we going, Will?" she asked.

Will didn't want to upset her, so he lied. "How 'bout we go to Clanton? Ya like to go to Clanton, don't ya?"

Stella's face lit up. "Yes, Will. I love going to Clanton. Can we stop at the hardware store while we're there? I need to buy a new axe. The old one has blood on it."

Will was beginning to believe Stella had more to do with Sudie's murder than earlier suspected. He decided to take the opportunity to ask her more questions concerning the situation.

"How did the axe get bloody, Stella?"

"I don't know, Will. I found it on the kitchen floor. It was all bloody, so I took it to the well to wash it. I tried to get it clean, but some of the blood was dry, and it wouldn't come off. So I put it back in the shed. John might get mad if he finds out his axe is dirty. I'll buy him another one, and then he'll never know."

Will was amazed at how calm Stella seemed to be now. Back at her house, in her bedroom, she was acting as if she'd gone mad. Now she was sitting beside him in his car as cool as a cucumber, her hands folded together nicely on her lap.

"Stella, did anybody drop by yesterday? A visitor, perhaps?"

"Why yes, Will. I heard Sudie talking to someone in the kitchen. It was probably one of her man friends what comes to see her when Dawson's gone. Sudie don't think I can hear her, but I do. She says mean things 'bout me all the time. She says I'm crazy. I ain't crazy. Do ya think I'm crazy, Will?"

Will looked at Stella again. She looked very sad.

"No, Stella. I don't think you're crazy. You're just different from the rest of us."

Stella smiled again. "There ain't nothing wrong with being different. Is there, Will?"

Will chuckled. "No, Stella. There ain't nothing wrong with being different."

By that time, the car had warmed up enough to run without shutting down. Will put the car in reverse and backed out of the yard. Ice crunched beneath the tires as he pulled out of the yard onto the narrow dirt road in front of the house. As they were driving north toward Clanton, they passed by several groups of men from the search party. They were walking back toward the house. Will didn't stop. He didn't want to upset Stella. He could see by the look on their faces that they hadn't found anything to do with the missing baby. Once the car reached the end of the dirt road, Will took a right onto Highway 31, going north toward Clanton. Just as they turned onto the highway, Will saw the sheriff's car approaching the stop sign. He was glad the sheriff was going to be there when they got to the jail. On the way, Will tried asking Stella more questions about the visitor, but Stella would say no more about it. She acted as though he never said a word. When they arrived in downtown Clanton, Will pulled into the city hall parking lot and turned off the ignition.

Stella looked around as though she were confused. "Why

are we stopping here, Will?" she asked. "I want to go to the hardware store. I told ya I need to buy John a new axe."

Once again, Will lied. "I need ya to come inside to see if ya can identify the visitor Sudie had yesterday."

Stella began to get agitated again. "I can't tell ya who he was, Will. I didn't see him. I only heard him talking."

"Well then we'll get him to talk, and maybe ya can identify his voice. Do ya think ya could do that, Stella?"

"What if he tries to hurt me?"

"We won't let him see ya. We'll hide ya so he won't know you're there."

Stella began to fidget. "I don't like this, Will."

Will got out of the car, went around to the passenger side, and opened the door. When Stella looked at him again, he realized she had that same crazed look on her face that he'd seen earlier that morning. He put out his hand to her.

"Come on, Stella. It'll be fine. I won't let nobody hurt ya."

Reluctantly, Stella took Will's hand and slid out of the car just as the sheriff pulled up beside them. Stella's eyes began to dart back and forth. She pulled her hand away from Will and began wringing them together. Will stood between her and the open door. Stella began shifting her weight from one foot to the other in a rocking motion. Sheriff Thornton got out of his car. Will spoke first.

"I told Stella she is here to identify the man she heard talking to Sudie yesterday morning, Sheriff."

The sheriff caught onto what Will was trying to do. "That's right, Stella. We need ya to come inside so ya can see if we've arrested the right man."

Stella continued to rock back and forth, her eyes darting from one side to the other. She was also mumbling something under her breath. Will could barely make out what she was saying.

"Be quiet!" she was saying. "I say be quiet. They will hear ya. I did what ya said for me to do. Now leave me alone."

Will stepped to Stella's side and placed his hand on her elbow, pushing her forward. Sheriff Thornton did the same on her opposite side. Slowly they led her inside the building. Several locals were sitting around the potbellied stove talking. When the sheriff and his guests entered, the men stopped talking and turned to see who was being escorted in. Stella stopped dead in her tracks. One of the men started to say something, but the sheriff motioned for him to keep quiet.

Will spoke to Stella, "We're going to put ya in one of the rooms with bars all around. You'll be safe there. Is that all right with ya? Ya do want to be safe, right?"

Stella nodded her head but said nothing.

The sheriff reached for the keys and opened an empty cell. Just as they were about to lead her inside, she went ballistic. She began screaming at the top of her lungs and pulling away. Will was amazed at her strength. She began hitting and slapping at them, trying to bite them even. It took both the sheriff and Will and one of the locals to subdue her. After ten minutes, they eventually had her safely in the cell with the door locked and secured.

Once she realized she was unable to get out, she sat down on the cot and began wringing her hands and mumbling to herself. Every so often, she would call out, "Shut up! Be quiet, I say!"

Frank England, the man who had helped Will and the sheriff subdue her, looked stunned.

"Who is she talking to, Sheriff?"

The sheriff looked at Frank and shook his head. "I have no idea whatsoever."

Will stood watching her for some time. "Sheriff, I think ya need to get a doctor in here as quick as ya can. It's plain to see she needs help. If she is the one who killed Sudie, it ain't likely she'll ever stand trial."

"Why do ya say that?" asked Frank.

The sheriff answered before Will could say a word. "Because ya can't try a crazy person, Frank. The law says they have to be able to understand the crime they've committed. I don't know if Stella even knows she's been arrested."

"She asked me to stop at the hardware store so she could buy a new axe for John," said Will. "I asked her why, and she said he would be mad if he found out the old one had blood on it. She even told me she was the one who took it to the well to wash it off. She was the one who put it back into the shed."

"Sounds to me like we have the guilty one locked up already," said Sheriff Thornton.

Will rested his hands on his gun belt. "It's hard to say, Sheriff, but it shore is looking that way."

Although Sudie had told Althea and Samson repeatedly about how crazy Stella was, they remained convinced Dawson had killed their daughter. Sudie's older sister, Massey, agreed wholeheartedly. Massey was a big-boned woman. She stood nearly six feet tall. Her square jawline and wide-set eyes made her look more like a man than a woman. She had never liked Dawson or any of his family. Massey drove over to her parents' house as soon as she heard about her sister's murder. Neither she nor her parents got very much sleep the night of Sudie's death. By four o'clock the next morning, both she and Althea were sitting at the kitchen table, drinking coffee, and discussing the situation.

"Mama," said Massey, "we need to start planning Sudie's funeral. And as far as I'm concerned, I don't want Dawson to be there."

"I feel the same way, Massey," Althea agreed. "We need to call the funeral home to see if we can keep him away from there. I know he killed her. I know he did."

Samson entered the kitchen where his wife and only living daughter sat talking.

"Ain't no call to do that. They'll just tell ya there ain't no way ya can keep him from being at his own wife's funeral."

Massey chimed in, "Even if he's the one what killed her, Daddy?"

Samson poured himself a cup of coffee and pulled another chair over to the table. "The only way anybody can keep him from coming to the funeral would be if'n he's in jail."

Althea spoke up, "Well that's exactly where he ought to be. I can't understand why the sheriff ain't arrested him yet."

Samson answered her, "Last night the sheriff said they ain't got enough evidence to arrest him."

Massey jumped up from the table so quickly, her chair slid across the rose-print linoleum-covered floor and hit the wall.

"How much more evidence do they need! They know he's mean, just like all them Huberts! They know he left his job at dinnertime and come back huffing and puffing like he'd been running a foot race. I just know he went through them woods, shot Sudie, chopped her up, and threw her body in the ashes. Then he ran back to work and told that tale 'bout getting hungry and going to Marbury to get him something to eat. Sounds like a lot of baloney to me."

Samson took a sip of coffee.

"Ya might be right, Massey, honey, but proving that's what happened is something altogether different."

Tears streamed down Althea's face. "If I knew I could get away with it, I'd get me a gun, go over there to his house, and blow his brains out!"

Massey leaned over and hugged her mother.

"Don't cry, Mama. The good Lord's gonna take care of

Dawson Hubert. It may not be in this lifetime, but he'll burn in hell if nothing else."

The phone rang and Althea and Massey jumped.

"I'll get it," said Samson.

Samson walked into the hallway. The heavy black telephone sat on a small table just inside the front door. It rang again, and he picked it up.

"Hello."

"Samson, this is Doug Turner. I shore am sorry 'bout your daughter."

"Thank ya, Mr. Turner," said Samson.

"I thought you might want to know they arrested Stella Hubert early this morning."

Samson could hardly believe what he was hearing. "Arrested Stella Hubert? What in tarnation for?"

"For killing Sudie."

"How do they know it was her?"

"All I know is they said she was acting suspicious."

"Well they're barking up the wrong tree. If ya want my opinion, they need to be arresting that sorry son-in-law of mine."

"Well, Samson, I don't rightly know what to say 'bout that. I just know they locked up Stella. I thought you would want to know."

"I appreciate ya calling me, Mr. Turner. Thank ya."

Before Doug Turner could say anything else, Samson hung up the phone and headed back toward the kitchen.

"Who was that?" asked Massey.

"It was Doug Turner. He called to tell us they arrested Stella Hubert this morning for Sudie's murder."

"Stella Hubert!" shouted Althea. "Has that sheriff gone stone-cold crazy?"

"He must have," said Samson. "I told him who killed Sudie. Dawson must'a paid the sheriff off."

Massey poured herself another cup of coffee. "Maybe it's 'cause Dawson's uncle is a constable. Ya know how them lawmen stick together. Maybe they arrested Stella to keep people from knowing Dawson done it."

"Well, they'll never convince me that Dawson is innocent," said Althea. "It's just a shame poor Stella has to take the blame for it. Just cause she's a little touched in the head don't make her a murderer."

Ed, Sudie's thirteen-year-old brother, walked into the room. Ed was a slim boy with curly, brown hair and a handsome face. He was the only member of the Newton family who actually liked Dawson.

"Well I don't think Dawson or Stella did it," he said as he sat down next to the fireplace.

Massey slapped at the back of his head with her open hand. "Okay, smarty pants, who do ya think did it?" she asked.

Ed rubbed at the back of his head. "I think it was some hobo. Ya know them hobos are always stopping by begging for food and money. I think one of them came by, asked Sudie for food or some money, and when she didn't give it to him, he killed her."

Althea balked. "Weren't no hobo what killed your sister, boy. It was Dawson Hubert what killed her."

Ed shook his head. "Think about it, Mama. It don't make no sense," he argued. "Dawson wanted that baby more than anything. He was excited 'bout being a daddy again. Why would he kill Sudie? He had no reason to kill her."

Massey sat back down at the table next to her mama. "Them Huberts don't need no reason for killing," she said.

"She's right, Ed," agreed Althea. "All the Huberts I know are mean folks. He might have killed her, cut the baby out of her, and hid it somewhere'."

Ed laughed. "Y'all don't know what you're talking 'bout. Dawson didn't kill Sudie. I know they didn't always get along, but he loved her. And as far as Dawson being mean, I can't see he's no meaner than most other folks I know."

"What about them times he hit her?" argued Massey.

Ed stopped laughing. "What about them times your husband hit ya, Massey? And I've seen Daddy hit Mama a few times too when he was mad. It didn't mean they was gonna kill you, did it?"

"Ya watch your mouth, boy," Samson scolded.

"I'm just saying, Daddy, I think y'all are jumping the gun accusing Dawson. I like him myself. And I don't think he would kill nobody, especially Sudie."

"Well, son, everybody is entitled to his or her opinion," said Samson. "It may not'a been Dawson what killed her. But I don't think it was Stella either."

"I don't know, Daddy," said Ed. "She's a strange woman. Sudie says … I mean Sudie said, she's crazy as a betsy bug."

Althea got up from the table, pulled out an iron skillet from under the counter, and placed it on the stove top. "Well I'd bet every last penny I've ever had that Dawson Hubert killed our Sudie. And nothing nobody can say or do will ever make me believe different."

Little Beth was left in the care of her grandma Cora. Everyone could tell she was traumatized by what she had seen. She didn't want to play. She only wanted to be held. Dawson was staying at his mama's house too. When he wasn't holding Beth in his arms, he was pacing the floor. All he could think about was Sudie and his unborn child. *Could my child be alive?* he wondered. *Could someone have killed Sudie just to get my baby? If that were so, then who was it and where had they taken the baby?* These were the questions that haunted him, making him unable to sleep.

After Will delivered Stella to the Chilton County jail, he stopped by Cora's house to give them the news. Dawson heard Will's car pull into the yard. He quickly grabbed his jacket and hurried out to meet him. Will turned off the ignition and got out of his car just as Dawson was coming out of the house.

Will called to him. "Howdy, Dawson. How are ya this morning?"

Dawson didn't answer his question but asked one of his own. "Has Stella told anybody who killed Sudie yet?"

Will took Dawson by the arm. "Let's go in the house, Dawson. It's too cold to be standing around outside."

Will and Dawson made their way back to the house. The wind was howling around the corner of the house. It was a bone-chilling cold. Will shivered as Dawson opened the door and stepped inside. Will quickly followed.

Cora and Lon were sitting by the fireplace. Beth was asleep in Cora's lap. "Morning, Will," Cora said, forcing a smile.

Will tipped his hat to each of them. "Cora, Lon," he said, "I've come to give y'all some news."

Will idled up next to the fire. "As I'm sure Dawson has told y'all the sheriff arrested Stella Hubert this morning," he answered.

"Well, sir," said Cora, "Dawson told us you and the sheriff took her away. I knew Stella was crazy. Did she confess?"

"No," answered Will. "But, the sheriff decided she was the most likely suspect, being she was the only one there. We tried to get her to talk, but all she would say was the voices made her do things she didn't want to do. She also said Sudie didn't deserve another baby. She said it was Sudie's fault the other baby was born dead."

Dawson was stunned. "My God!" he exclaimed. "I know Stella's a might touched in the head, but I can't believe she would actually kill anybody. What I don't understand is why Stella would say it was Sudie's fault that the other baby was born dead? She must be crazy. If only I had listened to Sudie, she'd be alive right now."

Will spoke again. "Well now, we don't know for sure she did it. The sheriff said the only way to know for sure is to have one of them head doctors take a look at her. Since John said he didn't have money to pay for a doctor, the sheriff said if he arrested her, the county or rather the state would pay for it."

Lon was more concerned about John than he was about Stella.

"How is John taking all this, Will?"

"Well, Lon, he was actually the one who suggested it might be Stella what done it."

Cora patted Lon on the back of his hand. "If she is guilty of killing Sudie, then John is better off without her. I think he was getting a might scared of her anyway. I know I shore don't trust her no further than I can see her."

Lon nodded his head in agreement. "Yeah, I suppose you're right, Cora. She could'a killed him that night she pulled that butcher knife on him."

Will looked at little Beth. She looked so peaceful sleeping in Cora's arms. "How is she doing?" he asked, nodding his head in Beth's direction.

Dawson answered for his mother. "She won't let us put her down. One of us has to be holding her all the time. I can't imagine my baby having to see what she saw done to her mama. I just hope it don't affect her for the rest of her life."

"It ain't likely," answered Will. "She's only two. Do you remember anything from when ya was two?"

"No," Dawson answered, "but I didn't see my mama get chopped up with an axe either."

Cora looked down at Beth, sleeping soundly in her lap. "Beth likes Stella. It would be shameful if she is the one who killed Sudie."

Dawson began to pace the floor. "I want to talk to Stella. Do ya reckon they'd let me talk to her?" he asked Will.

Will rubbed his hands together. They were finally thawing out. "It ain't likely, Dawson."

Cora got up from her chair and carried Beth over to the bed. Laying her down gently, she covered her with a quilt then turned to Dawson. "I could go in your place. I don't think they would keep me from seeing her. Just tell me what ya want to know. She might even talk to me quicker than she would talk to you."

Will turned around to warm his backside. "I think ya might be right, Cora. It'd be good if she would talk to somebody. It may be awhile before the doctors can talk to her. The sooner we know what happened, the sooner we can know who did this. I'd be glad to drive ya up there. Just let me know."

Lon got up and went over to the stove. "Ya reckon this coffee is still fit to drink?" he asked Cora.

Cora sat down in her chair near the fire. "I expect it's a might strong, but it's drinkable."

Lon looked at Will. "Ya care for a cup, Will?"

"Sounds good," he answered. "This cold weather's got me chilled slap to the bone. I ain't been completely warm since I got down in that well to look for the baby."

Dawson felt a pain in the back of his throat, and tears filled his eyes. The mere mention of his lost baby tore at his heart like a mad hungry dog tearing at a piece of meat. "Has anybody found any sign of the baby yet, Will?"

Will began to shake his head. "No," he answered. "I'm sorry, but they ain't found so much as a hair."

"I can't help but hope my baby is alive somewhere. I ain't much of a praying man, but I ask the Lord all the time that whoever killed Sudie might still have the baby, and we'll find him alive somewhere."

Although Will held very little hope for ever finding

Dawson and Sudie's baby alive, he didn't have the heart to tell that to Dawson. "A body never knows, Dawson. Miracles happen everyday."

Two days after Sudie's death and an autopsy had been performed, her body was placed in a wooden, pine casket and brought to Cora's house, much to the dismay of the Newton family. They tried very hard to take dominion over the body, but state law gave the right of burial to the spouse. Neighbors brought in food for the family and for those who would be sitting up at night with the dead. The mood in the house was somber. The casket remained sealed. A framed black and white picture of Sudie on her wedding day was placed on top of the casket next to a spray of pink and white carnations. Arrangements were made for the funeral. It was to be held two days later at New Prospect Church in the Marbury community. Reverend John Dewey was to preach her eulogy.

Over the next two days, people came and went. After condolences to the family, the main topic of discussion always turned to who could have killed poor Sudie. Some felt it was a vagrant looking to steal something. Most of Sudie's people were still convinced it was Dawson who had done it. And although Stella was known to act strangely at times, most thought her incapable of such a hideous murder. Everyone had an opinion, but none knew for sure.

The morning of the funeral was the coldest day of the year and a dampening mist filled the air. Cora, Lon, John, and Dawson stood near Sudie for the last time. Cora stood with her arm across Dawson's shoulder and cried. Dawson held little Beth tightly in his arms and wept. Beth touched her daddy's face with her tiny hand and wiped away the tear that rolled down Dawson's cheek. Dawson held his baby girl close. She put her arms around his neck and whispered in his ear. "Don't cry, Daddy." She was too young to understand what was happening. She had asked for her mama several times, only to be told her mama was in heaven.

Other mourners stood near the fireplace, trapping the heat with their bodies. The room felt almost as cold as it was outside. Around the room, sniffles and moaning could be heard as people mourned their loss.

At around nine thirty, a black hearse pulled into the yard. Two men dressed in long, black overcoats and black top hats got out of the hearse and made their way to the door. Dawson's aunt Ruth opened the door. The two men walked in, their faces solemn and drawn. One of them walked over to the casket and touched Dawson on the shoulder.

"Mr. Hubert," he said, "it's time to take the body to the church."

Dawson looked at him through bloodshot eyes and simply nodded his head.

"Are the pallbearers here?" the man asked.

Will and five other men stepped forward.

"We are the pallbearers," Will told the man.

The man in black nodded. "If you would, please, I will need three of you on one side and three on the other side."

Will, Sam Hawkins, and John Turner took their places on one side of the casket. George Honeycutt, Ralph Stanford, and Pate Kilgore took the other side. Together they lifted the casket from its stand and proceeded toward the door and into the yard. The second undertaker opened the back of the hearse, and the body was placed inside.

It was several miles to the church from Cora's house in the Mountain Creek community. Most people drove cars, but several sets of mules and wagons followed at a distance behind the parade of automobiles. A half hour later, the hearse arrived at the small white church. The pallbearers carried the casket inside and placed it near the front. The funeral directors brought in several sprays of flowers and placed them on either side of the casket.

Samson Newton and his family were already seated together on the left-hand side of the church. Dawson tried to speak to Samson and Althea, but both turned away. Massey looked at him with hate in her eyes.

"Stay away from us, Dawson," she said angrily. "We know ya killed Sudie. They may have arrested poor Stella, but they've arrested the wrong person. So just stay away from us, ya murderer."

Before Dawson could reply, Cora took him by the arm and led him over to the right side of the church. As other people entered, it was soon evident who believed what. Those who believed Dawson killed Sudie sat on the left side of the church. Dawson's family and friends sat on the right side. Soon the little church was filled to capacity.

Reverend Dewey took his place behind the podium. The reverend was a small man with a handlebar mustache and thinning white hair. His voice was high-pitched and his manner solemn.

"We are gathered here today to lay to rest a beloved friend, wife, mother, daughter, and sister, Sudie Mae Newton Hubert. Her death is a tragedy. For someone so young and full of life to be taken from us in such a horrible manner leaves all of us with questions. Why does God allow things like this to happen? I say to you, my friends, this is not God's doings. It is surely the work of the devil himself. Let us pray."

The congregation bowed their heads. Weeping could be heard from every pew and corner of the church.

Reverend Dewey began to pray. "Our heavenly Father, we ask you to bring comfort to those who are hurting. We pray you will take your child, Sudie Mae Hubert, into your kingdom so that she may walk on streets of purest gold. We pray her family will find comfort in knowing she is in a better place—a place where no evil can find her or misfortune can touch her. We also pray that the person who did this evil deed to poor Sudie will be found and punished. If not on this earth, Lord, in the fires of hell. We ask these things in Jesus's precious and holy name. Amen."

After the service was over, the pallbearers carried the casket to the cemetery, located next to the church. The mourners followed close behind. First was Dawson, who cradled Beth tightly in his arms. Next to him were Cora and Lon. Dawson's relatives and friends followed close behind. Behind them at a distance was Sudie's family and friends, those who believed Dawson to be Sudie's killer.

Ginny Honeysuckle sang "When the Roll Is Called Up Yonder" in her high-pitched soprano voice as people gathered around the soon-to-be resting place of Sudie Mae Hubert. Next to her was the grave of her baby boy, the one who had been still born a few years earlier. The marker on his grave read, "Baby Boy Hubert, Born Dead November 18, 1947."

A cold northern wind whipped across the graveyard, tossing dried, dead leaves into the air. Some landed against the larger grave markers, and some blew away to be forgotten like the unmarked graves of years past. A cold, misty rain coupled with tiny bits of ice began to fall. Onlookers pulled the collars of their coats up around their necks to help block the cold and rain. Others opened umbrellas and stood closer to one another.

Reverend Dewey kept the graveside service short. Once the crowd dispersed, the casket was lowered into the grave and Sudie Hubert was no more. Only her memory remained. Hers was a life short lived and a death beyond belief.

As Dawson, Cora, Lon, and Beth were getting into the car Dawson had borrowed from his boss, an angry woman's voice called out to him from across the churchyard.

"I hope ya rot in hell, Dawson Hubert!"

Dawson looked up. It was Althea Newton. She was shaking her clenched fist at him.

"I know ya killed her, Dawson," she yelled. "I hate ya! I hate all ya Huberts."

Dawson started to reply, but Cora discouraged him.

"Don't stoop to her level, Dawson. She's hurting. She's lost one of her young 'uns. Just let it be."

Dawson knew his mama was right. He was angry and hurting too. He'd not only lost the woman he loved, but he'd lost the baby he'd so looked forward to. Unless by some miracle his baby was found, he would never know if it was the son he so wanted or another girl like his precious little Beth. With a heavy heart, he slid into the driver's seat and closed the door. As they left the churchyard, Althea shook her fist at him one last time.

A week passed, and the search for baby Hubert was called off. Every inch of the woods around the house had been gone over time and again. If there ever was a baby hidden there, it had long since been eaten by wild animals or hidden so well it would never be found. Everyone had given up hope of ever finding the lost baby—everyone except Dawson. Every day he could be seen roaming the woods, turning over logs, moving dead limbs and branches, still searching for whatever might remain of his baby.

Two weeks passed, and Stella remained incarcerated in the Chilton County jail. Dr. Jacob Weber from Benton Mental Hospital was called in to evaluate Stella's mental condition. He arrived shortly after nine in the morning. The jailer was on break. However, Deputy Meed gave Dr. Weber Stella's file then showed him to her cell. As usual, she was pacing back and forth across the floor in front of the door.

Deputy Meed called to her. "Mrs. Hubert, I need ya to step back away from the door."

Stella stopped pacing and looked blankly at the two men. Dr. Weber spoke next, "Hello, my name is Dr. Weber. And you are?"

Stella did not answer but continued to stare at him with the same blank stare she had the day they found her sitting on the front porch in the cold.

Dr. Weber opened the file. "I see here your name is Stella Hubert. May I call you Stella?"

Still, there was no response.

Dr. Weber turned to Deputy Meed. "Please open the door now, Deputy."

The deputy slid the key into the lock and cautiously opened the door just wide enough for the doctor to pass. "Ya be careful, Doc," he warned. "She can turn violent at the drop of a hat."

The doctor stepped inside the cell next to Stella. "Shall we sit down, Stella?" he said, pointing to the cot.

To the deputy's surprise, Stella calmly sat down on the cot and the doctor sat down next to her.

"Can ya take me home now, Doctor?" she asked.

The doctor smiled at her. "Well, Stella, that all depends on you, now doesn't it? I need to ask you a few questions. Is that all right with you?"

She nodded her head in agreement.

"Do you know where you are?"

Stella looked around her cell. "I'm waiting for Will to come and take me to the hardware store. John will be mad when he sees there's blood on his axe. I have to get him a new one."

"How did blood get on the axe, Stella?"

"They did it."

"Who is 'they'?"

Stella's eyes began to dart back and forth. "The ones with the voices. I knew they would get her."

"Who did the voices get?"

"They got Sudie. Sudie's blood is on the axe. John'll be mad when he sees blood on his axe. When is Will coming back to get me? I have to get John a new axe."

The doctor ignored her comment. "Stella, did you see who killed Sudie?"

Stella's demeanor quickly changed. "I told ya the ones with the voices did it. I tried to warn her, but she wouldn't listen. She said I was crazy. I don't like Sudie. She killed my baby."

Stella stood up and began to pace back and forth across the cell. This alarmed Deputy Meed. "Do ya want to come out'a there now, Doc?" he asked.

Dr. Weber shook his head no.

"Stella, when Sudie killed her baby, what did she do with it?"

Stella stopped dead in her tracks and looked directly at Dr. Weber. "I told ya she killed my baby," she shouted. "Mine not hers!"

The doctor conceded. "What did she do with *your* baby?"

"I took it from her and hid it. I hid it from the voices too."

"Where, Stella? Where did you hide the baby?"

"I can't tell ya."

"Why can't you tell me?"

"It's a secret."

"You can tell me, Stella. I won't tell anyone. I'm good at keeping secrets."

Stella began stomping her feet and shaking her head from side to side. She hissed and growled. Her long, dark hair hung in strings across her face.

"No! No! No!" she yelled. "I can't tell anyone. They will kill ya if I tell. Now get out! I don't want ya here no more!"

Dr. Weber realized he was getting nowhere with Stella. He motioned for Deputy Meed to open the cell door. When he was on the outside of the cell, Stella calmed down. He decided then and there that Stella was definitely not competent to stand trial and he would not be able to get any information out of her about the murder or the baby. He recommended she be placed in the mental institution for an indefinite period of time.

When Cora got word Stella was to be transported to the mental hospital in Tuscaloosa, she decided to visit her. After all, she was her sister-in-law. Cora called her sister, Ruth, and asked her to take her to Clanton. Ruth agreed. The next morning, Ruth drove from Prattville to Cora's house at Mountain Creek. Cora hesitated about taking Beth, but she had no choice. Both John and Dawson had gone back to work, so she was Beth's main caregiver.

Ruth pulled her car into the yard and blew her horn to let Cora know she had arrived. Cora pulled on her coat, grabbed her purse, helped Beth with her coat, and quickly headed out the door toward the car. Ruth leaned across the passenger seat and opened the door. Cora lifted Beth onto the bench seat of the 1949 Chevrolet. Ruth took her hand and helped her get seated between her and Cora.

Cora spoke first. "I shore will be glad when this weather turns warmer," she said as she positioned herself next to the window.

Ruth pushed down on the clutch with her left foot and put the car into first gear. "You and me both," she answered.

"I appreciate ya coming all the way up here to give us a ride to Clanton."

"Well, I figured we needed to go see Stella before they took her away. Ya reckon she's really the one who killed Sudie?"

"It's hard to imagine, I know," replied Ruth. "But I don't reckon they would be putting her in the crazy house if she wasn't guilty."

"Will told me they was taking her there so they could determine if she could stand trial. Dawson thinks it was her."

"Well the Newtons sure don't."

"I know. They sent Dawson the ugliest letter you've ever read in yo'r life. It was just awful."

"I don't think they would believe Dawson didn't do it, even if Stella confessed."

"I don't think so either."

Beth was holding a small doll in her arms. The doll's eyes opened and closed each time it was laid back and then raised up.

Ruth noticed the doll. "I like your doll, Beth. What is her name?"

Beth looked up at Ruth and smiled. "Name Dolly," she said.

Ruth laughed. "That's a good name for a doll."

It was approximately twenty miles to the county jail where Stella was. The two ladies talked about Sudie's murder and little else. When they arrived, Ruth found a parking place out front. The three of them got out of the car. Cora carried Beth in her arms. Once inside she asked to visit with Stella. Sheriff Thornton told one of his deputies to escort them back to Stella's cell. They would have to talk through the bars, as the sheriff felt it was unsafe for them to be in the cell with her.

Beth was still holding her doll under her arm as they neared the cell. When they reached the cell, the deputy stepped to one side. Stella was sitting on her cot, her body rocking back and forth as though she was in an imaginary rocking chair.

Ruth and Cora stood directly in front of the cell door. Ruth spoke first.

"Stella, it's Ruth. How are ya?"

Stella stopped rocking and looked up. Her hair hung in oily strings across her face. Her eyes looked wild and distant. There was a distinct smell of body odor permeating through the room. For a moment, there was complete silence. Suddenly Beth's doll dropped to the floor. Then came a scream of sheer terror. Ruth looked toward Cora. Beth was attempting to climb over her grandmother's shoulder. She was acting as though she was scared to death.

Cora couldn't believe what was happening. Her grandchild was crying and screaming at the top of her lungs. Her shoes dug into the front of Cora's coat as her hands clawed at the air like a cat retreating up a tree while being chased by a vicious dog.

The deputy could see Cora was quickly losing control of the situation so he took a stance behind Cora. Beth literally dove into his arms. The deputy headed for the door, that led to the waiting area. Once they were through the door and Beth could no longer see Stella, she began to calm down.

Sheriff Thornton ran from his office to see what all the commotion was about. "What in tarnation is going on in there?" he called to his deputy.

"I don't rightly know, Sheriff," the bewildered deputy answered. "This little young 'un who came with the Hubert women went crazy when she seen our prisoner. She was doing her best to climb over her grandma like she was trying to get away from Stella."

Sheriff Thornton rested his right hand on the pistol, which hung low around his broad hips. "Looks to me like we've got the right person in jail after all," he said to the deputy.

A short time later, Cora and Ruth exited the prisoner's cell. Beth was calmer but still very upset. Cora took her from the deputy and comforted her grandchild as best she could. The sheriff stopped them as they headed for the door.

"Mrs. Hubert," he called.

Cora and Ruth stopped just short of the exit.

The sheriff patted Beth on the back. She hid her face in Cora's chest.

"What happened back there?" he asked.

Ruth and Cora explained what happened.

The sheriff scratched his head. "Well, ya know, I was worried we might have the wrong person in jail. But now...I think she may very well be the one who killed Sudie."

Beth turned her head toward the sheriff, looking at him through tear-filled eyes. Sheriff Thornton ruffled her hair. When he blinked, a tear rolled from the corner of his eye. His heart was full of sympathy for the poor, little motherless child.

Before leaving the warmth of the jail, Cora pulled the blue knitted cap, which hung behind Beth's neck, back onto her head. Beth put her small arms around her grandmother's neck.

"Go," she whispered.

Cora looked at the sheriff. "Sorry, but I think we need to get this young 'un home. She's been through enough for one day."

Sheriff Thornton nodded his head in agreement then added, "I think she's been through enough to last her a lifetime."

Ruth and Cora left the jailhouse and went directly to the car. Ruth opened the door for Cora and Cora slid onto the seat. Beth still clung to her like an ivy vine to a wall. Ruth closed the car door then hurried around to the other side. The cold wind whipped at her bare legs as she opened her own door. Neither of the women spoke until they were well out of town.

When Ruth looked toward Cora, she could see Beth

had fallen asleep. Only then did she speak of what had just happened.

"Cora, to be honest with ya, I had it in my mind that Dawson might have killed Sudie."

Cora waited a few minutes before she made a reply. "To be honest with ya, Ruth, I did too. I wouldn't want Dawson to know I said that. I know he's my son, and I love him dearly, but he does have a temper. The only thing that made me think he couldn't' a done it was the baby. Sudie would'a had to do something mighty bad for him to kill her and kill that baby."

"Yeah, I know what ya mean. He was really looking forward to the baby coming. Loftin thought maybe she birthed another dead baby and out of grief, Dawson killed her."

"Ya know, Althea and Samson believe it was Dawson. They've been chomping at the bit and wanting the sheriff to arrest Dawson."

"Well, frankly, I figured they would arrest him eventually. Even though he was supposed to be at work, he did leave for a while. But once I seen how that baby there reacted to seeing Stella, I don't think Dawson did it. I think the sheriff was right in saying he thought they had the right person in jail."

Cora stroked Beth gently across the back. "Poor little thing. She was shore scared when she seen Stella."

"I know. She climbed right out of your arms. It was a good thing that deputy was standing behind ya."

Cora stroked Beth again. "I won't be going back to see Stella no more. At least not while this young 'un is with me. I don't want to put her through that again."

"I don't blame ya. Besides, they're supposed to be shipping her off to Benton Hospital one day this week."

"Well if she's innocent, I hope they can help her. If she's guilty, I hope they keep her there till she rots."

Two days following the episode concerning Beth and Stella, an ambulance was commissioned to pick up Stella from the Chilton County jail. From there she was to be transported to Benton Hospital in Tuscaloosa. Two men dressed in white uniforms arrived at the jail around two in the afternoon. One of the men carried an envelope containing admission papers, that had to be signed by the officiating judge, Judge Leon Randall. The other man had a straitjacket draped across his arm. When the two men entered the building, Deputy Meeks was there to greet them. As soon as they were inside, he offered them his hand in greeting.

"Howdy, I'm Deputy Meeks. I sure am glad to see you fellers," he said, smiling. "That Stella Hubert is one woman I'll be glad to see go. She gives me the creeps."

The taller man stuck out his hand in response. "Glad to meet you, Deputy Meeks. I'm Roscoe Davis, and this is Melvin Roberts."

Melvin and the deputy shook hands next.

"Say, she's a might on the strange side, is she?" asked Melvin.

"You bet," answered Deputy Meeks. "Talks all the time like she's talking to somebody, except there ain't nobody there. She a might nasty too. We was gonna let her get a bath one day, but she came at us like a wild banshee. We ain't tried that since."

Roscoe laid the papers down on the desk by the front door. "Mentally ill people can be pretty tough to deal with. I could tell you some stories that would curl your toes."

Deputy Meeks shook his head and smiled. "I bet ya could at that."

Melvin picked up the envelope and handed it to the

deputy. "These papers need to be signed by the judge who ordered her into the hospital. Is he here?"

Deputy Meeks turned to Patsy Preston, the jail's secretary. "Can ya carry these over to the courthouse and have Judge Randall sign these forms?"

Patsy pushed her chair back from her desk and made a grunting noise as though she would do it but didn't like it. Her mid-length, straight skirt had a slit up one side, which touched just above her knee. Her strawberry-blonde hair fell in soft waves across her milky-white shoulders. Melvin took note of her robust yet curvy figure. When she noticed him looking at her, she smiled.

"Would you mind handing me my coat, sir?" she said in a slow, southern drawl. "It's hanging there on the rack behind you."

Melvin quickly reached for the coat and offered to help her put it on.

Patsy smiled sheepishly as she allowed Melvin to assist her. Then she looked at Deputy Meeks. "You deputies need to get some learning in manners from this one. He knows how to treat a lady."

Deputy Meeks took offense at what she was implying. "When I meet a lady, I'll keep that in mind," he snapped back.

Patsy stuck up her nose at Deputy Meeks and reached for the papers. As she brushed past Melvin, she leaned in and whispered something in his ear. Melvin turned a deep shade of red.

"Don't mind her, fellers," said Deputy Meeks. "She's about as nutty as Stella Hubert is."

After Patsy was out the door, Melvin and Roscoe asked to see their new patient. As soon as the deputy opened the door that led to the cells, they could smell her foul odor.

"Whew!" remarked Roscoe. "You were right about her

smelling bad. First thing we'll need to do when we get her to the hospital will be to clean her up."

Melvin agreed. "I expect we'll need to de-lice her too."

Deputy Meeks slid the key in the lock, but before he turned it, he looked at the two men standing beside him. "Now look here, fellers," he warned, "she ain't gonna take kindly to being bothered. Like I said, we ain't even been able to let her get a bath. Things will likely get somewhat nasty. Just be ready for anything is all I'm saying."

Melvin and Roscoe looked at one another then gave a nod to the deputy to let him know they were ready. The door creaked loudly as Deputy Meeks swung the heavy iron bars open. Stella saw her chance and took it. Faster than lightning, she jumped up from the cot and shot out the door like a bullet. Roscoe grabbed her by her arm, but she pulled loose from his hold. Melvin tried to wrap the straitjacket around her, but she managed to take it from him and tossed it on the floor.

Neither of the men could believe how strong she was. Deputy Meeks made little effort to help them, as he had dealt with Stella more times than he really wanted to; the long scratch mark down the side of his face was proof of how violent she could be. He decided he'd let them handle her.

As soon as Stella broke loose from Roscoe a second time, she headed directly for the door that led to the main entrance. Deputy Meeks had figured on them having problems and fortunately had locked the door behind them. When Stella realized she couldn't get out that door, she turned on the two men again, even angrier than before.

"Let go of me!" she yelled. "I have to get the baby! He's got the baby!"

This was the first time anyone had heard Stella mention the baby since Dr. Weber had visited several days earlier. Deputy Meeks called out to Roscoe and Melvin.

"Wait, fellers! Back off a minute."

The two men backed away from Stella. She continued yelling at them about getting the baby. Deputy Meeks decided to see if he could make sense out of what she was saying.

"Mrs. Hubert," he said in a calm, quiet voice, "who has the baby? Do ya know who has the baby?"

At that point, Stella calmed down a bit. She looked at Deputy Meeks, her eyes dull and empty. "He has the baby. The man has the baby."

"What man, Mrs. Hubert? What man has the baby?"

Stella began acting as though someone or something was about to jump at her out of the shadows. She was clearly frightened and even more confused. She ran back into her cell, crawled onto her cot, pulled the dirty, sweat-soaked blanket up around her neck, and hovered in the corner like a browbeaten dog. Deputy Meeks tried talking to her again.

"Mrs. Hubert, do ya know who has the baby?"

Stella's eyes darted back and forth from one corner of the cell to the other. Her teeth began to chatter, making loud clicking sounds. Suddenly she started humming. The three men listened intently to the melody. Roscoe was the first to speak.

"She's humming that lullaby song Mama used to sing to the babies."

Deputy Meeks agreed. "I think it's called 'Brahm's Lullaby.'"

"Well, I don't know what it's called, but that's what she's humming all right. That woman is one strange cookie."

"Do you reckon she seen somebody kill Miss Sudie and take the baby?" asked Melvin.

"Beats me," replied Deputy Meeks. "This case has been confusing from the start. First she tells her neighbor someone killed a woman and threw a baby down the well. But when asked, she don't know who the woman was that was killed. We checked the well, and there was no baby. Who knows? If you ask me, I think she's acting as crazy as a long-tailed cat in a room full of rocking chairs."

Roscoe scratched his head. "Well, then let's get her to the crazy house. Maybe some of the doctors at Benton can figure it out."

To their surprise, Stella did not put up a fight the second time. They placed her in the straitjacket and escorted her out of the jail house without further incident. Deputy Meeks was glad to see her gone. Now at least the cleaning lady who came once a week could clean out the cell, wash the dirty linens, and fumigate the place.

Two hours later, the ambulance arrived at Benton Hospital and Roscoe and Melvin delivered Stella and her paperwork to the admissions office. Up to that point, she had remained unusually calm and refrained. Shortly after she was admitted, she was taken to see the attending physician. There, her overall health was evaluated, and orders were written up for her care. Her first stop after leaving the doctor's office was the showers.

When first established, Benton Hospital was one of the finest mental hospitals in the South. However, with the onset of the Great Depression, the hospital was soon overrun with patients. More than five thousand mentally challenged people were housed there. Patients roamed the halls at will. Some were soaked with urine and smelled of feces. Clearly the hospital was inundated with more patients than the overworked staff was capable of caring for. Stella's caregiver, Bernice Stapler, towered over her a good eight inches. Stella looked up at Bernice as though she was about to cry. Bernice spoke to her in a deep stern voice, "First thing we've got to do is get you cleaned up, Mrs. Hubert."

"My name is Stella."

Bernice frowned. "Stella, huh? Well, Stella, I don't know what got you in this place, but God bless you honey."

Bernice escorted Stella to the shower room. Green paint was peeling off the walls in places. While Stella removed her clothes, Bernice turned on the water. The shower head was cracked, sending water spraying out in all directions. Reluctantly, Stella stepped under the water. It was barely warm but it felt good on her aching muscles. Bernice handed Stella a bar of soap.

"Don't forget to wash your nasty hair."

When bath time was over, Stella was given a gray cotton gown and a pair of house slippers. Bernice combed Stella's hair, pulled it back from her face, and secured it with a rubber band. She was then taken to her room.

Stella shared an eight foot by ten foot room with four other women. There were two cots in the room, similar to the army cots she'd seen in pictures. Four blankets and two pillows lay at the foot of each cot. The cots were occupied by two women who looked to be in their early forties. One of them was cradling a rag doll in her arms. She was rocking back and forth, humming softly to her doll. Her hair was dark on the ends, but at the scalp, it was almost solid white. She did not acknowledge their presence but continued to keep her eyes fixed on the doll in her arms. Stella looked at the woman on the other cot. Her arms were covered with deep scratches and scars. Drool dripped from the corners of her half-opened mouth.

"That's Mary," said Bernice. "She don't say much. Over there is Clara. She went insane when her baby died."

Someone came up behind Stella and started smelling her hair. Stella whirled around to see who it was. She was just a young girl with slightly slanted eyes and a peculiar look about her. She smiled at Stella. "He O," she said, her words unclear.

She reached for Stella's hair and began smelling it again.

Bernice could see she was starting to frighten Stella so she grabbed the girl's arm and pushed her to the floor. "Leave her be, Rose!" she demanded.

She handed Stella a pillow and two blankets. "You'll have to sleep on the floor. The cots are taken. Rose sleeps over there in that corner, and Zelda sleeps in the other corner. I don't know where they expect you to sleep. All I can say is find a piece of floor and make yourself comfortable. I don't know why they keep bringing people here. We don't have room for the ones we've got, but they keep sending them anyway."

Stella took the bedding and sat down in the far corner of the room between the wall and the cot where Mary was sitting. She could hear screaming coming from somewhere in the building. She could hear a dreadful moaning sound coming from somewhere down the hall. She lay down on the cold tile floor in a fetal position, put the pillow under her head, and covered her entire body and head with the blankets she'd been given. Beneath the covers, she found a feeling of comfort and resolve. She did not understand why she was in this awful place. These people were crazy. She wasn't crazy. She wanted to go home. She wanted to be away from the screaming, the moaning, and the stench. Huddled there in the corner, she eventually fell asleep.

At six o'clock sharp, Stella was awakened by an alarm that echoed loudly down the hospital corridors. The alarm was set to alert the patients that it was time to make their way to the dining area for supper. Those who were unable to make it on their own were occasionally helped by the attendants or by other patients, who in their own way had enough faculties about them to know what the alarm meant. However, there were always some who lingered behind, which meant doing without.

The dining hall was large with long, stainless-steel tables placed end to end. The benches were attached to the tables. Food was served by hospital employees dressed in white uniforms, some of which were dotted with various grease and food stains. Their hair was secured tightly to their heads with a dark brown hairnet. Their attitudes and demeanor toward the patients left much to be desired.

A rather short, corpulent woman with cropped, jet-black hair was the person in charge of the dining hall. Her name was Lucy Stinson. Everyone called her Mama Lucy. She ran her kitchen and her dining hall with a stern voice and a less-than-appealing manner. Under her were two black women cooks. Bell was a tall, slender woman with a missing front tooth, which had been knocked out several months before when one of the patients threw her plate of food at her. Flossie was an average-sized woman with a wide nose and large lips, which looked as though she had been stung by a swarm of angry bees. A young white girl helper by the name of Jesse rounded out the lot. She was pale and rather frail looking, and her thin, blonde hair smelled of cigarette smoke.

Both dinner and suppertime menus consisted mainly of beans, potatoes, cabbage, and fried cornbread patties. If a person was lucky enough to get meat, it amounted to no more than a small piece of fatback tossed in for a bit of flavor. Breakfast was mainly biscuits and white gravy or corn mush. Patients stood in line and were allowed a tin plate, a spoon, and a tin cup. As they walked the food line, Bell and Flossie dumped a helping of whatever the food of the day happened to be onto their plates. At the end of the line, Jesse filled their cups with water or milk when it was available.

When Stella awoke to the sound of the supper alarm, she slowly eased the covers off her head and peeked out to see what was happening. Rose was standing over her, looking down.

"Time ta eat," she announced, smiling. "Tome wif me. I stow ya."

Stella could hear her stomach growling. Slowly she emerged from beneath her blankets. Rose extended her hand to help her get up. Stella was unsure at first, but Rose reminded her of a little child. She reached out to her, and Rose helped pull her to her feet.

"Ollow me," said Rose.

Rose walked with an unsteady gait, as though one of her legs did not want to cooperate. As they moved down the hallway, Rose held tightly to Stella's hand. Soon the halls were filled with other patients making their way down the stairs toward the dining hall. Stella began to notice the people around her. One woman appeared to be picking something off her arms and would then toss it on the floor. Small streaks of blood, some dry and some fresh, lined the length of her arms and her legs too. Another woman pulled at her hair, twisting it around her finger until it was extracted from her scalp. She had no eyebrows, eyelashes, or hair on her arms. What little hair was left on her head was exceedingly sparse.

Some of the women talked to themselves, mumbling words unidentifiable by those around them. Others plucked at unseen objects in midair. Others cried; some moaned. One woman danced with an unseen partner as though they were in a ballroom, hearing music only she could hear. Some people were angry; others were sad; and still others appeared happy and carefree in a world of their own making. Again Stella wondered why she was here. *These people are crazy,* she thought to herself. *Surely they know I don't belong here. I need to get in touch with John so he can come and get me.*

The dining hall was located down a flight of stairs that led into the basement. When they reached the dining hall, a long line had already begun to form. Rose and Stella took their places behind a young man who looked to be in his mid-twenties. This was the first time Stella had seen a male. He was a rather short, thin man with dark hair and crooked teeth. He also appeared to have a large knot on his back, which made him look as though he was slumped over. She glanced around the room and realized there were many other men in the dining hall. They too had various oddities about them. The young man in front of them turned to Rose.

"Hi, Rosie," he said, smiling.

Rose flipped her shoulder-length brown hair with the edge of her hand and turned up her nose at him. "Me ame be Rose. No Rosie," she corrected him.

He smiled again. "I know, Rose, but I like Rosie better."

Rose raised her voice. "No Rosie! Rose!"

Mama Lucy caught wind of the conversation between the young man and Rose. "You two keep it down!" she yelled from behind the counter. "No talking in line!"

Rose put her finger to her lips and made a hissing sound. "E kuiete, Bud. Ma Ucy get mad."

Bud turned around and picked up a plate from atop the stack of plates then handed it to Rose. Instead of keeping it, Rose passed it to Stella. He and Rose did the same with the spoons and cups. When each of them had what they needed, they moved down the food line. That night's menu consisted of navy beans and cabbage. Bud pushed his plate toward Bell. She dipped a large spoonful of beans onto his plate.

"Thank ya," he told her.

"Yeah, yeah," replied Bell. "Move along, move along."

Next Flossie dipped a spoon of cabbage onto his plate and placed a piece of fried cornbread on top.

"Thank ya," said Bud.

Flossie smiled. "You're welcome, Bud."

At the end of the line stood Jesse. Tonight was a water night. The milk truck that delivered milk to the facility had not shown up that day, so Jesse filled Bud's cup with water. Behind him, Rose became agitated.

"No 'ater. Rose 'ant 'ilk."

"I'm sorry, Rose," Jesse said. "There is no milk tonight. Maybe tomorrow."

Again, Rose declared her wants even louder than before. "Rose 'ant 'ilk. No 'ater!"

Bud tried to console Rose, but she was adamant about her desire for milk.

"Rose 'ant 'ilk!" she cried.

Mama Lucy motioned for one of the guards. It so happened Roscoe, the guard on duty, was one of the men who had escorted Stella to her new home. As Roscoe made his way toward the food line, Rose continued to insist on having milk and not water. She began to stomp her feet and even threw her plate on the floor, Other patients were becoming agitated by the disruption. By the time Roscoe reached her, she was in a full-fledged temper tantrum.

Mama Lucy shouted to Roscoe, "Get her out'a here! Take her back to her room!"

Roscoe grabbed one of Rose's arms and forced it up her back. Rose cried out in pain.

"Me be 'ood! Me 'rink 'ater! Me 'ungry. No go 'ack to 'oom!"

Mama Lucy offered her no slack. "Get her out'a here, I said."

Roscoe escorted Rose out of the dining hall and back to her room. By the time they reached her room, she was crying. Roscoe felt sorry for her, but there was nothing he could do.

"Sorry, Rose. You stay here now and mind your manners. You don't want to end up in the padded room, do you?"

Rose shook her head no but continued to weep. "Me 'ungry, 'Oscoe," she said between sobs.

Roscoe walked away without looking back.

Bud motioned Stella to follow him over to one of the tables where several others were already seated. Stella eased onto the bench and placed her plate and cup in front of her. When Bud sat down beside her, she leaned close and whispered, "Where did they take Rose?"

Since they weren't supposed to talk while eating, Bud whispered back, "They took her to her room."

"Will they give her some food?"

"No. She will have to wait till morning to eat."

Stella's eyes scanned the room to make sure no one was watching, then she reached for a piece of fried bread and slipped it into her pocket. After that, she picked up her spoon and began to eat the beans and cabbage. They needed salt and a bit of pepper, but there was none to be seen on any of the tables. Despite the bland taste, Stella ate everything on her plate. When she was finished, she took her plate, cup, and spoon, and placed them alongside the other dirty dishes waiting to be washed. Then she made her way back to her room.

When Stella got to her room, the door was closed. She could hear Rose crying softly. She opened the door and went inside, closing the door behind her. Mary, Clara, and Zelda were still not back from eating. Stella walked over to where Rose sat crying in her corner of the room.

"Rose."

Rose looked up. Her eyes were red and swollen. "Rose 'ungry."

"I know, child. I have something for ya."

Stella reached into her pocket and took out the piece of cold fried bread and handed it to Rose.

"It ain't much, but maybe it will hold ya over till morning."

Rose took the bread, and a wide grin replaced the tears. "I 'ove 'ou, Tella."

Stella didn't respond. Instead, she walked over to her corner of the room and sat down, covering herself with her blanket. Before pulling the blanket up over her head, she looked at Rose.

"Ya eat up now, Rose. Everything's gonna be all right. Stella will take care of ya. Just don't ya cry no more."

A month had passed since Sudie's murder and the house where the murder took place had been abandoned. Dawson and Beth remained at his mama and daddy's house. John had moved in with his sister, Vera, in Vida. For fear he would have to pay for Stella's psychiatric care, he had also filed for a divorce from Stella.

Although Stella was a probable suspect in the murder, there were still those who were convinced Dawson was the culprit. Everywhere he went, people stared while others turned their backs to him. When Dawson or any of his family walked into a room, whispers and strange looks replaced "good mornings" and welcoming "hellos." Dawson's boss had even decided to lay him off when some of the other men refused to work with him.

Once the crime scene was released, Dawson decided to see what pieces of furniture and belongings, if any, he could salvage. As springtime approached, an early warm spell replaced the chill associated with winter months in the South. Dawson decided it was as good a time as any to face the scene where Sudie's life had ended. Cora asked him if he wanted her to go along, but he refused her offer, saying he felt it would be easier facing it alone.

Rube Morrow loaned Dawson his pickup. Dawson arrived at the house around ten that morning. He pulled into the yard and shut off the engine. Next to the house, near the steps, he noticed there were daffodils starting to bud out. He thought back to the day when Sudie planted the bulbs. She loved the bright yellow blooms. She said they were her favorite flowers because it meant warmer weather and spring were just around the corner. *She would have loved seeing them in bloom,* he thought to himself.

Slowly, Dawson got out of the truck and headed for the front porch. Both doors on either side of the porch were closed. He opened the screen door and then the wooden door. When he stepped into the room he had once shared with his wife and daughter, he became instantly light-headed, much like the day he'd walked past the room and smelled death. It was a reaction he had not expected. He looked at the floor. Dried, caked-up blood covered the floor in the area near the dresser and in front of the fireplace. Bloody footprints from several adults led from the bloody scene into the kitchen and back again. Smaller footprints, which he knew to be that of his little girl, were also intermingled with the larger ones. As he stood looking at the scene, he began tracing the blood splatter up the side of the wall. As it neared the ceiling, he noticed a clump of tissue with a thick strand of dishwater-blonde hair hanging from it. Sudie's hair. He broke down and began to cry. He quickly retreated out the door and onto the porch.

Whatever is left in the house will just have to remain there, he thought as he headed toward the steps. His head was spinning and beginning to pound. He was about to leave when he remembered the one thing he did want to keep, not for himself, but for his little girl. Regardless of how he felt, he had to go back inside. He had to get the ballerina. It was very special to Sudie, and Beth loved it too. He wanted to save it for Beth so she would have something that belonged to her mama.

Taking a deep breath, Dawson returned to the blood-spattered room. Sudie kept the ballerina on the table beside their bed. He would get it and get out as quickly as possible. However, when he reached the table, the figurine was nowhere to be seen. He knelt down and searched under the bed. He looked behind the couch, under the table, behind the dresser, on the mantle. Clearly, it was gone—gone like the baby he had hoped for, gone like the woman he had loved.

The next morning Stella was awakened again by the sound of a loud clanging alarm. To her surprise, she had slept all night with no voices to hinder her sleep. She actually felt refreshed for the first time in months. When she pulled the covers off her head, Rose was standing over her, looking down.

"'Ood 'orning, Tella," she said cheerfully, extending her hand to her newfound friend. "'Et's go eat."

Stella allowed Rose to help her up again. Upon standing, she realized her body was sore and stiff from sleeping on the hard floor. She would have to remember to put one of the blankets on the floor to act as padding. Together, she and Rose walked hand in hand to the stairway and down the steps to the dining hall. Before they walked into the hall, Stella stopped Rose.

"Remember, Rose. No talking in line. We don't want ya to git in trouble again."

Rose put her finger to her lips and pretended to zip her mouth shut. Stella smiled as they both walked to the end of the line. Morning breakfast was the same as usual: hard, cold biscuits and water gravy. Fortunately for all concerned, the milk truck had run early that morning. Rose was able to get her milk. The two women went to the table where Bud was sitting and took their seat across from him.

Rose smiled at Bud. "Hi, Bud."

Stella cautioned Rose about being too loud. They finished their meal in silence. The only noise in the hall was someone banging a spoon on the table. After a few minutes, Mama Lucy ordered the morning guard to remove that person from the hall, whereupon the person was promptly escorted back to his room. When breakfast was finished, they were allowed to go to one of two day rooms. The rooms were located at the far end of the building on the second and third floors. Stairs went from the first to the third floor. The business offices and doctors' quarters were on the first floor. Women were housed on the second floor and men on the third floor. The day rooms could be used by either men or women. It was the only time, other than when they were eating, that they were allowed access to the opposite sex. The day room on the second floor had several tables with chairs along the outer walls. A nurses' station was located to the right of the entrance door. Medicines were dispensed to patients as soon as they came into the room.

Stella liked the day room. Tall windows at the end of the room let in a lot of light. Sometimes the windows were left open to let in fresh air. Heavy bars had been installed over the window openings to make sure no one could jump out. There was also an old piano in one corner of the room. An old, gray-haired gentleman sat playing "Chopsticks" over and over until one of the guards closed and locked the piano. The old man laid his head down on the piano and cried.

Stella, Rose, and Bud were looking out the window at a beautiful redbird making its nest in the eve of the building. It would fly away in search of building materials. Shortly afterward, he would return with a twig or piece of string, hand it to his mate, then fly away again in search of other useful materials. While he was gone, the female would busy herself with the making of the nest.

"Stella Hubert," a voice called from the far end of the day room. "Stella Hubert. I need you to come to the nurses station."

Stella looked toward the nurses station. A rather tall, thin woman with steel-gray hair and horn-rimmed glasses pushed low on her nose was calling her name.

"I wonder what she wants," Stella said to no one in particular.

Bud spoke first. "Maybe she wants to give ya some medicine. Rose and I get medicine. They say it keeps us from acting crazy."

Rose continued to watch the incoming redbird hand off another twig to his mate. "It 'akes me sheepy."

Stella thought about ignoring the nurse, but she had seen what going against the rules could do. Slowly she started toward the nurses' station.

"Ee ya' 'ater, Tella," called Rose.

Stella did not look back but raised her hand to let Rose know she had heard her. When she reached the nurses' station, she noticed the nurse was holding a clipboard with a long list of names on it.

"Are you, Stella Hubert?" she asked.

Stella nodded yes.

"Fine then. My name is Nurse Edna. Dr. Weber wishes to have a session with you in his office."

She pointed to a big black man with a shaved bald head and massive arms.

"Moses will show you where it is. Just follow him."

Moses opened the day room door without saying a word and proceeded to the stairway. Stella followed at a safe distance. When they reached the first floor, Moses walked down the corridor and stopped in front of a closed door. A brass sign on the door read "Dr. Jacob A. Weber." Moses knocked, and a voice inside bid him to enter. Moses opened the door but did not go inside. Instead, he stepped aside and motioned for Stella to enter. Cautiously, Stella stepped into Dr. Weber's office.

Dr. Weber sat behind a large oak desk. On his desk were pictures of a pleasant looking woman and two young children. Stella assumed they were most likely his wife and children. There was also a stack of manila folders at least two feet high and a black desktop telephone. Along one wall was a bookcase with more books than Stella had seen in her entire life. On another wall were graduation certificates from universities where Dr. Weber had studied to become a doctor. Dr. Weber stood up from his tall-backed, brown, leather chair to greet Stella.

"Mrs. Hubert, nice to see you again. Please have a seat on the couch."

Stella looked toward where the doctor was pointing. Along the other wall was a long, brown, leather couch matching the chair. She moved toward the couch and eased down onto the sofa. She found it to be very soft and very comfortable.

Dr. Weber walked over to where she was sitting.

"Are you comfortable? Would you like to lie down? You may if you wish."

Stella declined.

Dr. Weber pulled up a chair next to the couch and sat down.

"I'm sure you're wondering why you are here. I will answer that question for you. You are here to determine if you are responsible for the murder of Sudie Hubert and her unborn baby. You are also here to determine if you are sane enough to stand trial for that murder."

The mere mention of Sudie's murder sent Stella into a deep state of anxiety. Her eyes became blank and began darting back and forth, looking from one side of the room to the other. She began to wring her hands and tremble. A deep furrow formed across her brow.

Dr. Weber could clearly see the intrusive effects the mentioning of Sudie's murder caused. "There is no need to get upset, Stella. It is all right if I call you, Stella?"

She did not answer or look directly at him at any time.

The doctor opened his notebook and took a pen from his white lab coat. "I'm going to ask you some questions, Stella.

Answer them as clearly and thoughtfully as possible. Is your name Stella Hubert?"

No answer.

"Do you live on Mountain Creek Road?"

No answer.

"Is your husband's name John Hubert?"

Stella stopped wringing her hands and dropped her head. "I need to get John a new axe. He's gonna be mad something fierce when he finds out there's blood on his axe. Will was gonna take me to the store to get a new one, but he lied. He didn't take me to the store. He took me to jail. Now y'all done brought me here. Ya think I'm crazy, but I ain't."

"Well, Stella, that is what I'm here for. I have to determine if you need to stay here or go back home. If you go home, you'll be tried for murder unless you can tell me what happened to Sudie Hubert. Can you do that, Stella? Can you tell me in your own words what you saw the day Sudie Hubert was murdered?"

Stella's eyes began darting back and forth. "I told ya already. The voices killed her. The voices shot her. They hit her in the head with a stick of stove wood. Then they chopped her open and stole the baby. My baby. I tried to stop him, but it was too late. He threw my baby down the well. I wanted to get him out, but it was too deep. If only Sudie had listened to me. She should'a never let him in. I knew what he was up to. I knew he was gonna kill her. She should'a listened."

"Stella, did you see the person who killed Sudie? Can you describe him to me?"

Stella got to her feet and began pacing the floor. "No, I didn't see nobody, but I heard him all right. I been hearing him for a long time. I knew he was just waiting till it was time for my baby to be born. I tried to warn her, but she wouldn't believe me."

"Do you know where he took Sudie's baby?"

Stella suddenly became enraged. "I told ya it was my baby. Mine! She didn't have no business with another baby. She'd just kill it like she done the other one."

Dr. Weber could see they were getting nowhere with his line of questioning. Although hers was an interesting case, there were twenty-five more cases to attend to before he could go home to his family for the day. He scribbled some orders for medicine on a pad, closed Stella's folder, and returned to his chair behind the desk.

"That will be all for today, Stella. You may go back to whatever you were doing. We will come back to this at a later time."

Stella opened the door. Outside the door, Moses was waiting to escort her back to the day room. Before they walked away, Dr. Weber called to Moses.

"Moses, take these orders to Nurse Edna. Make sure she understands that Mrs. Hubert is to get started on her medicine today."

Moses took the paper from Dr. Weber.

"Yes, sir. I shorely will."

Moses stepped out into the hallway. Stella was leaning against the wall, waiting for him. As they were making their way back to the day room, Moses turned to her.

"How did your first session go, Mrs. Hubert?"

"That doctor's as crazy as a betsy bug."

Moses laughed. "I 'pect you're right, Mrs. Hubert. I 'pect you're more right than ya think."

Dawson decided to look for a job in the nearby larger city of Montgomery. He applied at several places, including a trucking company. He had never driven a big eighteen-wheeler, but he figured it couldn't be much different than the big logging trucks he'd driven when he worked for the sawmill. While job hunting, he also looked for a house where he and his family could be close to his work. He found such a place on Hull Street. It was a big two-story house with a small front yard and a sidewalk running along the edge of the street. The back-yard was big and spacious and was fenced. He liked that. He also liked the fact it had an indoor toilet and running water. No more going outside to the outhouse or drawing water from a well. The rent was twenty-five dollars a month plus utilities. That was twice what they'd been paying at the old place. Still, he figured if he did get the job at the trucking company or one comparable to it, he could easily afford the added cost. Mrs. Williams, the lady who owned the house, asked for ten dollars upfront to hold it for him. It was his last ten dollars, but he didn't want to miss out on renting the property. A week later, he was hired by Seamon Trucking Company. His base start-ing pay was forty-five dollars a week plus mileage. That was more money than he had made working an entire month for the sawmill. That very weekend he moved his mother, father, and little Beth into their new house. Behind him he left the rumors, accusations, and taunting stares of a small, tight-knit community.

The day they moved into their new house was sunny and bright. Dawson felt as though he had left his old life behind him. To be sure, it would be a totally different existence from the country living he was used to. The few pieces of furniture his parents owned barely filled the downstairs bedroom. The spare bed was placed in an upstairs bedroom. Beth would have to sleep with Dawson until he could afford to buy her a new one. He thought about going back to their house in Mountain Creek again to try and salvage some of the furniture he and Sudie had shared. However, the thought of going back into that house sent shivers down his spine. Once he got on his feet, he would buy Beth a new bed. He would give her a new life, a better life.

As Dawson was spreading sheets on his bed, he heard the laughter of a small child. He walked over to the window, that faced the backyard. There he saw Beth playing with a small black-and-white kitten. The kitten was chasing a long piece of what looked like an old window cord. Beth was pulling the cord along as the kitten pounced forward to catch it. Each time it did so, Beth giggled loudly and pulled the cord away. Dawson smiled. It was good to see his little girl laughing again. In his heart he felt he had done the right thing by getting away from the place that had caused them so much pain. When Dawson finished making the bed, he went downstairs to the kitchen. Cora was putting away her dishes and cooking utensils. When he walked into the room, he smiled.

Cora was pleased. "It sure is good to see ya smiling again, son."

Dawson handed her a dish from the box she was unpacking. "It feels good to smile again, Mama."

"I know living in the city will take some getting used to, but with your new job and all, I think it will be a wise decision."

"I think so too, Mama."

When the box was empty, Dawson walked to the back door and looked into the yard. Beth was nowhere to be seen. Instantly he panicked. The thought of losing Beth too was unthinkable. If something happened to her, he would have no reason to live.

"Oh my God!" he yelled. "Where did Beth go?" In a flash he was out the door, down the steps, calling her name. "Beth! Beth! Where are ya?"

"Here me, Daddy," a small voice called from behind the steps.

Dawson whirled around. "Beth, ya scared me. What are ya doing under there?"

"Me find kitty."

Dawson walked over to the steps. There were ten wooden steps that led from the back door down to the ground. It was a perfect place for a little girl to play and hide away from the rest of the world. He thought to himself, *If only I had a place I could go to hide for a while. To be alone. To forget.* His thoughts were disrupted by the sound of not one but several kittens meowing. He bent down to look. Sure enough, there was not just one kitten but a litter of six. They appeared to be around six or seven weeks old. There were three black-and-white spotted ones, two solid black ones, and one solid white one.

"Well," said Dawson, "looks like a mama cat has left us a surprise."

Beth picked up one of the black-and-white kittens around its neck and came walking out from behind the steps. The kitten was hanging limp in her hands. Dawson took the kitten from her.

"Beth, don't hold the kitties around the neck, honey. You'll choke them. Hold them like this."

Dawson showed Beth how to carry the kitten by cradling it in her arms. The little kitten meowed his approval.

"Me kitty," said Beth.

"We'll see," said her father. "Let's take it inside and give it some milk."

Beth pointed to the other kittens. "Need milk too, Daddy."

Dawson smiled. "Okay, but we'll bring a bowl outside for the other kittens. I don't think your grandma would like having a whole litter of kittens under her feet while she's trying to get things unpacked."

Dawson watched as Beth gently carried the little kitten up the back steps. *So innocent,* he thought. *If only her mama was here to see her. She would be so proud.*

Stella and Rose spent most of their mornings in the day room. Stella would watch Rose as she danced clumsily around the room while the old man at the piano continued to play "Chopsticks" over and over again. One morning, Bernice was attending a rather sickly looking woman sitting at the table next to Stella.

"Bernice, how come that old man don't play something different? Is that the only song he knows?" Stella asked.

Bernice wiped the drool from around her patient's mouth before answering. "That old man was once a classical pianist. They say he used to play concerts up in New York City. Then he had a nervous breakdown. Ever since then, he just plays the same thing over and over again."

"What's his name?" Stella asked.

"Mr. Joseph Bice. But he likes to be called 'Bojangles.' Don't ask me why, 'cause I have no idea."

Stella decided to try to talk to him. She crossed the room to where the old piano was. It was obvious the piano had seen its better day. The varnish was cracking, and the stain was faded on one side where the sun shown through the window. Stella walked up to the piano and touched the man on his shoulder. He stopped playing and looked up at her.

"Howdy," she said. "My name is Stella Hubert. Bernice said ya liked to be called Bojangles."

He nodded his head in agreement.

"How about ya play something besides what ya been playing. That tune is getting a might old."

Once again the old man nodded his head in agreement then turned back to the piano. He raised both hands to the keys as if he was about to play something magical. Instead, he began banging out "Chopsticks" again.

There shore is a bunch of crazy folks in this here place, Stella thought to herself. *Glad I ain't one of them. Then again, maybe I am and just don't know it.* As she turned to walk away, she danced a little jig and smiled.

Part Three

The year was 1989. Stella had spent most of her adult life in the institution. She would soon be turning eighty. She had long since resigned herself to dying in the institution. Her longtime friend, Rose, had died in her sleep two years earlier. Stella was glad she died in her sleep. She felt that a soul as sweet and innocent as Rose should never have to suffer. Rose had no family, so the hospital buried her in the paupers cemetery in a grave marked with nothing more than a number on a small stone, placed at the foot of her grave. Stella figured she would be buried there too. She asked Bernice to make sure when her time came that she would be buried beside her friend.

It was seldom Stella saw any of her family anymore. It was as though she'd been forgotten by all who once knew her. The only people who ever came to see her anymore were her sister, Ida, and Ida's husband, Jack. Neither of them was in the best of health. As time had gone by, their once-a-month visits had turned into twice-a-year visits.

There were times when Stella could no longer remember why she was in the institution. Some days she waited by the front window for Will to come and take her to the hardware store. She worried that John would be really mad if he saw blood on his axe. She needed to get him a new one before he found out. She would often ask Bernice when Will was coming. Bernice would smile and say, "I'm sure he'll be along in a little while."

A week shy of Stella's birthday, she began to feel ill. Her lower back hurt terribly, and she had begun to run a fever. She had not been eating well for quite some time, and her weight had dropped considerably. All she wanted to do was lie in bed. Dr. Leon Lambert, the medical physician there at the institute, was called in to take a look at her. A complete physical exam and a battery of tests later, the diagnosis was confirmed to be cancer. It seemed to be a widespread cancer that affected her liver, kidneys, and stomach. The institute contacted the only relative it had on file, her seventy-two-year-old sister, Ida Jones.

Although Ida and Jack were barely able to take care of themselves, they agreed to take her in. Arrangements were made to have Stella released from the hospital and sent to Ida's house to live out her remaining days on earth.

Three days after her diagnosis, she was released into Ida's care. Bernice wheeled her to the front door in a wheelchair. In her lap was a brown paper bag that contained what few worldly items Stella owned. Ida and Jack were waiting for her in the lobby. They exchanged hugs and kisses. Stella looked weak. Dark circles surrounded her hollow eyes.

"How are ya?" Ida asked sadly.

Tears formed in Stella's eyes. "I'm fine."

Bernice felt a lump forming in her throat. She'd been Stella's nurse since the beginning. She was glad to see her leaving, but she felt sad too. She and Stella were not only nurse and patient but also had become friends. When Rose died, she and Stella were the only two people in the institution who cried. When Bojangles was released from the institution some five years earlier, it seemed as though she and Stella were the only ones who missed his music.

"You take care of yourself, Miss Stella," she said. "Don't go getting into anymore trouble."

Stella smiled. Jack tried to take the brown paper bag from Stella, but she pushed his hand away. Feeble but overjoyed, she walked out of the institution as a free woman.

Because she had neither income nor health insurance, she was referred to the Mount Vernon Health Clinic. Her caseworker was a rather handsome man by the name of Jake Tillery. He was tall with dark brown hair slightly graying at the temples and intense sky-blue eyes. He was polite and seemed truly concerned about getting Stella the best care possible. As she entered his office, he stood up and escorted her to the black folding chair which sat in front of his desk.

"How are you feeling today, Mrs. Hubert?" he asked.

Stella stopped as though she were surprised that he would ask how she was feeling. She grinned a weak but sincere smile. "I reckon I'm fair to middling," she answered.

Once Stella was comfortably seated, he went around to the other side of his desk and took a seat. A stack of files cluttered his desktop. He reached for Stella's file and began to read it to himself. He found it to be quite interesting.

From the moment Stella saw him, she thought about how

familiar he looked. She dug deeply into her memory to try and recall where she had seen him before but to no avail. His eyes looked especially familiar. She sat quietly while she waited for him to speak first. Eventually, he looked up from her file and smiled.

"My name is Jake Tillery. I will be your caseworker. I have arranged for you to see Dr. Robert Glazier. He is an outstanding cancer doctor. He will be working with you and your home care nurses to make you as comfortable as possible. Do you have any questions or concerns you would like to talk about today?"

Stella cocked her head to one side. "How come ya look like I ought to know ya? Have I seen ya before?"

Jake shook his head no. "I don't believe so, Mrs. Hubert. I guess I just have one of those faces."

"No, I've seen ya somewhere. I just can't place where it was."

"Well, I'm sure you'll think of it later. Now let's get you set up with an appointment to see the doctor."

"How come ya can't be my doctor?"

Jake chuckled. "I'm not a doctor, Mrs. Hubert. Although there are times I wish I was. I know the pay is certainly better."

"Ya ain't gonna send me back to the crazy house, are ya?"

"Of course not. You don't ever have to go back there again."

"Good. Them folks are crazy."

Jake smiled as he flipped through the rotary index sitting on his desk to find the number for Dr. Glazier. He picked up the phone and dialed the number. Stella continued to try to remember where she had seen him. After talking a few minutes with the doctor's receptionist, he covered the receiver with his hand and leaned across his desk.

"Will next Monday be okay?" he asked Stella.

"I reckon so. I ain't got nothing better to do."

Jake verified the date and time with the receptionist,

thanked her, then hung up the phone. He reached for one of his business cards, flipped it over, wrote the information on the back, and handed it to Stella.

"Once you have seen the doctor, his office will notify me. I will then make arrangements to have a home healthcare nurse come to your sister's house at least twice a week to take care of your personal needs. Be sure to keep your appointment, Mrs. Hubert. If there is a problem with transportation, give me a call, and I will make arrangements to have someone pick you up. Any questions?"

Stella looked at the card. "I don't reckon so."

Jake got to his feet. "Good. Shall I see you out to your car?"

"It's my brother-in-law's car," Stella corrected him. "I don't drive. Never learned how."

Jake moved around to the other side of his desk and helped Stella to her feet. "Of course. Well, with all the crazy drivers there are out there, there are times when I wish I had never learned to drive."

Stella rose to her feet. "Not as many as there were in the institution. Them folks there were crazy for shore."

Jake chuckled at her quick response. Carefully and slowly, he helped her into the hallway where Ida and Jack were waiting. When Jack saw them exit the office, he helped Ida to her feet.

"I'll pull the car around," he told her. "You and Stella wait by the front door."

Ida shook her head to let him know she understood.

Jake handed Stella over to her sister. Stella took Ida's hand, and they began their long walk down the hallway to the front of the building. Jake watched as they idled along. Neither of them was in the best of health. Ida walked stooped over from the osteoarthritis in her back. The two of them shuffled along at a snail's pace.

Beth pulled her metallic-blue, restored 1965 Ford Mustang into the driveway. On the other bucket seat, her daughter, Kayleen, sat with her arms folded across her chest in protest. Kayleen was a fifteen-year-old girl who thought she was twenty. She was Beth's only child and somewhat spoiled. She had shoulder-length blonde hair and stark blue eyes. Her premature, well-developed body made her look older than she actually was.

Mama Cora was standing just inside the screen door, waiting for her arrival.

"I don't know why I have to stay with Mama Cora," she protested. "I'll be sixteen in less than six months from now. I don't need a babysitter."

Beth put the car in park and turned the ignition to the off position. "Kayleen, we've been over this a dozen times. I am not leaving you alone by yourself. There are people out there who could hurt you, even kill you."

"I'm not a baby, Mama. I can take care of myself," Kayleen shot back.

Beth pounded her fists on the steering wheel. "No, Kayleen you're not a baby. But you are my daughter … and you will do what I tell you to do. So lose the attitude. Mama Cora is old, and she doesn't need the grief."

Kayleen watched as her great-grandmother opened the screen door and walked slowly across the porch. She waved her hand and smiled.

"Got time for a cup of coffee this morning?" she called to Beth.

Beth leaned her head out the window. "Sorry, Mama Cora. I'm running late, and I need to drop off some clothes at the dry cleaners. I'll see you after work."

She turned her attention back to Kayleen. "Behave yourself today, Kayleen. Help your grandma with her housework. She may not be with us much longer. I owe her my life, and I will not have you acting like a spoiled brat around her." She leaned over and kissed Kayleen on the cheek. "I love you, honey. Gotta run. I'll see you this afternoon."

Kayleen opened the car door and got out. Before her mother pulled away, she leaned down and said to her, "I love you too, Mama."

Beth smiled, put the Mustang in reverse, and pulled out of the driveway. As she was leaving, she stuck her arm out the window and waved a final good-bye. Kayleen waved back then headed for the porch. As she approached the steps, she called to her great grandmother.

"Morning, Mama Cora."

Mama Cora smiled. "Good morning, sweetheart. Have ya had breakfast yet?"

Kayleen reached the top of the steps. Mama Cora wrapped her arms around her great granddaughter and kissed her on the cheek.

"Ya look so purdy this morning. Did ya get a good night's sleep?"

"No, I haven't had breakfast yet. Thank you. And yes, I got a good night's sleep," she answered her great grandmother's questions consecutively.

Mama Cora put her arm around Kayleen's waist and pointed her toward the door. "All right, then let's get ya fed first thing. Then I need ya to help me take down the living room curtains. They need washing something awful."

"Actually, Mama Cora, I'm not hungry."

"Nonsense," Mama Cora protested. "You're a growing girl. Ya need to eat breakfast. It's the most important meal of the day. I heard that report on the *Today Show* just this morning."

Kayleen knew there was no use in arguing with her

grandma. At fifteen, Kayleen was a foot taller than Mama Cora, She wrapped her arm around her grandma's shoulder. Side by side, they made their way back to the kitchen.

"Ya sit down at the table, honey, and I will get ya some eggs cooked," said Mama Cora.

She walked over to the refrigerator.

"How many would ya like, and how would ya like them cooked?"

Kayleen pulled a wooden chair out and sat down at the yellow oilcloth-covered table.

"Just one scrambled will be fine," she answered.

"How about some grits and a sausage to go with your egg?"

"Sure. That would be great, Mama Cora."

As Mama Cora was heating the iron skillet, Kayleen put her elbows on the table and propped her chin in her hands. "Can I ask you a question, Mama Cora?"

Mama Cora smiled. "Of course, ya can ask me anything. Ya know that."

"What happened to Mama's mother? I know she died when Mama was young, but she never wants to talk about it."

Mama Cora placed a sausage patty in the hot skillet. Immediately it began to sizzle and pop. She looked beneath the pan and adjusted the flame to a lower temperature. Then she turned to look at Kayleen. "Your grandmother Sudie did not die, Kayleen. She was murdered."

Kayleen dropped her hands into her lap.

"Murdered?" she replied. "How? Who murdered her?"

Mama Cora broke an egg into the pan alongside the patty and stirred it with a wooden spoon. "Let me get your breakfast cooked, and I will tell ya all I know about it."

Kayleen sat quietly, pondering what her great-grand-mother had just told her. *Murdered*, she thought to herself. *No wonder my mother is afraid to leave me alone at home.* She could hardly wait for her breakfast to be finished so she could learn exactly what had happened.

Within minutes the sausage and egg were cooked. Mama Cora took a plate from the cupboard and slid the egg onto it. She dipped grits from a pot onto the plate next to the egg. From the oven she took out a leftover biscuit and added it to the plate. Lastly, she placed the sausage next to the grits then set it on the table in front of Kayleen.

"Would ya like milk or orange juice?" she asked.

"Milk is fine."

Mama Cora took a small glass from the cupboard and filled it with ice-cold milk from the refrigerator. She set the milk down next to Kayleen's plate then put the remainder of the milk back into the refrigerator. Only then did she sit down herself.

Eating the food her great-grandmother had prepared was the last thing on Kayleen's mind. She wanted to hear about her grandmother's murder.

"Okay, Mama Cora. Tell me about the murder."

Mama Cora laid her wrinkled arms on the table in front of her then clasped her hands together, one finger over the other. Dark age spots dotted her thin, fragile skin. Several dark bruises just beneath the skin looked worse than they actually were.

"Your mother was only two years old when Sudie was killed. I don't expect she even remembers anything about it. When she was younger, she would ask about it, but your grandpa Dawson didn't like to talk about it neither. It was nineteen fifty-one. The weather was freezing cold. Sudie and Dawson shared a house with your great-uncle, John and his wife."

"You mean Aunt Milly?"

"No, not Aunt Milly. Milly is John's second wife. His first wife's name was Stella. She was a rather peculiar woman."

Kayleen took a bite of grits and egg. "Peculiar how?"

"Well today the young 'uns would say her bread wasn't done."

Kayleen chuckled.

"Anyhow, I was giving Sudie a baby shower that afternoon."

"Grandma Sudie was pregnant?"

"Yeah, she was. As best we could figure, the baby was due in less than a month. Dawson was at work at a sawmill not too far from their house. She fixed his breakfast that morning. They talked about the shower and the baby coming soon. Dawson was hoping it was a boy. He wanted a boy real bad. Before Beth was born, Sudie had a baby boy, but he was born dead. It like to have killed the both of them. When yo'r mama was born, she was Dawson's pride and joy. Still, everybody knew he secretly wished for the new baby to be a boy."

"I never knew Mama had a brother who died."

"I expect there's a lot ya don't know about, Kayleen. That's why I'm telling ya now. So you'll know … now let me see, where was I?"

"Grandma Sudie cooked breakfast," Kayleen reminded her.

"Oh yeah. Well soon as Dawson was done eating, his boss come by to pick up him and John and take them to work. Dawson was almost to the car when he realized he'd forgot his wallet. He ran back to the house to get it. Sudie was standing just inside the door, waiting to hand it to him. She handed it out the door and waved to Dawson's boss man. That wallet is probably what kept your grandpa from being arrested for Sudie's murder."

"Grandpa Dawson?" said a surprised Kayleen.

"Yes, honey. Ya see, Dawson and Sudie fussed and argued a lot. He had a bad temper back then. Sudie left him one time and took Beth with her. 'Course Dawson wouldn't have none of that. Soon as he found out she was gone, he went to Samson and Althea's house and got her back. He told Sudie she could stay there if she wanted to, but Beth was coming home with him. I took care of Beth for nigh onto a week before Sudie come back."

Kayleen swallowed her last bite of grits. "I can't believe Grandpa Dawson used to have a temper. He's so docile now."

"He got that way after Sudie was killed."

"Tell me about the murder, Mama Cora," Kayleen insisted.

"Samson was the first person to find Sudie. Him and Althea was gonna bring Sudie, Stella, and Beth to the shower. When they got to the house, Stella was sitting on the front porch. They said she was just sitting there rocking back and forth with a strange look on her face. Samson spoke to her, but she didn't say a word, just kept on rocking. He knocked on the door, but nobody answered. He said he could hear Beth crying, so he opened the door and stepped inside. Sudie was laying in a pool of blood. She'd been shot, her head was bashed in, and the baby she was carrying was gone. Cut from her womb with an axe."

Kayleen's eyes filled with tears. "Oh my gosh, Mama Cora. That is terrible. Who could have done such a thing?"

Mama Cora patted Kayleen on her shoulder. "The first suspect was your grandpa. Everybody knew him and Sudie was bad to argue. The sheriff thought it was him for shore. So did Samson and Althea. That's one reason ya ain't never had much to do with them. They hate all us Huberts."

"I know. I never understood why they never come around. I think I've only seen them once or twice in my whole life."

"They wanted the sheriff to arrest Dawson. The thing that saved him was going back for his wallet. They knew she was alive when Dawson left for work, because his boss seen her wave to them out the door."

"So did they ever find out who killed her?"

"They arrested Stella Hubert."

"Uncle John's first wife?"

"Yep."

"What happened to her? Did they put her in jail?"

"She went to jail for a short time. Then they sent her to Benton Mental Institution."

"The crazy house?"

"As far as I know, she's still there. She'd be quite old by now. She may be dead, for all I know."

"Why did she kill Grandma Sudie? What was her motive?"

"I don't think anybody ever knew why. Like I said, she was a peculiar somebody. She threatened to kill me one time when I told one of the young 'uns I was gonna spank them."

"You're kidding me!"

"She pulled a knife on John one time too. I guess she was just a killing waiting to happen."

"Did they ever find the baby?"

"No, they never did. Stella told one of the neighbors it was thrown down the well. They sent your great-uncle, Will down there to see, but all he found was a dead chicken."

Kayleen crinkled up her nose. "Gross."

"Sudie's death liked to have killed Dawson. He couldn't go back to the house where it happened, it was just too painful. Later on he got laid off from the sawmill."

"Why?"

"Some of the other men who worked there refused to work with him anymore. There were a lot of folks who believed he was the one who killed Sudie. Ya wouldn't believe the things they said about him and about our family. It got so bad he decided we needed to move. He got a job driving trucks, so we moved here. He rented the house at first, but then he bought it later on down the road."

"And he never remarried."

"Never did. Oh, he had girlfriends here and there along the way, but he never remarried."

Kayleen sat in silence for more than five minutes. When

she spoke again, her mood was somber. "Had Stella not killed Grandma Sudie, Mama would have had a brother or sister."

"Yeah, she would. But I reckon some things are just not meant to be."

Stella met with Dr. Glazier at her appointed time. He was a short, stocky gentleman with a Hitler-style mustache, bushy eyebrows, and dark green eyes. He was bald on top of his head but obviously trying to hide it by doing a comb-over with what little hair remained on the side of his head. Stella reasoned to herself he might fare better at covering his head if he used his eyebrows, as they were much thicker than that on his head. As she envisioned this she chuckled at the prospect. When she did so, Dr. Glazier looked up and smiled politely, and then he went back to reading her chart. When he was finished reading, he closed the file and laid it on his desk.

"Mrs. Hubert," he said, looking rather distraught, "after reviewing your medical charts, I am sorry to report there is very little I can do for you. Your cancer is in the last stages. You might live a month. You might live six months. However, your prognosis is not good. Are you in much pain?"

Stella's thoughts were still focused on his balding head and how he could cover it.

Dr. Glazier realized she was in another world.

"Mrs. Hubert," he said loudly, "I said are you in pain?"

"Pain?" she asked, refocusing her attention to the moment at hand. "Yes, I suppose I'm in pain. Mostly my lower back and stomach. Are you?"

Dr. Glazier looked puzzled. "Am I what?" he asked.

"Are ya in pain?"

"No, I'm not in pain."

Stella smiled. "Good. I'm glad. Pain hurts, ya know."

Dr. Glazier shook his head. "Yes, well, I am going to prescribe some pain medicine for you. We want to try and keep you as comfortable as possible."

"That would be nice," she said.

Dr. Glazier took a prescription pad from his desk and began to scribble something down. When he was finished, he leaned over the desk and handed it to her. "You take one of these every four to six hours as needed. They will fill it for you at the clinic."

Stella took the piece of paper from Dr. Glazier and looked at it. A deep furrow formed across her forehead. "I shore hope they can read this chicken scratching. I can't tell hide nor hair of what it says. And I went all the way through the sixth grade in school."

Dr. Glazier became somewhat amused by her statement. "You can rest assured they will be able to read it, Mrs. Hubert. I will see you in a month. The receptionist will give you an appointment time to come back."

Stella stood and turned to leave. Suddenly she stopped and looked back at the doctor. "I'll be here if I live that long."

Without another word, she walked out of his office.

Jack was waiting for her in the waiting room. The receptionist handed Stella a card with her next appointment time.

"Have a good day, Mrs. Hubert," she said, smiling.

"Yeah, ya have a nice day too," answered Stella.

Jack took Stella's hand, and they walked out of the doctor's office and into the bright sunlight. The warmth of the sun felt good. Flowers were blooming along the edge of the walkway.

"Where's Ida?" Stella asked as she stopped to pluck a yellow iris from the flower bed.

"She's at home, Stella," Jack answered. "Don't you remember? She didn't feel up to coming with us today. And I don't think you're supposed to pick them flowers."

Stella chuckled. "What they gonna do to me? Put me in

the crazy house again? I'm dying. They ain't gonna put me back in there. That nice young man at the clinic said so."

"I reckon you're right about that," Jack agreed. "They kept you all them years, now they don't want you no more."

"That's cause they knew I'm dying. I ought'a just keep on living for the meanness of it."

Jack laughed. "You're something else, Stella. That's sounds just like something you'd do, all right."

When they reached his blue Impala automobile, Jack opened the door for Stella. Slowly she got onto the seat and tried to buckle her seatbelt. Jack decided to help her. He took the strap from her hand and pulled it across her frail body. That was when he noticed the paper in her hand.

"What's that you got there in your hand?" he asked.

Stella looked at the paper again. "It's a prescription for some pain medicine, I reckon. Looks like a bunch of hen scratching to me. He said they would know what it says down at the clinic."

Jack fastened her seatbelt securely. "Well then I reckon we best take it to the clinic so they can fill it for you."

Jack got into the car and carefully pulled out of his handicap parking space. The clinic was several blocks from the doctor's office. On the way there, they passed several fast-food establishments. Up ahead, Stella noticed one with golden arches out front. A neon sign below the arches read, "Over two million hamburgers sold."

"That place must make some good hamburgers if they've sold two million of them," Stella commented.

"Yeah, that's McDonald's. Me and Ida gets us one of them hamburgers on grocery shopping day. I like their French fries too. You ever ate a McDonald's hamburger?"

"I don't reckon so. We had what they called a hamburger ever' once in a while when I was at the crazy house. I can't say much for them. They was dry and didn't have much taste if you ask me."

Immediately, Jack put on his right blinker and slammed on his brakes. The car behind him came to a screeching halt just in time to avoid hitting the back of the Impala. The driver put his fist out the side window and shouted obscenities at Jack. Jack acted as though he were oblivious to the near accident. Instead, he made a right turn into the McDonald's parking lot.

"What say we get us a hamburger and some French fries?" Jack suggested.

Stella nodded her head in agreement. Jack found a parking space near the door and parked. After turning off the ignition, he went around to the passenger side and opened the door for Stella. Stella slowly got out of the car, and the two of them went inside. Jack escorted Stella to a nearby table. Once she was seated, he went to the counter and ordered two hamburgers, two fries, and two small Cokes. In minutes he had his order. He placed the tray on the table and divided its contents between the two of them.

Stella unwrapped the burger and took a bite. She smiled. "This is good, Jack. Nothing like them dried-up hamburgers at the crazy house. The bread is nice and soft too."

"Glad you like it. Eat up then. Try the French fries. They're good too."

As they were enjoying the meal, a tall man with dark hair and intense blue eyes walked into the restaurant. When he saw Stella, he walked over to the table.

"Well, hello, Mrs. Hubert," he said. "Good to see you out and about."

Stella looked up from her hamburger. "Do I know ya?" she asked.

"Yes, Mrs. Hubert. I'm your caseworker, Jake Tillery."

"Oh yeah," she said. "I remember ya now. Do ya like hamburgers too?"

Jake smiled. "Yes, as a matter of fact, I do. My wife says I eat too many of them. She says that's why I'm getting fat."

"Ya don't look fat to me. I need some fat." She held up a flabby arm. "I ain't much more than skin over bones."

"How did your doctor's appointment go?"

Stella wiped her month then reached into her dress pocket. "He give me this here prescription. He said y'all would fill it for me at the clinic; that is, if ya can read it."

Jake took the piece of paper from Stella. "I know what you mean. Doctors aren't known for their handwriting. Would you like me to have it filled for you? I can drop it by your sister's place on my way home from work. It's on my way."

Stella looked at Jack. Jack nodded.

"That's mighty nice of ya, Fate," said Stella.

"It's, Jake, Mrs. Hubert. Jake, not Fate."

"Okay, Fate. Ya go on now and let me eat my hamburger."

Jake smiled then walked away, leaving Jack and Stella to their meal.

The day was long and tiring for Beth. It felt like everybody and his brother were having problems with their mortgage payments. As manager of her department, it was her job to smooth over frustrated and often angry customers. When five o'clock arrived, she was more than happy to switch the calls to the answering service. She would deal with those late callers tomorrow. For the time being, all she wanted to do was go home, take off her shoes, and relax for a few precious minutes before starting supper.

Hopefully Kayleen will have changed her attitude, she thought to herself as she prepared to get into her car. Dealing with her daughter's teen years had definitely been hard. *It would be so wonderful if Kayleen would just be a little more understanding.*

Surely I didn't give Mama Cora as hard a time as Kayleen has given me this past year. Beth inserted the key into her locked car door. She tried to turn the key, but it wouldn't budge. *Great!* she thought. *Now what?*

She pulled the key out of the lock and stepped back to survey the situation. Only then did she realize she was trying to open the wrong car door. She was so tired, she had to laugh to keep from crying.

To her surprise, when Beth pulled into Mama Cora's drive, Kayleen was there to greet her.

"Hi, Mom," she called happily.

Beth reluctantly smiled back. In the back of her mind she was thinking, *What is she up to? She must be wanting something.*

Kayleen opened the door. Beth got to her feet. Before Kayleen shut the car door, she hugged her mother around the neck.

"Glad you're back, Mom. How was your day?"

"Tiring," she answered honestly. "How was your day?"

"Great."

Puzzled, Beth started toward the house.

"I made you some fresh lemonade, Mom. It's chilling in the fridge."

"Okay. Now you want to tell me why you're being so nice?"

Kayleen turned serious. "Because I love you, Mom."

Beth smiled. "I love you too, Kayleen."

Beth and Kayleen made their way inside. Mama Cora met them as they entered the front door. In her hands were two tall, frosty glasses of freshly squeezed lemonade. She handed one glass to Beth and the other to Kayleen.

Kayleen picked up a magazine that was lying on the seat of the brown leather recliner. "Sit here, Mom, and prop your feet up."

Beth gladly sat down. Kayleen pulled the lever on the side of the recliner. The foot rest popped out and up. She even took off her mother's shoes for her. Beth laid her head against the back of the recliner for a minute or so and closed her eyes.

"I don't know if I can stand all this pampering," she said before opening her eyes again. "There must be something you're wanting. Go ahead and spill the beans, little girl. Is it a new outfit?"

Kayleen smiled. "No, Mom. I don't want a new outfit."

"You want to go to the movies tonight with your friends," she guessed.

"No, Mom. I really don't want anything. I just thought I would be nice for a change."

Mama Cora sat down on the couch. Her blue floral-print dress lay just over the edge of her knees, revealing her calf-length rolled-down stockings.

"Now, Beth, what have I taught ya about looking a gift horse in the mouth?" she said to Beth.

Although still skeptical, Beth laid her head back and closed her eyes again, relishing the few minutes of relaxation. "Well, all right then," she said. "I'll just enjoy it while it lasts."

A few more minutes passed without anyone speaking. Finally, Kayleen could stand it no longer. "Mama, why didn't you ever tell me about Grandma Sudie's murder?"

Beth's head popped up like a jack-in-the-box. "Who told you Mama was murdered?"

"Mama Cora."

Beth gave her grandmother an I-dare-you look. "I thought we said we would wait until she was old enough to tell her about Mama's murder."

Kayleen quickly defended her great-grandmother. "Mama, I'm almost sixteen years old. I'm not a baby anymore. When were you going to tell me? When I get to be as old as you?"

Beth let the foot rest down until she was sitting upright. "You're right, Kayleen. I suppose you are old enough to know the facts. It's just that...." She paused, and tears filled her eyes.

"It's okay, Mama. Mama Cora told me all about it. It must have been terrible for you. I can't imagine how I would feel if someone killed you."

Beth wiped the tears from her eyes. "Actually, Kayleen, I don't remember anything about that day. I was so young. All I know is what people have told me. Daddy didn't like for anyone to talk about it, especially in front of me."

"Mama Cora said they arrested Stella Hubert for the murder."

"That's right. They did. In fact, she never went to trial. She was sent directly to Benton Mental Institution. As far as I know, she's still there."

Kayleen sat down on the arm of the recliner. "What I don't understand is what happened to the baby she was carrying."

Beth laid her hand on Kayleen's knee. "No one really knows for sure. I expect she threw the body in the woods, and the wild animals devoured it."

Kayleen shivered. "That's gross, Mama."

Mama Cora spoke. "Dawson used to have dreams about a little boy. He said the little boy looked just like he did when he was a child. He could see him through a tall iron gate. The boy would be running and playing in a playground with other little boys and girls. In his dream, he called to the little boy. The little boy would stop playing and start walking toward him. Just before he would get within reach, the dream would end. Dawson would wake up crying."

Once again, Beth's eyes filled with tears.

"Daddy wanted a little boy so badly. Don't get me wrong, he loved me with all his heart and soul, but when their first baby was stillborn, it broke both their hearts. He was so in hopes the new baby would be a boy. Then the murder happened. I used to find him sitting out there on the front porch in the swing. He would be crying. When I asked him what was wrong, he would say he was just thinking about his baby boy.

He never gave up the hope that one day he would find his son, but of course, that was never to be."

"What if he is still alive?" asked Kayleen. "What if the wild animals didn't eat him? That would mean you have a brother out there somewhere."

Beth patted Kayleen on the leg. "Honey, that is never going to happen. Whether it was a boy or a girl, it is gone."

She rose to her feet and slipped her shoes back on her feet. "Enough of this morbid talk. Let's go home so I can fix us some supper."

"Oh!" Kayleen spouted. "I almost forgot. I made dinner for us."

"What?" Beth asked in shock.

Kayleen ran to the kitchen and came back with a container of food. "Mama Cora and I made your favorite, chicken and dumplings."

"Wow! How wonderful. This is a surprise," said Beth as she took the container and smelled its contents. "Smells delicious."

Mama Cora slowly rose to her feet. "Why don't y'all stay here and eat supper with me and Dawson? He's supposed to get home from his haul tonight."

Beth leaned over and kissed Mama Cora on the cheek. "Sorry, we can't tonight. Luke gets home from his business trip tonight too. In fact, his plane should be arriving right about now. He'll be hungry for some home cooking. He always is when he's been eating hotel food for a few days."

"All right then," said Mama Cora. "Tell him I'm glad he's home safe. I always worry about Dawson and Luke when they're off somewhere. By the way, when ya reckon Luke's gonna ask ya to marry him? Y'all been living together for close to ten years now. Ya know I don't like y'all living in sin like ya do."

"It ain't Luke, Mama. He would marry me in a New York

minute. I just don't want us ending up like Kayleen's daddy and I did. Besides, you always say when it ain't broke, don't fix it."

Mama Cora shifted in her seat. "I wasn't referring to the two of y'all when I said that," she corrected her granddaughter.

Kayleen knew it was time to exit before the conversation got too intense. She kissed Mama Cora too. "Thanks for telling me about Grandma Sudie. And thanks for helping me with the chicken and dumplings. I can't wait to hear if Mama and Luke like them or not."

Beth chuckled. "I'm sure I'll like them simply because I didn't have to cook them. I love chicken and dumplings, but I hate rolling out and cutting the dough."

Stella had been home several weeks. Her appetite had actually improved since moving in with Ida and Jack. Ida still remembered her sister's favorite foods and did everything she could to make sure Stella ate well. She would not talk to Ida or Jack about her experiences at the hospital. However, she did talk a lot about Rose. Although Rose was a grown woman, she had been childlike in many ways. As far as Stella knew, she had no family. If she did have family, none of them ever came to visit. After a year or so, Rose had started referring to Stella as "Mama." Because she could not say "Mama," it came out "Ama," but Stella knew what she was saying and gratefully accepted the role of mother.

When Stella spoke of Rose, it was usually in a joyful way. She would talk about her silly antics and how she would dance around the room while Bojangles played "Chopsticks." She told them about Bud and how he took a shine to Rose and how Rose rejected him for ever so long. Finally one day, he told her he was going to find him another girlfriend if she didn't start being nicer to him. So she kissed him on the cheek. After that, finding another girlfriend was never mentioned again.

One day Ida found Stella sitting by the window looking somewhat depressed. She was staring out the window as though her mind was a thousand miles away. Ida pulled a chair up beside her sister and touched her on her knee. Stella jumped.

"Sorry I scared ya," said Ida. "Are ya all right? Ya look sad."

Stella patted Ida on her hand. "I was just thinking about Rose. Today would have been her birthday. She died on her birthday, ya know."

"No, Stella, I didn't know that."

"The last thing she said to me was on the night before she died. I'd taught her the prayer our mama taught us when we were children: 'Now I lay me down to sleep. I pray the Lord my soul to keep. If I should die before I wake, I pray the Lord my soul will take.' Ya remember that prayer, don't ya, Ida?"

"Yes, Stella, I do."

"Well, she said her prayer. Then she said, 'Ama.' She couldn't say mama so she called me Ama. She said, 'Tomorrow's my birthday. Don't forget. Okay?' I said I wouldn't forget. She giggled and said, 'Night 'Ama. I love ya. I told her I loved her too. The next morning when she wasn't there to wake me up, I knew something was wrong. I went over to her cot, and sure enough, she was gone. It broke my heart. I loved that little gal. She was one of God's angels sent down to help me get through all those long days and the even longer nights I spent in that god-forsaken place."

Ida hugged her sister. "I'm so sorry."

"It wasn't long after that when they told me I had cancer. I'm glad she went before I did. I don't think Rose could have dealt with me leaving her. I reckon God knows best. I shorely do miss her though."

Ida decided it was time to change the subject. She didn't

like seeing her sister so upset. "Ya have an appointment today to go see Jake."

"Is it today?" she asked.

"Yes."

"What time?"

"Ten."

"Is Jack gonna take me?"

"Jack isn't feeling well today. I called Jake, and he is sending a special bus to pick ya up. They'll be here in about an hour."

"I like Jake."

"He certainly is a handsome young man."

Stella laughed. "I know. If I was forty years younger, I'd be chasing him across barbwire fences as high as his head."

Both of them laughed. Ida got up and headed toward the kitchen.

"Ya won't do, Stella Hubert. Ya just won't do."

The bus arrived at nine thirty. The driver parked the bus on the street then walked up the sidewalk to the door. He started to knock, but Stella opened the door before he could do so. The driver was a rather short, stocky man with cropped hair and piercing gray eyes.

"Good morning," he said to Stella. "I am here to pick up Stella Hubert."

"I'm Stella Hubert."

"Good. Are you ready, Mrs. Hubert?"

"Ready as I'm gonna be."

Stella turned toward the kitchen and called out to Ida. "I'm gone. I'll be back when they're through with me."

Ida peeked around the doorway. "Okay. Be careful."

The driver offered his arm for Stella to lean on. Stella laid her hand on his forearm and slowly ambled out to the bus. On the side of the bus was a sign that read, "Jefferson County Public Transportation." When they reached the bus, the driver pushed a button on the side of the bus. The door opened, and a pair of automatic steps moved out to accept them. Stella was amazed.

"Now ain't that something," she remarked.

The driver smiled. "Nothing's too good for our passengers," he replied.

Stella stepped aboard. There were several other passengers on the bus already. An older lady in a bright pink shift-style dress and blue straw hat began laughing as soon as she saw Stella. Stella looked at the driver.

"What's she laughing at?"

As the driver escorted Stella to an empty seat, he replied, "Don't mind Mrs. Peacock. She's a little on the strange side. She don't mean nothing."

Stella took her seat several rows behind the pink lady. *Seems like everywhere I go, there's crazy people,* she thought to herself. *And they say I'm crazy.*

Stella was looking forward to meeting with Jake again in hopes she would remember where she'd seen him before. The shock treatments and medications she took while at Benton Hospital had not only rid her of the voices, but also removed much of her memories from the past. The drugs she continued to take after leaving the hospital kept her demons under control but they also interfered with her thought process. Still, as she looked out the window of the bus at her new surroundings, she searched her memory banks for something, anything, that would tell her why Jake looked so familiar. After picking up several more passengers, the bus arrived at the clinic. One by one, they filed out of the bus and were escorted by the driver to their individual destinations. As it so happened, the lady in pink was one of Jake's clients also. While the two of them sat in the waiting area, the pink lady started talking to Stella.

She talked extremely fast and in short, choppy sentences. "Are you crazy too? I am, you know. Crazy as they come. Crazy like a fox. I like Jake. He's handsome. Do you think he's handsome? He's my boyfriend. Is he your boyfriend? We're getting married today. Are you getting married today? Do you like my dress? It's pink. I like pink. Do you like pink? Do you like my hat? I like my hat. I wanted a pink hat. My hat is blue. Do you like blue? I like blue. I like pink more. Do you like pink more?"

To Stella's relief, the door to Jake's office opened. He and an older gentleman with bright red hair and a long, scrappy beard walked out together. Jake shook his hand and told him he would see him next week. He then turned to the ladies.

"Hello, Mrs. Hubert. I see you've met Mrs. Peacock," he said, smiling.

He bent over until he was eye-level with the pink lady.

"How are you today, Mrs. Peacock?"

Mrs. Peacock giggled like a young adolescent at her first boy-girl party. "Are we getting married today?" she asked.

Jake looked at Stella and winked. "Not today, Mrs. Peacock. Mrs. Hubert and I have to visit for a while. You sit here and behave yourself. Okay? I'll be back to get you in a little while."

As Stella and Jake disappeared into his office, Mrs. Peacock called out to him, "Then can we get married?"

Jake looked back over his shoulder. "We'll see."

Jake led Stella to the chair in front of his desk and helped her get seated. "Sorry about Mrs. Peacock. She really is a nice lady. She just has a few mental problems. She really should be somewhere she could be cared for and watched more closely. However, with all the government cutbacks, she was released from her regular care facility. I never know when she will even show up for her appointments." He stopped himself. "I'm sorry. That is not your concern, is it? So how have you been doing at your new home?"

"Good," she answered. "My sister and I get along real good. Jack is nice too. I like my room. I do miss my friend, Rose. She liked me to tell her a bedtime story every night. Ida is a good cook too. I've been eating better since I got there. I told her she's gonna make me fat if she don't quit feeding me so good."

Jake smiled. "I'm glad to hear you're happy, Mrs. Hubert."

Stella stopped him. "Please, call me Stella."

"Okay, Stella. And you can call me Jake."

"Jake? I thought your name was Fate."

"No, it's Jake."

"Good! I never did like the name Fate. I had an uncle by the name of Fate. He was a mean feller. When he got drunk, he used to beat my poor aunt half to death."

"That's terrible!"

"Yeah. One night he passed out on the railroad track and got hit by a train. Course I don't reckon ya care bout hearing none of that."

Jake quickly changed the subject.

"What about the voices, Stella? Do you still hear the voices?"

"No. I haven't heard the voices in some time now. They finally went away. I'm glad too. I didn't like what they told me to do."

"What did they tell you to do, Stella?"

"Different things. But I don't want to talk about that anymore."

"Stella, I was wondering. I've been studying your file very closely. You were sent to Benton Hospital because you were accused of killing your pregnant niece. Is that correct?"

"I reckon. To tell ya the truth, I ain't quite shore. Will was supposed to be taking me to get a new axe for my husband, John. I knew he'd be mad if he seen blood on his axe. I was gonna buy him another one. But instead of going to the store, Will took me to the jailhouse and just left me. Never did come back. I don't rightly know what become of the axe that feller had."

Jake looked at Stella curiously. "What fellow would that be, Stella?"

Stella looked shocked at Jake's question. "Why, the one what killed Sudie. That's what feller."

"Stella, are you saying you saw someone else kill Sudie?"

"Ya better believe I did. I tried to tell Mrs. Faulkner, but she wouldn't listen. Wouldn't nobody listen. The voices kept telling me to keep my mouth shut. So I did. They didn't like Sudie. They tried their best to get me to kill her myself, but I couldn't do that. I knew if I killed Sudie, it'd kill the baby too. That was my baby she was carrying. I'd done planned on taking the baby and running off with it once it was born."

"Who did you see kill Sudie?"

"I don't rightly know his name for shore. I heard him talking to Sudie that morning after John and Dawson left for work. I listened through the door. I think I heard him say his name was Silas, but I wouldn't swear to that. He's the one what done it. I heard the gunshot. I heard Beth crying. I wanted to help her, but the voices told me to let it be."

Jake could tell by Stella's demeanor that she was becoming quite agitated. "It's all right, Stella. Calm down. Take your time. No need to get upset. Anytime you need to quit, you just let me know."

Stella looked Jake straight in the eyes. "I ain't got much time left on this earth, Jake. I need to tell someone about what I seen. I need to tell somebody about the baby. He's out there somewhere. Somebody needs to find him."

Jake was shocked. "Do you mean to say the killer took the baby?"

"He shorely did. After the gunshot, I heard the back door slam. I peeped through the keyhole. I could see Sudie lying on the floor. Beth was standing beside her, crying. Sudie was moaning."

"You mean she was still alive?"

"Yeah. She was bleeding real bad, though. I was fixing to open the door when I heard the back door open again. I stayed real quietlike. I could see he had a stick of stove wood in his hand. He shoved Beth down on the floor and went to beating Sudie in the head After the first couple of blows, she stopped moaning. After he hit her with the stove wood, he went outside again. In just a little bit, he come back with John's axe. That was when he chopped her open."

By then, Stella was in tears and shaking violently. Jake came around his desk to where she was sitting. He knelt down in front of her and took her hands in his. "Are you sure you want to keep going, Stella?"

"Let me finish, Jake. I need to finish my story."

Jake nodded his head in agreement.

Stella continued on. "When he got her cut open, he reached inside her stomach and pulled out the baby. I thought it was shorely dead. But then I heard it start to cry. Then he stuffed it inside his coat like you'd put an old rag in a knothole. I thought for a minute he was gonna kill Beth too. But he just looked at her and says, 'There ya are, little missy. Now ya ain't got no Mammie. That's what ya get for sassing old Silas.' With that, he turned and walked out'a the room, like what he'd done happened everyday. I heard the back door open and close again. I got the gun John bought to protect me from the voices. Slowly and quietly, I sneaked over to the kitchen window. He was standing at the well and that's when I seen him throw something into the well. I thought to myself, 'Oh, Lord, don't let it be that baby.' He started to come back in the house. I was afraid he was coming back for little Beth. I opened the back door, pointed the gun at him, and shot. I was so scared, I was shaking like a leaf. I reckon I missed 'cause he lit out'a there like a possum with a blue tick hound on his tail. When I turned around, I saw the bloody axe lying on the floor. I knew John would be mad if he seen his axe all bloody so I took it to the well and washed it as best I could. Then I put it back in the shed."

Jake could barely believe the story Stella had told him. When she was finished, he handed her his handkerchief and sat down flat on the floor. He was also shaken. "Why didn't you tell the police this story, Stella?"

"I told ya. The voices told me not to."

"I'm sure had they known the truth they would not have sent you to the mental hospital. You would have been a free woman all these years."

"I might'a been free from the hospital, but I wouldn't been free from the voices. Being in the hospital wasn't so bad. I got fed. I had Bernice and Rose. The medicine they gave me made me feel better. I expect I would'a died there if I didn't get this cancer. I reckon they didn't want to have to pay for my funeral, so they sent me away."

Jake's mind was reeling. He hardly knew what to say next. He stood to his feet and reached across his desk for Stella's file. Quickly he flipped through the paperwork, looking for transcript papers from her trial. There were none.

"Stella, did you go to trial?" he asked while still searching through the papers.

"What do ya mean a 'trial'?"

"Did you go to court? Did a jury find you guilty of the murder of Sudie Hubert?"

"No. I never went to no trial. As best I recall, I went straight from jail to Benton Hospital."

Jake began to pace back and forth from one side of his office to the other, deep in thought. After several minutes, he stopped and looked at Stella. "Stella, I need to find out more about your case. Do you think it's possible Sudie's baby survived?"

"I don't rightly know, Jake. I was sure he threw it down the well. John told me Will looked for it, but all he found was a dead chicken."

"It seems I read something about a dead chicken in your paperwork. What was that about?"

Stella dropped her head. "I done that. I killed all the chickens. They quit laying, so I killed them. Sudie fussed at me 'bout it. So I hung one of them on Sudie's door."

"Why would you do that?"

"The voices told me to do it."

"How did it get down in the well?"

"I done that too. Dawson threw it in the woods, but I found it and pitched it down the well."

Jake started to ask Stella why. Instead he answered his own question, "The voices."

Stella shook her head. "The voices."

"Wouldn't it be something if the baby did live?" He paused and looked out his office window toward the street. "Unbelievable."

"Well I don't know 'bout that, but I do want to thank ya, Jake."

Jake looked puzzled. "Thank me for what?"

"I've held this story inside a me for nigh onto forty years. I feel like a weight's been lifted off my shoulders."

A tear came to Jake's eye. "You're welcome, Stella. I'm glad I was able to help."

Stella stood up. "Can I go home now?"

"Yes, of course. Let me help you out to the bus."

"I'll be fine, Jake. I can make it alone now. I ain't felt this good in years. I may go out juking tonight." She laughed. "Besides, I think ya got a wedding to attend."

"What? A wedding?"

Stella pointed toward Mrs. Peacock. Jake chuckled.

"Oh yeah, a wedding. Right."

Jake hugged Stella. "I am going to see if I can find out

what happened to Sudie's baby. I know it would be a miracle, but I'm sure going to try."

Stella touched Jake tenderly on his cheek. "Good luck to ya. You're a good boy."

As Stella was walking away, Jake called after her, "See you in two weeks. Same time."

Stella did not answer. Instead, as she continued on her way, she threw up her hand to let him know she had heard.

Jake pulled up to the front of the Chilton County jail the following day, around ten in the morning. Several deputies were standing out front in the shade of an enormous oak tree. One of the men looked to be in his early to mid-sixties. Jake got out of his blue, used 1985 Chevrolet Malibu and walked over to where the men were talking.

"Hello," he said, extending his hand to the older gentleman.

He noticed the badge on his shirt pocket read, "Deputy Coy Rucker."

"Deputy Rucker, my name is Jake Tillery. I am here to try to get information on a patient of mine. Her name is Stella Hubert."

A look of shock came over Rucker's face. "Stella Hubert?" Deputy Rucker replied. "Ya mean that crazy woman is still alive?"

Jake found his attitude to be rather uncaring. "I'm assuming you knew Mrs. Hubert?"

"Yeah, I knew her. She was the one who killed Sudie Hubert and her unborn baby."

The other deputies acted as though they knew nothing about Stella's case. Deputy Rucker knew the younger men had little if any knowledge of the case, so he told them about it and the day that Beth saw Stella in prison.

Jake wondered if it was such a good idea to be talking to the deputy. It seemed to him he was certainly convinced of her guilt. However, he needed to find out for himself whether or not Stella was, in fact, guilty.

"So you never found the baby?"

"No, I'm sorry to say. I don't know what she did with it. It liked to have drove Dawson Hubert crazy. He was Sudie's husband."

"I see. Deputy, did you know there was another person in Sudie's house that day?"

Deputy Rucker looked at Jake like he was insane. "What do ya mean 'another person'?"

"Stella told me there was a man who showed up after John and Dawson went to work."

"Stella Hubert told ya that? That's impossible. Stella Hubert has been at Benton Mental Hospital ever since the murder."

"She *was* at Benton Hospital," Jake corrected him. "She was released several weeks ago. She is living with her sister in Jefferson County. I am her caseworker."

"Really? So you're telling me there's a killer on the loose?"

"I don't believe she is a killer," said Jake. "Besides Stella has cancer. She'll be lucky to live six months. In our last session, she told me something she said she had never told another living soul." Jake went on to tell the deputy the story Stella had told him.

Deputy Rucker shook his head. "That's some story, all right. And I don't believe a word of it."

"Well I do, and I'm going to prove it. Stella Hubert may have had mental problems, but she is no killer. I'm going to try and find the baby too."

"Well, good luck, buddy. Sounds like you're wasting time, if ya ask me."

"I'd like to get the addresses of those people involved with the case. Is that possible?"

"I ain't sure where most of them are. Sheriff Thornton died several years back. Will and Delta Deason live somewhere in Billingsley. Sudie's mama and daddy, Samson and Althea Newton, live in Prattville. Dawson lives somewhere in Montgomery. That's about all I can tell you. Sheriff Meed might can tell ya more. He was another deputy on the case. He's the sheriff now. 'Course, he ain't here today. He's gone to Shiloh to pick up an escaped prisoner."

Jake scribbled down names and towns. He put his hand out. Deputy Rucker reluctantly extended his hand. As they shook hands, Jake thanked the deputy for his information then bid him and the others good day. Getting back in his car, Jake wondered what he'd gotten himself into. Still, he could not let it go without investigating further. Since Prattville was the nearest town, he decided to visit Sudie's parents first.

When he arrived in Prattville, it was nearly noon. His stomach was telling him it was time to eat. At the edge of town, he discovered what appeared to be a mom-and-pop restaurant called Jim's. The parking lot was full, which implied the food must be pretty good. He pulled into the lot and found a parking place near the rear. When he got inside, there were several people ahead of him waiting to get a table. Booths lined the front of the room next to the windows facing the parking lot. Next to the booths were tables. Before long, the people in front of Jake were escorted to a booth. Since there was only one of him, the waitress asked if he would mind sitting at the counter. He agreed and was immediately seated.

The waitress was wearing a black gathered skirt and a starched, Oxford-collar white shirt. She had dark hair pulled away from her thin, pale face and secured in a bun. Her name tag read simply, Betty. She handed him a menu and placed a glass of water on the counter in front of him.

"What can I get ya to drink?" the waitress asked with a long Southern drawl.

"I'll have sweet ice tea," Jake answered.

Jake looked at the menu. The special of the day was fried chicken, mashed potatoes, green beans, turnip greens, and corn muffins. The dessert was banana pudding, all of which sounded good to Jake. Betty placed a huge glass of tea on the counter.

"What'll ya have?" she asked.

Jake smiled. "The special sounds good to me."

Betty turned toward the kitchen, which was directly behind the counter. "I need a special, Jim," she yelled.

A voice from the kitchen called back to her. "One special coming up."

The seat beside him was empty. A bell hanging above the entry door signaled the arrival of another mouth to feed. Without being asked, the middle-aged man eased himself onto the empty seat. Jake looked over at him and nodded his head as a simple greeting. The man was much older than Jake. The deep-set wrinkles in the man's face and under his eyes led Jake to believe he must have lived a hard life. Betty was pouring tea into a glass at the other end of the counter. She called out to him, "Howdy, Mr. Newton. The usual?"

"You bet," the man answered.

Newton, thought Jake. *Could he be Samson Newton?* Although he looked older, Jake didn't think he looked old enough to be the man he was looking for, but he might know Samson Newton. He put out his hand to him.

"Hello, my name is Jake Tillery."

The man beside him did the same. They shook hands.

"Ed Newton."

"Say, you wouldn't happen to know Samson Newton, would you?"

Betty set a cup of strong black coffee in front of Ed and

answered for him. "Yeah, I'd say he knows him." She laughed. "Samson Newton is his daddy."

"Unbelievable," said Jake. "What luck."

"Do ya know my daddy?" asked Ed as he poured a large amount of sugar into his coffee.

"Not really," answered Jake. "I would like to talk to him though."

"Ya ain't with the IRS, are ya?" Ed asked.

"No, no. I'm a social worker of sorts. I'm trying to get some information about his daughter, Sudie's, murder."

Ed took a sip of coffee. "I reckon I can tell ya most anything ya need to know. Ya ain't apt to get much out of Mama. Daddy died two years ago. Daddy didn't like to talk about it. Both of them were convinced the wrong person was accused. To this day, Mama will swear it was Sudie's husband, Dawson, who did it."

Jake was curious. "And what do you think?"

Ed scratched his head. "I was around fifteen when Sudie was killed. I never thought for a minute Dawson did it. 'Course, I didn't think Stella did it either. I believe to this day it was a transient, some hobo riding the rails. Them kinda folks were always begging food off the people who lived near the tracks. It used to make Dawson mad, but Sudie always shared whatever they had. Sometimes it wasn't nothing more than an old, cold biscuit, but she shared."

"What do you think happened to Sudie's baby?

"I like to think it lived."

"How's that?"

Again, Ed scratched his head before answering. "Could be the hobo stole the baby and then sold it on the black market. Folks who couldn't have babies of their own back then were known to buy babies. It was easier for some folks than going through an orphanage and adoption procedures."

Jake thought of his own adoption. For years he wondered

why he looked so different from either of his parents. Both of them had blond hair and light green eyes. His hair was dark, and his eyes were blue. When he turned sixteen, his parents told him he was adopted. When he asked who his parents were, they told him his paternal parents were both dead. His thoughts were suddenly interrupted when Betty placed a large plate of food in front of him. It smelled wonderful. His stomach growled loudly. Jake put his hand on his stomach and blushed.

"Sorry about that. I guess I'm hungrier than I thought I was."

Betty refilled his glass with tea. "Well, eat up," she said. "Just save room for the banana pudding."

Jake picked up a fried chicken leg from his plate and took a bite. With his mouth still full, he commented, "Really good."

Betty smiled and walked away.

Ed spoke again. "Ya know, come to think of it, ya remind me of Dawson when he was younger."

"Oh really," said Jake.

"He was tall, dark, and quite handsome in a rough kinda way."

"Do you have a picture of Dawson?"

"No."

"Do you think your mother would have one?"

"If she ever had one, I'm pretty sure she destroyed it long ago. She hated Dawson. Still does, as far as I know."

Betty retrieved a tuna fish sandwich and potato chips from the kitchen and placed it in front of Ed. "There ya go, Mr. Newton, the usual."

"Thanks, Betty," he replied.

By the time Jake finished his lunch, he was so full, he felt as if he would pop. He rose to his feet and extended his hand to Ed. Ed responded with a hardy handshake.

"Thank you, Ed. I have got to be going. You've been quite helpful."

"If you'd like to talk to Dawson, he lives with his mama, Cora Hubert, in Montgomery. I know he drives a big eighteen-wheeler for Seamon Trucking Company, so he's on the road a lot. Ya might ought to call before ya go, just to make sure he's home."

"I would like very much to meet Dawson, but I have to get back home. I took a personal day from work to come here today. I would, however, like his phone number if you have it."

Betty overheard their conversation. She quickly reached for the Montgomery phone book, which was stashed under the cash register counter. She handed the book to Ed. Flipping through the book, he found the "H" listings and ran his finger down the page. There was not a listing for Dawson Hubert or Cora Hubert.

Ed closed the phone book and handed it back to Betty. "Sorry, I guess they aren't listed."

Jake placed a ten-dollar bill on the counter. "Thanks anyway, Ed, Betty. Y'all take care."

Betty picked up the ten. "What about your change?"

"You keep the change, Betty, and tell Jim his food is delicious."

Betty put five dollars in the cash drawer to cover the lunch ticket and the other five in her pocket. It was the best tip she'd made all day. "*Nice guy,*" she said to herself.

Ed followed Jake to the door. As Jake was pulling out of the parking lot, he looked toward the café. Ed was standing just inside the screen door, waving good-bye. Jake threw up his hand and waved back. *Nice guy,* he thought to himself.

All the way home, Jake kept thinking about what Ed had told him. His words made Jake wonder, *Had Stella spent all those years in a mental hospital for something she didn't do? Certainly she had mental problems, but to be placed in an institution without so much as a hearing or a trial was inconceivable.* He had to know the truth. Somehow he had to find out for himself who really did kill Sudie Hubert. Was it Stella Hubert? Was it Dawson Hubert or, like Ed suggested, a passing hobo, which would certainly coincide with the story Stella told him?

When Jake arrived at work the next morning, there was a message from Stella on his answering machine. "Jake, I need to talk to ya 'bout a dream I been having. I used to have the same dream a long time ago. It went away when they did them shock treatments on me. I hadn't had it in years, but I've dreamed about the same thing two nights in a row now... Ya call me. I'll tell ya 'bout it."

Jake had a stack of files on his desk that needed his immediate attention. He decided he would wait to call her after work. Perhaps he could go by her place on his way home. He picked up the top file and opened it. He looked at the first page in an attempt to read and comprehend what he needed to do with it. Regardless of how hard he tried to concentrate on his job, his mind kept going back to Stella and the murder of Sudie Hubert. He laid the file down and reached for his briefcase. Inside he found Stella's file. Once again, he scanned its contents for some thread of evidence that would show Stella's innocence or guilt. Most of what was in Stella's file were notes from the doctors at Benton Institute. However, one page caught his attention. It was an interview with Stella about the dream she was having. Jake read the note:

> Stella Hubert speaks of a recurring dream in which she sees the baby of Sudie Hubert alive and well. In her dream, she also witnesses a hobo she calls "Silas" killing Mrs. Hubert. She speaks of floating above the crime scene, watching him commit the murder. She says he shoots her first, but Sudie doesn't die. Then he leaves the room and comes back with a piece of stove wood and an axe. He hits Sudie in the head with the stove wood. Then he cuts the baby

from her womb and stuffs it into his coat. I believe she continues to be delusional. She cannot accept the horrific crime she has committed. The dream is her way to justify what happened to Sudie Hubert. I believe it is easier for her to blame the crime on a fictitious character she has made up in her mind than to admit to being the murderer.

This sounded like the story Stella had told him at their last meeting. Yet she said she had never told another living soul. Could it be it was just a dream? Was he wasting his time trying to discover who really killed Sudie when it was Stella all along? He threw the file back into his briefcase and once again picked up the file at hand. He had to put Stella Hubert out of his mind if he wanted to get done what needed to be done. Perhaps he would think about it later.

By the end of the day, Jake was dog tired. All he wanted to do was go home to his wife, pour himself a shot of Jack Daniels, and relax in his recliner. He didn't want to think about work. He didn't want to think about appointments. And he certainly didn't want to think about Stella Hubert anymore. Still, when he neared the turnoff to her sister's house, he couldn't seem to help himself. Where Stella was involved, there were too many questions and not enough answers. He turned on his right-hand turn signal and headed down Cedar Street toward Jack and Ida's house.

To his surprise, Stella was sitting on the front porch in a rocking chair, quietly rocking back and forth as though she were waiting for him. He pulled his car into the driveway and turned off the ignition. He didn't bother with his briefcase. Instead he reached for a small flip pad and a recently sharpened #2 pencil. As he was making his way across the yard, Stella called to him.

"Howdy, Jake. Ya look tired."

Jake made his way up the steps. When he reached the top

step, he sat down. "I am tired, Stella," he answered. "It's been a rough day."

"I bet ya wish I'd go on and die so ya wouldn't have to fool with me no more," she said matter-of-factly.

Jake replied quickly, "Don't say that, Stella. I don't wish that for you or anybody else. I like you. You're an interesting person. Your case is challenging. I want to hear about this dream you're having. Is it the same dream you were having when you were in the hospital?"

"No, it ain't the same. In this dream, I'm following a man. He has dark hair and is very tall. I can't see his face 'cause he's always ahead of me. I feel like I should know him. I try to run to catch up to him, but I can't. He's too fast. I try calling to him, but he don't act like he hears me. There's also a little blonde-haired girl in my dream. She's crying and very frightened. I want to pick her up, but she acts like she's scared of me. I call to her to come to me, but she runs to the man instead. He picks her up, and she stops crying. The dream ends. What ya reckon it means, Jake?"

"I don't rightly know, Stella. I wish I did."

Stella stopped rocking and became very serious. "Jake, did I kill, Sudie?"

Jake looked deep into Stella's eyes. "Honestly, Stella, I don't know. One thing I do know is I'm going to do my best to find out."

"I need to know too, Jake. I'm at my jumping off place in life. I don't want to spend eternity in hell. I spent the last thirty-nine years in hell already. If I did kill her, then I deserve it. But if I didn't kill her, maybe I stand a chance at going to heaven."

Jake felt so sorry for Stella, he wanted to cry. Here was a woman who had spent most of her life in a mental hospital. Everyone she had known in her past hated her. She knew she was dying and wanted to be forgiven. Yet without knowing the real truth, she could not forgive herself. He leaned forward and touched Stella on her knee.

"I promise you this, Stella Hubert, if it is at all possible, I will find out who killed Sudie, and I will find out what happened to Sudie's baby. You just hang in there. Okay?"

Stella smiled. "Thank ya, Jake. You're a good man."

Jake rose to his feet and kissed Stella gently on her forehead. "Try not to worry, Stella. I'll get to the bottom of this, if it is the last thing I ever do."

Stella reached for Jake's hand and patted it gently. "If I would'a had a son, I would've wanted him to be just like ya."

"Thanks, Stella. I've got to go now. Try not to worry. I'll call you when I find out anything."

As Jake was backing out of the driveway, Stella leaned back in her rocking chair and began gently rocking back and forth.

Dawson arrived home around seven thirty. He'd been on the road driving an eighteen-wheeler for nearly two weeks. His lower back hurt something fierce. He was glad to be off work for a few days. As soon as he walked in the back door, Mama Cora handed him a tall glass of iced tea. She had prepared his favorite meal: fried chicken, mashed potatoes, biscuits, and sawmill gravy.

Although he was hungry, the first thing he wanted was a hot bath. Mama Cora had the bath water running, so he didn't let any grass grow under his feet. In a matter of minutes, he was easing himself down into the tub. He laid back with his head rested on the edge of the tub and closed his eyes. He could smell the lavender-scented salts his mama had added to the water. He could instantly feel the tension leaving his muscles. A half hour later, Dawson was sitting at the kitchen table, enjoying his dinner when the phone rang.

"If it's for me, I ain't here," he said.

Mama Cora walked into the living room and picked up the phone.

"Hello. Yes, this is Mrs. Hubert. Did ya say this is Ed Newton? Lord, help me. I ain't heard from ya in years. How in the world are ya?"

Ed explained how he got her phone number from her sister, Delta. He also told her about Jake Tillery and about Stella being released from Benton Mental Hospital. When he was finished, she thanked him, told him it was good to hear from him and to drop by sometime to visit. After hanging up the phone, she went back into the kitchen where Dawson was finishing his supper.

"Who was that on the phone, Mama?"

"It was Ed Newton."

"You're kidding me. Why I haven't heard from him in years. What did he want?"

Mama Cora told her son about their conversation. Dawson could hardly believe what he was hearing.

"They let that crazy woman out of the hospital?"

"I reckon so. He also said a feller by the name of Jake something wants to talk to ya about Stella."

"Well did ya tell him I have no intentions of talking to anybody about Stella, Sudie, or anything else that has to do with the murder?"

"I guess this feller is some kind of social worker. He told Ed that Stella is dying of cancer."

Dawson rose to his feet, picked up his plate, and carried it over to the sink.

"Well I hope she rots in pain."

"Dawson Hubert," Mama Cora scolded. "What an awful thing to wish on anybody."

Dawson turned and looked directly at his mother.

"That's how I feel, Mama. She took my wife and Beth's

mama. She took my unborn child from me. Whatever pain she suffers will never be good enough."

The next morning was Saturday. Jake got up early in order to cut the grass before breakfast. At the breakfast table, he and his wife, Vicky, were discussing what they wanted to do the rest of the weekend.

They met while still in high school, attended the same college, and married the day after they graduated. Vicky earned a degree in journalism and immediately went to work for the local newspaper, *The Birmingham News*. Jake knew what he wanted to do that day, but convincing Vicky to ride with him to Montgomery to investigate a forty-year-old murder case might not be easy. He was hoping her love for investigative reporting might kick in to help convince her. Jake took a sip of his coffee and cleared his throat.

"Vick, do you remember a few weeks ago when I was telling you about one of my clients, Stella Hubert?

Vicky poured herself a glass of orange juice and grinned. "Yes, I remember. She was the one who was put in the mental hospital without so much as a hearing. Right?"

"That's the one. I'd really like to talk to the family of Sudie Hubert. I had to go to Prattville a few days ago to follow up on one of my other clients. Just by chance, I met Ed Newton, Sudie's brother, at a restaurant there in town. He doesn't think Stella killed Sudie either. He believes it was one of the transients who often frequented that area. His theory goes hand in hand with Sudie's story about the man she calls Silas."

Vicky interrupted. "And you want to spend our weekend playing detective on something that happened nearly forty years ago."

Jake paused a moment before answering. He ran several

responses through his mind that he felt might influence his wife's approval, none of which seemed appropriate. Instead he answered simply, "Yes."

"You're really into this Stella woman's situation, aren't you?"

Jake took another sip of coffee. "There's just something about the entire scenario. I can't get it out of my mind. Maybe if I can talk to these people on a personal basis, I can better understand what and how it all happened. And the baby ... what happened to the baby?"

"Jake, you do realize you may never know the answer to that question?"

"I know. I know. But what if the baby was stolen and lived? What if I could find him or her?"

Vicky had a worried look on her face. "Jake, does this have anything to do with your being adopted?"

Jake pushed away from the table, stood up, and walked over to the window. Silence engulfed the room as he peered out the window.

"Every child should know who their real parents are. I know my real parents are dead, but there could be a person out there who has at least one parent who is still living."

Vicky walked over to the window and placed her arm around Jake's shoulder. "You do know the chances of finding that person is slim to none."

"Yes, I know," he answered as he turned to face her. He put his arms around her waist. "But, Vick, I have to try. Can you understand that?"

Vicky kissed Jake gently on his cheek.

"I do understand. When do you want to leave?"

Jake became very excited. "Right away. It only takes a couple of hours to get from Vestavia Hills to Montgomery If we leave now, we could be there before lunch. In fact, why don't we pack an overnight bag? We could get a hotel room and make a weekend of it."

"Okay," agreed Vicky. "Help me get the dishes in the dishwasher, and I'll pack the bag while you go get the car filled with gas."

Dawson was glad to be home in his own bed. Sleeping in the cab of his eighteen-wheeler was okay, but there was nothing like the comforts of home. When he awoke, he glanced at the clock on the nightstand beside his bed. It was a quarter past eight. He hadn't slept that late in a while. He could smell bacon frying. He knew Mama Cora would have him a big breakfast with grits, fried eggs, and homemade biscuits. He loved her biscuits. Nobody could make them like his mama. He slowly sat up on the side of his bed. The pain in his left knee felt like a toothache. The doctor said it was arthritis. He opened the nightstand drawer and took out a tube of Bengay. It smelled strong, but it seemed to help ease the pain. As he was rubbing his knee, he heard Mama Cora call to him from the bottom of the stairs.

"Dawson! Your breakfast is ready. Get on down here now 'fore it gets cold."

Dawson pulled on his jeans and his favorite blue-plaid shirt with pearl buttons down the front. Beth had given it to him for Father's Day. He could hardly wait to see her and Kayleen. It seemed like every time he was gone, Kayleen grew at least two inches. He wanted to spend the entire day doing nothing but relaxing, visiting with his daughter and granddaughter, and watching his favorite baseball team, the Atlanta Braves.

Dawson had barely sat down at the table when a car drove

up in the driveway. Mama Cora pulled the blue ruffled curtain back and looked out the window to see who it was.

"It's Beth and Kayleen," she announced. "They shore didn't waste no time getting over here to see ya."

Within a minute, the two of them were rushing through the front door, through the living room, and into the kitchen. Kayleen was the first to reach her grandpa. She threw her arms around his neck.

"Papa!" she yelled excitedly. "I missed you so much."

"I missed ya too, honey," he said.

Beth hugged her father too. "How are you, Dad?" she asked. "How's your knee?"

"Ahh, It's fair to middling. Can't complain. Don't do no good no way."

"Have y'all had breakfast yet?" Mama Cora asked.

Beth answered first. "No, and I could sure use a cup of coffee."

"Well help yourself, sugar. How 'bout some eggs too? There's grits on the stove and bacon. Got plenty of biscuits too. I figured y'all would be coming by early this morning."

Beth got two more plates from the cupboard and a cup for her coffee. She dipped grits onto each of the plates and handed one of them to Kayleen. "Here, get whatever else you want."

After filling their plates, they sat down at the table across from Dawson.

"What do you want to do today, Papa?" asked Kayleen.

Dawson chuckled. "I don't want to do nothing I don't have to."

Beth spoke next. "I have to go into work for a little while. I have some stuff I need to catch up on. I figured you and Kayleen can hang out for a while, if that's all right."

"Hang out with her? No way," Dawson teased.

"Oh, Papa. You know you love hanging out with me."

"Sure I do." He grinned.

Beth looked at her watch, gobbled down a few bites of the food on her plate, and grabbed her keys from off the table. "I'd better get going if I plan on getting back by lunchtime."

She stood up, kissed Kayleen, her dad, and Mama Cora good-bye. "I'll see y'all around noon."

In a flash, she was gone.

When the rest were through eating breakfast, Kayleen helped her great grandmother clean up the kitchen, and then she and her grandfather went out onto the front porch and sat down on the swing next to each other. Kayleen laid her head on Dawson's broad shoulder.

"Papa, can I ask you a question?"

"Sure, honey. Ya can ask me anything. What ya want to know? I am a genius, ya know."

"Oh, Papa." Kayleen giggled. "You're so silly."

"What ya want to ask me?"

"Papa, what was Grandma Sudie like?"

Dawson was shocked. He leaned slightly forward and looked at Kayleen very seriously. "Why in the world would ya ask me about Sudie?"

"Well she was my grandmother, Papa. You never talk about her. I've never even seen a picture of her. What was she like? Mama Cora told me she was murdered. I never knew that. I just want to know something about her. Was she nice? Was she pretty? Did you love her?"

Dawson leaned back against the swing and began to slowly move back and forth. "I loved her very much, Kayleen. That's not to say we didn't have our share of troubles. Ya see, I had a pretty bad temper back then. She left me one time, but she came back. She was pretty enough in a simple kind of way. The Great Depression left its mark on a lot of folks back then. I wanted to give her nice things, but that never happened. I worked at a sawmill back then. I was only making two dollars a day. That barely paid the rent and bought food for her and Beth. I don't know if Mama told ya, but she was pregnant when she was killed."

"She did tell me. That must have been terrible for you."

"I thought my world had ended. But I still had Beth. Your great-grandma stepped in and helped me take care of her. I don't know what I would'a done without her."

"How come you all moved to Montgomery?"

"There were folks on Mountain Creek who figured I was the one who killed Sudie. Everywhere I went, they looked at me like I was the killer. I decided it was time I got on with my life. I came down here, got a job driving trucks, and rented this here house. We lived here 'bout a year when the lady who owned it died. I bought it from her kin. Been here ever since."

"Do you have a picture of Sudie?"

"I have one. It was taken the day we got married. It's the only picture I've ever seen of her. Folks didn't take pictures much back then."

"Can I see it, Papa?"

"I reckon so. It's upstairs in my closet on the shelf above the clothes. It's in a green tin box with a picture of a dog on the front. Go see if ya can find it. I'll wait here."

Kayleen hurried up the stairs and into her grandpa's bedroom. There was a cane-bottom, chair sitting next to the chest of drawers. She pulled it over to the closet and opened the door. She climbed onto the chair and began pushing things aside, looking for the box. In the far back corner, she spied it. It was a small green box about the size of a cigar box. She retrieved it from its hiding place and looked at the picture on top. The picture was faded, but she could see a dog. It appeared to be a golden retriever. In the background was a field. There was a man in the field plowing. The plow was being pulled along by a large, white horse. Kayleen tucked the box under her arm, put the chair back in its place, and closed the closet door. In seconds she was back with Dawson on the front porch.

"Is this it, Papa?" she asked, handing him the box.

Dawson took the box and opened it. "Yes, this is it."

There were several papers in the box. Dawson took out the one on top. "This is your mother's birth certificate."

Kayleen took the yellowed four-by-six-inch card and began to read, "Elizabeth Cora Hubert. Born January 29, 1949. Weight: seven pounds, three ounces. Length: nineteen inches. Father: Dawson Jackson Hubert. Mother: Sudie Anne Newton Hubert. Wow. I didn't know your middle name was Jackson, Papa."

"Yeah. I was named Jackson after your great-great-grandpa on your great-great-grandma's side of the family."

The next piece of paper was a copy of Sudie's death certificate. Dawson carefully unfolded it. The time of death was written up as the early morning hours of February 20, 1951. Cause of death: gunshot wound and beating by unknown assailant.

"Mama was only two years old when her mother died," said Kayleen.

Jake corrected her. "She didn't die, Kayleen. She was murdered. There's a big difference."

Kayleen squeezed her grandpa's arm. She could see this was very difficult for him. "I'm sorry, Papa. I know it must have hurt you deeply."

Dawson did not answer. Instead he began moving things inside the box, searching for the picture. Near the bottom of the stack, he found it lying facedown. He picked it up. On the back it read, "Sudie Newton Hubert. March 1, 1946. My wedding day." Dawson turned the picture over. On the flip side was a black and white photo of a young girl with light-colored hair, wearing a white, lacy dress and heels. In her hand was a bouquet of daffodils. She was standing on the front steps of what appeared to be an old courthouse. She was smiling.

"This is your grandmother Sudie, Kayleen."

Kayleen took the picture from her grandpa's hand and studied it carefully. "I think she's beautiful, Papa."

"Yeah," he agreed. "I guess she was at that. I'd almost forgotten what she looked like. A lot of water's gone under the bridge since that picture was taken."

"Is this a courthouse in the background?"

"Yeah. That's the Autauga County courthouse. Her mama and daddy didn't want us to get married. We had to elope. She borrowed that dress and them shoes from your great-aunt Emma. There was a man standing out in front of the courthouse when we came out. He wanted to take our picture."

"Why aren't you in the picture, Papa?"

"Well, he said it cost a dollar to take a picture of just one of us and two dollars for both of us. After paying for the marriage license, I didn't have but a dollar left, so we settled on just a picture of Sudie."

"You should put it in a frame, Papa, and set it out so everyone can see it."

"Yeah, I reckon I should. It was a long time before I could stand to look at it without breaking down and crying. When I cried, it upset Beth, so I just put the picture away so I couldn't see it."

"How about we go to the store right now and buy a frame for it?"

"Ya want'a go right now?"

"Sure, Papa. Why not? We don't have anything else to do. Let's go now."

Dawson smiled at his granddaughter's enthusiasm. "Well, all right then. Let's go."

Jake and Vicky got into Montgomery around ten o'clock. They found a hotel near the downtown area and checked in. The hot summer sun was beginning to play havoc on Vicky's pale, delicate skin. She sunburned easily and had forgotten to pack the sunscreen. She knew if she was going to be outside all day roaming the streets of Montgomery, looking for who knows who, she'd better find a new bottle quickly. A Walgreens was located down the street from their hotel. She and Jake found the aisle where the sunscreen was on display. Vicky was looking at them, trying to determine which one to buy. A male voice from two aisles over caught Jake's attention.

"Dawson Hubert," the voice called loudly. "How in the world are you, son?"

The name Dawson Hubert rang in Jakes's head like a church bell on Sunday. He could hardly believe his ears. *Surely not*, he thought to himself. *It can't possibly be the Dawson Hubert I'm looking for. But how many Dawson Huberts could there be?* He at least had to take a look. As he rounded the corner on the second aisle over, a young girl was coming around the other side at the same time. They collided, almost sending the blonde-haired girl to the floor. Jake grabbed her and quickly began to apologize.

"I am so sorry. I wasn't looking where I was going. Are you okay?"

The girl smiled. "I'm okay. No harm done. It's my fault too. I wasn't looking where I was going either. Say, you wouldn't happen to know where the picture frames are, would you?"

Jake answered, "No, I'm sorry I don't. My wife and I are from out of town. This is the first time I've been in this store. I just heard someone call out the name 'Dawson Hubert.' I'm looking for a Dawson Hubert who used to live up in Mountain Creek."

Kayleen looked surprised. "Dawson Hubert is my grandfather."

"Wow, you're kidding me." Jake laughed. "I can't believe this."

"Come on. I'll introduce him to you," Kayleen offered.

"Hang on. Let me get my wife, Vicky. She won't believe this. We thought we'd be looking all day. Vicky, come here quick."

Vicky grabbed a bottle of sunscreen and quickly made her way to the end of the aisle. "What is it, Jake?" she asked.

"You're not going to believe this. This is ... I'm sorry. What is your name?"

"I'm Kayleen."

Vicky smiled. "I'm Vicky. Vicky Tillery."

"Yeah," said Jake. "I guess I should introduce myself also. I'm Jake Tillery."

"Glad to meet you, Jake, Vicky."

Jake turned to Vicky. "Would you believe Kayleen is Dawson Hubert's granddaughter?"

Vicky looked doubly surprised. "You're kidding me."

"No, I really am," said Kayleen. "He's right around the corner. We were here looking for a picture frame. Come with me."

Jake and Vicky followed Kayleen around the corner. Two men were standing face-to-face talking. Kayleen walked up behind her grandfather and touched his arm. He looked down.

"Joe, this is my granddaughter, Kayleen. Kayleen, this is Joe Turner. We went to school together back when."

"You mean they had a real school way back then?" Kayleen teased.

Dawson ruffled her hair and laughed. Jake and Vicky laughed too. Dawson noticed the couple standing behind him.

"Sorry, I didn't see y'all there. Do ya need to get by?"

Kayleen spoke first. "Papa, this is Jake and Vicky Tillery. They are from out of town, and they're looking for you."

Joe poked Dawson in the ribs. "I told ya the law would catch up to ya sooner or later."

Jake put his hand out. "Oh we're not the law. I'm a social worker for Jefferson County. I came here to try and talk to you about your wife's murder."

Dawson turned solemn and did not offer his hand in greeting. "What about my wife's murder? That was a long time ago. Why would a social worker want to be talking with me?"

Jake looked at Vicky then back to Dawson. "Stella Hubert is a client of mine. She told me a man by the name of Silas killed your wife."

The hair on the back of Dawson's neck stood on ends. He could feel the anger rising up inside him. The muscles in his jaw tightened.

"And ya believed her?"

"Well, I believe her to a point. As best I can tell by reading her files, she was shipped off to Benton Hospital but was never convicted of anything. There is no record showing there was ever a trial, a hearing, or anything. I think that is rather strange, don't you?"

"Ya weren't there, Mr. Tillery," said Dawson. "Stella Hubert was my aunt. I didn't want to believe it either. Besides, all this is in the past—a past I've spent years trying hard to forget. What difference does it make now? What's done is done. I suggest ya let sleeping dogs lie."

Dawson turned back to Joe and extended his hand. "It's been good seeing ya, Joe. Sorry I have to cut our visit short, but I need to get out of here. Call me sometime and we'll catch up on old times."

The two men shook hands and Joe promised to call his old friend at a later date. Without another word to Jake or

Vicky, he reached for Kayleen's hand and quickly headed out the door. Jake started to follow him but Joe stopped him.

"Listen, mister," said Joe, "I've known Dawson Hubert for years, and now is not a good time to try and talk to him about his wife's murder. Give him a little time to cool off and maybe then he'll be willing to talk."

Vicky agreed. "I think he's right, Jake. He seemed to be getting rather angry."

Jake thanked Joe, then he and Vicky paid for the sunscreen and left the store. Across the street was a hotdog stand. They decided to have lunch there then go back to the hotel room and nap.

At a quarter till two, Jake woke Vicky from her nap. "Time to get up, honey. I still want to find where Dawson lives. I can't leave here without talking to him first."

Vicky got up, brushed through her hair, and even applied a dab of lipstick on her lips. When she was finished, she called to Jake, "Ready, let's go."

When they were in the car, Vicky turned to Jake. "Where do you plan on starting your search?"

"I'm not rightly sure. While you were asleep, I looked in the phone book, but there was no Dawson Hubert listed. I didn't see the two of them get into a car when they left. So perhaps they live within walking distance of downtown. I suppose we could drive up and down a few streets on the chance we might see them in the yard. I know it's a slim chance, but I don't know what else to do."

Vicky buckled her seatbelt. "Okay, then let's give it a shot."

They spent several hours driving up and down the city streets to no avail. They stopped at a mom-and-pop grocery store on the corner of Lawrence Street to ask if they might know where Dawson lived, but the elderly lady behind the counter could not help them. It was getting late. Jake was about to give up when an idea came to him.

"You know, Vick. It seems to me that I remember Ed Newton saying that Dawson drove an eighteen wheeler for some company here in town."

"Do you remember the name of the company?"

Jake searched his memory bank. "If I remember correctly it started with an S."

"Well, how many trucking companies could there be in this town starting with an S?"

"You're right, Vick. We need to find a phone booth."

As they were driving down Commerce Street, Vicky spied a phone booth.

"There, Jake. There's a phone booth. Pull over."

There was a parking space not far from the phone booth so Jake pulled into it and stopped. While Jake went to check the phone book, Vicky put a nickel into the parking meter. When Jake got to the phone booth he discovered an empty black phonebook cover. Obviously, someone needed a phone book and just took it. Disappointed, he went back to the car. Vicky was standing by the parking meter waiting for him.

"Did you find the trucking company?"

Jake shook his head. "No. The phone book is missing."

Vicky looked around. "I think I see another phone booth two blocks down."

Jake took her hand. "I think you're right. Let's go."

When the two of them reached the phone booth, it too had been vandalized. It was dusk dark and the downtown stores were beginning to close for the day. As they were walking back to their car, an older gentleman came out of one of the stores and was about to lock the door when Vicky got an idea.

"Excuse me sir. I was wondering if you might know of a trucking company here in town that starts with the letter S?"

The old man smiled. "No, not right off hand I don't," he replied. "Why? Do you need to rent a truck?"

Jake extended his hand to the old man and introduced himself.

"We need to find out about a man who works for a certain trucking company."

Jake quickly summarized the story about the murder and why he was looking for Dawson. The old man listened intently. When Jake was finished the old man replied, "That's quite a story, young man."

Vicky mentioned their search for a phone book.

"Well now, I might can help you with that. I have a brand-new phone book inside. Got it just this week. You kids come on in and I'll get it for you."

Jake smiled at Vicky as the two of them followed the old man into the store. Just inside the door, the old man switched on the lights. He then went behind the counter and pulled out the shiny new book. On the front cover was a photograph of the state capitol building. Jake took the book from the old man and quickly turned to the yellow pages under trucking companies. There were several listed. As he scanned down the list he came to Seamon Trucking.

"That's it!" he shouted happily. "Seamon Trucking. They're located on the Mobile Highway. Thank you so much, mister."

"You're welcome," he replied. "Glad I could help. Do you want to use my phone to call them?"

Jake thought for a minute. "No, we've taken up enough of your time. I think it would be better just to go out there and talk to whoever is onsite. But thank you again and you have a good evening."

Jake and Vicky shook the old man's hand and quickly hurried to the car. Once they were on their way, Vicky looked at Jake.

"What if they are closed? Maybe we should have called first."

"Usually there is always someone at the loading docks of most trucking companies. If it's a big company, they have trucks coming and going at all hours of the day and night."

By the time they reached Seamon Trucking Company, it was pitch dark. There were several eighteen wheelers parked around back. A small sign on the corner of the building pointed toward the office. He parked the car and the two of them got out. As they were walking up to the door, Jake could see a dim light shining through the blinds. A man was sitting behind a paper-cluttered desk talking on the phone. Jake knocked.

A voice from inside answered loudly, "We're closed."

"My name is Jake Tillery. I need to talk to you about one of your employees."

Vicky touched Jake on the arm. "Maybe we should come back tomorrow."

"No. I need to know tonight."

Once again he knocked on the door. "Please, mister. I promise to only take a few minutes of your time. It's very important. It could mean life or death."

"Jake!" warned Vicky. "Don't tell him that."

"I'll tell him the world is about to end if it will get him to the door."

Jake could see the man hanging up the phone. The look on his face was not a pleasant one. When he stood up, Vicky noticed how tight his blue-plaid shirt was drawn across his massive chest. To say the least, he was not a small man. When he reached the door, he stopped before opening it.

"What is it ya want?" He asked in a deep raspy voice.

Jake answered with a question. "Do you have a Dawson Hubert working here?"

"Yeah, I know Dawson. What about him?"

"I need to know where he lives. I have something very

MURDER AT MOUNTAIN CREEK

important I need to discuss with him. It's about his murdered wife."

Jake heard the door lock click as it was being opened. Curiosity had gotten the better of the big man inside. The door swung open and he motioned for them to come in. Vicky clung to Jake's side as they entered the dimly lit room.

"Take a seat," he said, pointing to two rickety metal chairs.

Jake and Vicky sat down while the man went behind the desk and sat down himself. Once he was seated he leaned back on the chair's back legs and put his hands together behind his head.

"What is this about a murdered wife?" he asked.

Jake told him enough of the story to satisfy the man's curiosity. When he was finished, the man let his chair back down and reached for a pad and pencil. He scribbled Dawson's phone number and address on the paper and handed it to Jake. Jake reached for it, but before the man would turn it loose, he said to Jake, "ya didn't get this from me. Understand?"

"Yes. I understand. And thank you. This is a big help. We appreciate it very much."

The man released the paper. Jake folded it and put it in his pocket. Without another word, the man pointed toward the door. Jake and Vicky took that as meaning he was ready for them to leave. Without hesitation they walked to the door and headed straight for the car. When they were safely inside, Vicky looked at Jake.

"I would hate to run into him on a dark street corner."

They both laughed.

"Let's get back to the hotel. I want to call Dawson tonight. Maybe he's had time to think about the situation and will be willing to talk to us."

Dawson did not say a word to Kayleen all the way back to the house. She tried to talk to him, but he refused to discuss it. When Dawson and Kayleen arrived home, Beth had returned. She and Mama Cora were sitting on the front porch. Dawson did not stop to speak to either of them but went inside, slamming the door behind him.

"What's wrong with, Daddy?" Beth asked.

Kayleen sat down on the top step and began telling them about meeting Jake and Vicky at Walgreens. "Papa got so upset he just stormed out of the store. Said he didn't want to talk about it."

"Oh dear," said Mama Cora, "why do folks want to stir up something that happened forty years ago?"

Dawson went straight to his room, threw the picture of Sudie on the bed, and laid facedown on his pillow. But, when he closed his eyes, all he could see was the bloody scene where Sudie's murder took place. The taste of iron filled his mouth. He felt sick to his stomach. He sat up and opened his eyes. There at the foot of his bed was the picture of Sudie on their wedding day. He picked it up. Tears welled up in his eyes. *If only you could tell me what happened that day,* he thought to himself. *Was it Stella? Could it have really been someone else?* He threw the picture on the nightstand beside his bed. *Why now after all these years?*

Dawson spent the rest of the afternoon alone in his room. Beth tried to talk to him but he refused to talk to anyone. Kayleen had just finished setting the table for supper when Dawson finally came down the stairs. As soon as she saw him, she ran to him crying, throwing her arms around his waist.

"Papa, I am so sorry for all this. I didn't know how much

it still hurts you to talk about my grandmother's death. Please forgive me."

Dawson pulled Kayleen away from him far enough that he could look into her eyes.

"My dear sweet Kayleen, Papa ain't angry with you. I guess deep down inside I knew the day would come when the cream would rise to the top of the milk. All these years I've tried to forget, to act like it never happened. But it did happen. After thinking bout it this afternoon, I wish now I had talked to that feller we met in Walgreens."

"Oh, Papa, I was so worried about you. I love you so much."

From the kitchen, Beth heard her father and daughter talking. She walked to the dining room door. "Are you okay, Dad?"

"I'm fine. I just needed some time to think and to be alone."

Mama Cora walked by Beth with a bowl of mashed potatoes and sat it on the table next to the country fried steak. "I fixed one of your favorite meals. Soon as the biscuits come out of the oven, we'll be ready to eat."

Dawson smiled and took his seat at the head of table. After the blessing was asked, everyone filled their plates and began to eat. Nothing further was said about the events of the day. Just as they were finished eating, the phone rang. Kayleen jumped up to answer it. She went into the living room and picked up the receiver.

"Hello. Yes, this is the Hubert residence."

"I wonder who that could be this time of night," said Beth.

Mama Cora stood up and began clearing the table. "Probably some salesman. They're always calling here wanting me to change phone companies. I tell them I've been with AT&T for nearly forty years and I don't intend on changing now."

"Just a minute please. I'll have to go and ask." They heard Kayleen say.

Kayleen put the phone down and walked into the dining

room. She had a very somber look on her face. Before she could say anything, Mama Cora spoke up.

"If it's a salesman child, tell them we don't want whatever it is they're selling."

Kayleen looked directly at her grandfather. "Papa, it's Jake Tillery. The man we met at Walgreens. He wants to talk to you."

Beth became instantly offensive. "Tell him your papa doesn't want to talk to him and not to call back ever again."

Kayleen started to turn around but her grandfather stopped her. "No, Kayleen. I do want to talk to him. It's time I faced my demons."

Dawson went into the living room and picked up the phone. "Hello. This is Dawson Hubert—Yes I remember ya — Tomorrow? Yes tomorrow will be fine—Around two is good. That will give us time to get home from church and have our dinner—Yes. Good-bye."

Jake drove down Hull Street while Vicky looked at the mailbox addresses.

"One oh three, One oh five, One oh seven, One oh nine. There it is," she said, pointing to the white, two-story, older home.

Jake pulled alongside the curb. Kayleen was sitting on the front porch waiting for their arrival. As soon as she saw their car, she ran out to meet them.

"Hi, Jake. Hi, Vicky. Y'all get out and come in. My mother's here too. I should tell you, she's a little concerned about bringing up the subject of grandma's death."

Vicky and Jake got out of the car and walked up the sidewalk to the porch. Kayleen opened the door and escorted them inside. Dawson, Beth, and Mama Cora were seated in the living room. Mama Cora spoke first.

"Y'all come on in and have a seat. I'm Dawson's mama. Everybody calls me Mama Cora. This here is my granddaughter, Beth. She's more like a daughter to me than a granddaughter. I raised her after her mama got killed. Can I get y'all something to drink? I got tea, or I got a pitcher of fresh lemonade. Y'all go on and sit down. Make yourselves at home. I think we could all use a glass."

Vicky and Jake took a seat next to one another on the overstuffed, red floral couch. Kayleen sat down on the arm of the couch. Dawson was sitting in the matching armchair, and Beth was sitting across from him in a cane bottom chair. Everyone seemed to be at a loss for something to say. Vicky finally broke the silence.

"You all have a very nice house. I love these tall ceilings."

Dawson looked up as though he had never noticed the ceilings being tall. "I reckon so," he muttered.

Jake Dawson spoke next. "I understand you drive an eighteen-wheeler. That must be very exciting work."

Dawson did not respond to Jake's comment but rather asked him a question. "How did ya know I lived in Montgomery?"

Jake shook his head. "Well, you see, I was in Prattville last week and ran into Ed Newton at Jim's Restaurant. He told me you lived in Montgomery. I've never spent much time in Montgomery, so I wasn't sure we could find you. I tried to look you up in the phone book, but you aren't listed. It was by pure coincidence we ran into you and Kayleen at the store."

Mama Cora came back into the room with a tray full of lemonade. Kayleen helped her pass the glasses out to each of them. Jake immediately took a long, slow drink. He was glad she had made it, as his throat felt like he was trying to choke down a mouthful of cotton.

Dawson set his glass on the coffee table without taking a swallow. "Ya said ya wanted to tell me something about Stella."

Jake set his glass down too. "Yes, that's right."

Beth spoke for the first time. "I can't believe they let her out of the hospital. Mama Cora said she heard Stella has cancer."

"Yes, I'm afraid so," answered Jake. "She doesn't have long to live. On our last visit, she told me a story she said she had never told anyone before." Jake recounted the story Stella told him in his office.

When Jake looked at Beth. Tears rolled down her cheeks. Kayleen knelt down beside her mother and held her hand. Dawson's eyes were flooded with tears also.

"I know it must be hard for all of you to hear this again but"—he paused—"I don't know. I just felt like you needed to know. If her story is true and the baby did live, then you could have a child out there somewhere."

Dawson put his head in his hands and propped them on his knees. "I've always hoped and prayed my young 'un was out there somewhere. I looked everywhere in the woods around the old house. I never found not even a hair from its head. I always felt like there would have been something, blood, bones, something."

"That is why I wanted to talk to you, Dawson. If Stella's story is true and the baby was stolen, you might very well have a son or daughter. I know if I were he, I would want to meet my real mother and father. Of course, he can't meet his mother but he could meet you, Dawson."

Beth got to her feet. All at once she became angry. "This is ridiculous," she snapped. "The chances of finding a baby born forty years ago are next to impossible. In fact, it is impossible. I wish you wouldn't have come here with this crazy story. You've upset all of us."

Vicky spoke in defense of her husband. "I know this is hard for all of you, but Jake is only trying to do what he thinks is right. He's lain awake many nights over this. We are using our days off to come here. Please try to understand his side."

"I think it's a noble thing you're doing, Jake," said Kayleen. "If it were my child, I would want to find it no matter how bad it hurt. Don't you realize, Mama, you could have a brother or a sister you don't even know about?"

Beth was still upset. "Sometimes it's best to let sleeping dogs lie," she countered.

Dawson lifted his head. "We're not talking 'bout a dog here, Beth. We're talking 'bout a human being. Our flesh and blood."

"I know, Dad. I just don't want to see you get your hopes up."

"Ya let me worry 'bout that." He turned his attention back to Jake. "What do ya need to know that will help ya find my baby?"

Jake wasn't sure what he needed, but he needed to give them some kind of answer. Suddenly it came to him. "Do you have a picture of Sudie?"

"Yes," answered Dawson. "It's upstairs laying on the night-stand next to my bed. Will ya get it for him, Kayleen?"

Kayleen ran up the stairs and found the picture. When she returned, she handed the picture to Jake.

"Great. Now, how about a picture of you, Dawson? One taken around the time you turned forty."

Beth spoke up again. "What good will a picture of Daddy be in finding this illusive child?"

Jake began to explain, "I have a friend who works for the FBI. He is an artist. Hopefully he can take these two pictures and come up with a composite drawing of what the person would look like today. We'll also have him run it through the FBI database. If the person has ever been in trouble or I don't know … It's a long shot for sure, but it's worth a try."

Mama Cora spoke up next. "Well by George, I say give it a

try. Nothing ventured, nothing gained, I always say. I'll get the picture album. I'm sure we've got a snapshot of my handsome boy in it somewhere."

Before Jake and Vicky left later that evening, they had collected several snapshots of Dawson, Mama Cora, Beth, and Dawson's deceased father, Lonnie. They also took along the one and only picture they had of Sudie. Hopefully Jake's friend would be able to put together a near likeness of the missing child. Only now, he or she would be a grown man or woman.

Jake gave his friend, Russell Andrews, a call from their hotel room that evening as they were packing to leave. Russell listened to Jake's outlandish story but agreed to help them. Jake and Vicky would drop off the pictures on their way home. Russell promised he would have the sketch back to them as soon as possible.

A week passed. Jake was beginning to get antsy. He could hardly keep his mind on his work. He was looking forward to seeing what Russell was going to come up with. Stella was due to come in for her next appointment in two days. He hoped Russell could get the drawing back to him by then. As he was pondering the possibility, his phone rang and made him jump.

"Hello, this is Jake Tillery. How may I help you?"

"Jake, my boy. The question is not how you can help me but how I can help you."

Jake recognized the voice as being his friend Russell. "Hey, Russ. How's it hanging?"

"I'm good. I've got your sketch ready. How about we do lunch at Martin's?"

"Sounds good to me. I really appreciate your help. Lunch is on me."

Russell laughed. "You bet it is."

"How's eleven thirty sound?"

"I'll be there with bells on."

Jake laughed. "Please, man, wear more than just bells."

"Yeah, yeah. You're no fun at all."

The morning seemed to drag on forever. Jake kept watching the clock. It felt like twenty minutes had passed, yet the clock showed only five. During the morning. he met with two clients and caught up on some paperwork. By then it was a quarter after eleven. The restaurant was just around the corner from his office. Since he still had plenty of time to get there, he decided to walk rather than take his car. He arrived at Martin's just as Russell pulled into the parking lot. Jake watched and waited at the door for Russell to join him before going inside. Once they were inside, the hostess seated them right away.

Martin's was a locally owned family business. The food was excellent and the atmosphere relaxing. Jake frequented it at least twice a week. He and Martin had become friends, so he always gave Jake an extra-large helping.

The hostess placed the menus on the table. "Steve will be your waiter today. Enjoy your lunch, gentlemen."

Jake thanked her then looked directly at Russell. "Okay, Russ, let's have it."

Russell looked surprised. "Let you have what?" he teased.

"The sketch, Russ. The sketch."

Russell held up a manila envelope. "You mean this sketch?"

Jake tried to grab the envelope from Russell's hand, but Russell pulled it away.

"I need to talk to you about it first. How about we put in our order, then I'll show it to you?"

As if on cue, a waiter came over to the table. He was a tall, thin man with slicked-back hair and a pencil-thin mustache. "Good morning, gentlemen," he said. "I am Steve. What can I get you to drink?"

Jake ordered sweet tea. Russell ordered a Miller Lite. They also ordered the special of the day, beef stroganoff and a green salad.

"Okay, Russ, what's the holdup?"

Russell opened the envelope and pulled out the sketch. "Before I show you this, Jake, you have to understand something. This drawing is based on a forty-year-old photo of the woman and a twenty-year-old picture of the man."

"I know that, Russ. But it might give us an idea of what the person would look like. Did you run it through your database?"

"I did."

"Did you get a hit?"

"I did."

"You're kidding. You got a match?"

"I got a match."

"Who was it? Was it a man or a woman?"

"It was a man, all right."

"Unbelievable. Do you have a name and an address?"

Russell did not answer. Instead he turned the sketch around so Jake could see it clearly. Jake was stunned. He wanted to speak, but nothing would come out. The waiter came back with their drinks. He set the tea in front of Jake and the beer in front of Russell, and then he too looked at the picture.

"Great drawing," he said to Jake. "Looks just like you. I wish I could draw. I can't draw a stick man and make it look like anything."

Jake looked across the table at Russell. "Is this some kind of joke, Russ?"

"It's no joke, my friend," Russell answered.

Jake looked up at Steve. "I think I'll have a drink after all. Scotch and soda. Make it a double."

Russell handed the drawing to Jake. "I don't know what to say, Jake. They say everybody has a double. He could be your twin brother."

Jake continued to stare in disbelief. "This just blows my mind. It can't be. I mean, I know I was adopted, but my parents were killed in a car accident. This is just too weird. What do I do, Russ?"

"I have no idea," answered Russell. "Do you think it is at all possible you could be this person?"

"I don't see how ... I think the first thing I need to do is talk to my mother again."

"Are you going to tell the Hubert family about this?"

"Not yet. I will have to be completely convinced of it myself before I present my findings to them. They've had enough disappointments and sorrow in their lives. And who knows, it may turn out to be just like you said, my double."

Steve brought Jake his drink. Before the ice had settled in the glass, he snatched it up and gulped down half of it. Within minutes, their food was served. Although it was delicious, Jake could barely swallow. He felt like his throat was stuffed with a six-pound lead weight. Russell had no trouble eating at all. Jake thanked Russell for the sketch, paid the bill, and told Russell good-bye. On his way back to the office, his mind was whirling in every direction possible. He needed to call Vicky. Most of all, he needed to call his mom.

Jake decided he would take the rest of the day off. He called his mother and told her he was coming by. She asked him if there was something wrong. He lied and told her no, but he knew she could tell he was lying. He asked Vicky to meet him at his mother's house at two o'clock. He didn't tell her what it was about, just that it was important.

Jake arrived at her house a few minutes early. He sat in the car, trying to decide how he should go about asking his mother for more details about his adoption. No matter how hard he tried, nothing he came up with seemed appropriate. When Vicky arrived, he got out of the car to meet her. They kissed.

"What's going on, Jake?" she asked. "Why did you want me to meet you here?"

"I guess I just need you for moral support. You'll under-stand when we get inside."

"Does it have something to do with the drawing Russ did?"

"How did you know it was finished?"

"For some reason, Russ called me first to say it was done. I told him to call you at work. I'm assuming that he did."

"Yes, we had lunch together. I have the sketch here."

He held up the manila envelope.

"Can I see it?" she asked.

"I'll show it to you when we get inside. Mom is waiting on us."

They made their way up the flower-lined sidewalk to the front door. Before Jake could knock, his mother opened it.

"Come in, come in, you two. This is such a pleasant sur-prise." She hugged and kissed both of them. "Let's go into the den. I made us a nice, cold glass of tea with fresh mint from the garden. Jake, do you remember when you put mint leaves in Tabby's food?"

She sat down in a soft yellow chair next to the window.

"Tabby was a cat we used to have," she explained to Vicky. "When I asked him why he did it, he said because her breath smelled like fish, and he thought the mint would make it smell better. I never knew what he was going to do from one minute to the next."

Vicky chuckled. "He hasn't changed a bit. I never know what he's up to half the time, either."

Jake sat down across from his mother. Vicky sat down next to him. As his mother was pouring tea into the glasses, he looked at her—truly looked at her for the first time in a long time. She had always been a very youthful-looking person. Her light brown hair was more gray now than brown. He noticed the deep-set wrinkles around her eyes. Had this all happened since his father died? He felt bad he had not spent more time with her recently. She'd been a good mother to him. His father had been a good dad. A thought flashed across his mind: *How would my life have been different had I known and been raised by my real parents?*

"Jake," she called to him. "Here's your tea, son."

Jake reached for the glass. "Thanks, Mom."

Mrs. Tillery sat back in her chair and sipped her tea. "Now what is it you want to talk to me about, dear? Do you and Vicky have something you need to tell me? Say, for instance, I'm going to be a grandmother?"

Shocked, Jake and Vicky looked at one another then back at Mrs. Tillery.

"No. No," they said in unison.

"No babies. At least not yet anyway," added Vicky.

"Too bad. Wishful thinking, I suppose."

Jake took the lead. "Mom, do you remember when you and Dad told me I was adopted?"

"Well, of course, I remember, Jake. Your father didn't want to tell you, but I felt you deserved to know."

"You also told me my real parents had died in a car accident."

Mrs. Tillery dropped her head. "Yes that's what we told you."

"Mom," Jake said earnestly, "did my parents really die in a car accident?"

Mrs. Tillery's eyes filled with tears as she looked directly at Jake. "No, son, they did not."

"Do you even know who my real parents are?"

"Not really. You see, when I was told I couldn't have any children, I was devastated. So was your father. I was in my late thirties by then. Your father was almost fifty. Most adoption agencies wouldn't even talk to us about adopting. I cried for weeks on end. Then one day, your father came home with the most wonderful surprise of my life. You were wrapped in an old, bloody coat. You'd never even been cleaned up from being born. When I asked your father where you came from, he said you were a gift from God and that was all I needed to know. At first I was afraid he had stolen you. I read the paper every day from cover to cover to see if someone reported a missing child. After a while, I guess I just convinced myself you were a gift from God and let it go."

"In the years that followed, I asked him several times about where he found you, but he never would say. It was a secret he carried to his grave. When you were turning sixteen, I convinced him we should tell you about being adopted. That was when he made up the story about your parents being killed in a car accident. To be honest with you, Jake, I have no idea who your real parents were. However, I do know this, no one in the world could have loved you any more than your father and I loved you."

Jake got up from the couch and knelt down in front of his mother's chair. "I know that, Mom. You and Dad were and still are the best parents anybody could ever ask for. I love you very much. I loved Dad, too."

Mrs. Tillery patted him on the hand. "I know you do, son. You've always made us proud. I wish I could give you better insight into who your real parents are. The only thing I have, which might help, is something that was wrapped up in the coat with you."

"What do you mean, Mom?"

"I saved it all these years. It too was covered in blood, but I cleaned it up and put it away. There's been many times I wanted to give it to you, but I didn't quite know how to go about it. I'll get it for you now."

Mrs. Tillery got up from her chair and went straight to her

bedroom. Jake couldn't imagine what she could possibly have that might help him discover who he was or where he came from. A few minutes later, she returned carrying a figurine.

"This was in the coat with you," she said, handing it to him.

Jake held up the figurine.

"It's a dancing ballerina," said Vicky. "That's an odd thing to give to a little boy baby. Maybe it belonged to the mother. Maybe she was a dancer."

Jake turned it over and looked on the bottom. "It says it was made in Occupied Japan. It's not an expensive piece. Probably purchased at a five and dime."

"I'm sorry. That is all I have. That and the coat you were wrapped in. I washed it and kept it too. Would you like to have it?"

"Yes, Mom," he answered. "I would like to have it."

Mrs. Tillery put her hands on each side of Jake's shoulders. "Jake, I hope you don't hate me for keeping this a secret all these years. I just didn't know how to tell you."

Jake hugged his mother tightly. "I could never hate you, Mom. I love you with all my heart, and you will always be my mother."

Dawson lay awake in his truck's sleeper bed, thinking about what Jake had said. Could it be the son he'd always hope for was out there somewhere? He had always been in his dreams. Some of his dreams were nice dreams. He would be playing catch with his son, or they'd be rolling around on the ground, wrestling with each other. Then there were the bad dreams. In the bad dreams, his little boy was being swept away by the darkness. He would look for him, but he was always just out of reach, being swallowed up by some unknown force. The dreams started shortly after Sudie's death. Every night he was haunted by them. Over the years, the dreams had almost stopped coming. In a way he was glad. Like his dreams, his hopes of ever having a son had faded too. Now someone had given him new hope. If only he could be sure Jake was right. All he could do was wait and see.

Beth and Kayleen were anxious about the situation too, Kayleen more than Beth.

"Mama, do you think it's possible you might actually have a brother or sister somewhere out there?"

Beth put down her dishcloth and looked at Kayleen. "I think there's a better chance of my having a brother or sister in one of the towns Dad delivers to than there is of finding my mother's dead baby still alive."

Kayleen laughed. "Mama, I can't believe you said that. Papa would never do something like that. Mama, do you think Jake is a good-looking man?"

Beth finished wiping off the table, rinsed out her dishrag, and hung it across the gooseneck faucet to dry.

"I suppose. I didn't really look at him that closely."

"I think he is very handsome. Too bad he's married. He would be just about the right age for you."

"Hey, girly, don't go matching me up with another man. Luke is as close to being my husband as any man is ever gonna be. Besides, Jake is already married to Vicky. They seem like they care for each other a lot."

"I saw Dad the other day. He has a new girlfriend."

Beth flopped down across the couch. "That's nice."

"Don't you want to know what she looks like?"

"No."

"She looks okay, but she's not nearly as pretty as you are."

Beth flipped her hand through her hair and flung her leg in the air. "Of course not. I'm the most beautiful and sexiest woman in the world. How could anyone be as pretty as me?"

Kayleen

Beth threw a pillow at her mom. "You're so crazy."

Beth threw it back at Kayleen. "And the craziest woman in the world. That's me."

The phone rang. Kayleen picked it up.

"Hello. Oh, hi, Jake. We were just talking about you." She covered the receiver with her hand. "It's Jake."

"What does he want? Did he find out anything?"

"Tomorrow. Just a minute, I'll ask Mom. He wants to know if he can come down tomorrow."

Beth shook her head. "Of course. Tell him tomorrow is fine."

"She said tomorrow is fine ... Around ten o'clock. Yes, ten is good ... I'll tell her ... We'll meet you at Mama Cora's at ten. Thanks. See ya."

"Did he say if he found out anything?"

"No. He just said he needed to see us as soon as possible. He also asked me to call Papa. He said he tried to call but couldn't get anyone."

Beth sat upright on the couch. "That's right. Dad is out of town. Mama Cora said he wouldn't be back till sometime tomorrow. I wonder where Mama Cora is."

"You forget, Mama. Tonight is the night she plays bingo at the community center."

"That's right. I always forget about her bingo night. You would think I would remember. She's been playing there every Friday night for the past five years."

"I guess it's just old age setting in," teased Kayleen.

Jake crawled into bed beside Vicky. She had the manila envelope in her lap and was looking at the picture Russell had compiled.

"This is so weird, Jake. This picture looks so much like

you. I thought your mother was going to have a heart attack when you showed it to her."

"I know. It'll be interesting to see what Dawson has to say and if he knows anything about the figurine. I thought about showing it and the coat to Stella. She had an appointment with me this afternoon. She's really going downhill in a hurry. Jack was having to push her in a wheelchair. I'm sure I'll have to go to her house from now on. I don't think she'll be able to make the trip to my office. I wanted to tell her about everything, but I just couldn't bring myself to burden her with anything else. Once I know for sure, then I'll tell her."

"What time do you want to leave in the morning?"

"I told Beth we'd meet them at Mama Cora's house at ten."

Vicky chuckled. "She's got you calling her 'Mama Cora' too."

"I know. It's weird, Vick, but I feel like I've known these people all my life. Plus, Mama Cora is one of those people anyone would want to claim as their grandmother."

Vicky reached inside the envelope and pulled out the picture of Sudie. Jake lay his head on her shoulder.

"Sudie was a pretty woman," she said.

Jake stared at the picture for several minutes before responding. "Yes, she was." Suddenly he sat straight up in the bed. "Vick, do you realize we could be looking at a picture of my real mother?"

Vicky smiled and placed her hand on Jake's shoulder. "Yes, sweetheart. I do realize that, and I worry about how it's going to affect you emotionally."

Jake fell back onto his pillow. "The truth is, Vick, Mom is the only mother I've ever known. Sudie is gone. If it turns out she is my biological mother, the only way I will know anything about her will be what those who knew her can tell me."

"I know, Jake. But if she is your real mother, that makes Dawson your real father. And he is still alive."

Jake rolled over and turned the switch on the lamp to the off position. The room went dark on his side of the bed. He fluffed his feather pillow, turned toward the wall, and closed his eyes.

"I can't think about that now. I have to get some sleep if we're going to get out of here first thing in the morning."

Vicky put the drawing and Sudie's picture back into the envelope. She laid the envelope on the nightstand and flipped off the light. She leaned over and kissed Jake on the cheek.

"Good night, sweetheart. I love you."

"I love you too, Vick. Good night."

Jake was awake by five o'clock the next morning. He made coffee, scrambled each of them two eggs, and made toast. He put the eggs, toast, coffee, and small glass of orange juice on a tray and carried it into the bedroom where Vicky was still sleeping.

"Wake up, sleepyhead," he called to her. "Breakfast is ready."

Vicky rolled over and sat up in bed. She looked at the clock. "Jake, it's five fifteen. We don't need to leave here till around eight."

"I know but I woke up and couldn't sleep, so I made us breakfast." He placed the tray across her lap. "Eat up while I pack our suitcase."

Vicky leaned back against the headboard and reached for the cup of coffee. She took a sip. It was so strong, it could practically stand by itself.

"Jake, honey, how many scoops of coffee did you put in the coffeemaker?"

"Ahhh, I don't know. I just put some in there. Why? Is it too strong?"

"*Strong* isn't the word for it." She laughed.

"Well, drink your OJ. I know it's not too strong. What do you want to take to wear?" Jake stepped out of the closet, holding up a pair of green jeans and an orange shirt. "How about these?"

Vicky smiled. "I don't think so, Jake. You pack what you want to wear and let me worry about packing my stuff. We've got plenty of time. It only takes a couple of hours to get to Montgomery from here."

"Okay. I just don't want to be late."

Vicky ate the breakfast Jake prepared for her, except for the coffee. That she poured down the bathroom sink. After taking a quick shower, she packed what she would need for an overnight stay. By that time, it was barely six thirty. She made the bed then went downstairs. Since Jake had made breakfast, she was expecting to see a messy kitchen. To her surprise, Jake had already cleaned up the kitchen, straightened the living room, fed the cat, and took out the trash. She couldn't believe her eyes.

"Wow," she said, quite shocked. "You've been busy this morning."

Jake walked over, kissed her on the cheek, and took the overnight bag from her hand. "I'll put this in the car. You call Jess and make sure she knows to feed Socks this evening. Tell her I opened a new bag of cat food. It's in the pantry on the bottom shelf."

"Jake, it's not even seven o'clock. I'm not going to call Jess on a Saturday morning and wake her up. I'm sure she was out late last night with her friends. The last thing she wants to hear is the phone ringing at this hour. We'll call her when we get down the road a ways."

"Yeah, I guess you're right. I just don't want to be late getting to Mama Cora's house." He thought for a minute. "The pictures. Did you get the pictures?"

"Yes, Jake. They're in the overnight bag."

"Did you get the ballerina?"

"Yes. It's in the overnight bag."

"Did you wrap it in something to make sure it doesn't get broken?"

"Yes, Jake. I wrapped it in tissue paper and put it in between my pajamas and my T-shirt. As long as you don't bash the overnight bag against the wall, I'm pretty sure it will be safe."

"I would feel terrible if something happened to it."

"I know, Jake. I would too, but I think it will be fine."

"Well, shall we get on the road?"

"We're going to be early getting there."

"Better early than late, I always say."

Vicky laughed and grabbed her purse as the two of them headed out the door. "I can hardly wait to hear what Dawson and Mama Cora have to say about the picture and the figurine," she said as they got into the car.

Jake put the key into the ignition. "I know. My stomach feels like it's tied up in fifty knots."

Jake and Vicky arrived in Montgomery around nine o'clock. They drove up in front of Mama Cora's house, expecting to sit there until their appointed meeting time. Instead, they discovered they weren't the only ones early. Beth and Kayleen were also there. Kayleen ran out to meet them even before Jake had time to turn off the engine.

"Hey, y'all," she yelled as she bounced down the steps. "I could hardly wait for y'all to get here."

When Jake and Vicky got out of the car, Kayleen hugged each of them.

Vicky laughed at her enthusiasm. "We're glad to see you too, Kayleen."

"What did you find out?" she questioned Jake.

"All in good time," Jake answered. "All in good time. Is Dawson here?"

Kayleen wrinkled up her nose. "No, but he's supposed to be getting home any time now."

Jake looked a little concerned. "Well, that might be best anyway. It'll give Mama Cora and Beth a chance to give me their opinion of what I found first."

Kayleen was so excited, she could hardly stand it. "Great, then hurry and get inside so you can tell us all about it."

"Okay," said Jake. "Just let me get our overnight bag. It contains some pictures I want to show everyone."

Jake and Vicky followed Kayleen into the house. Mama Cora was sitting on the couch, and Beth was coming from the kitchen with a tray full of coffee cups filled with hot, steaming coffee for everyone. She set it on the coffee table then hugged Vicky and Jake.

"Good to see ya," she told them. "Have a seat. How 'bout a cup of coffee?"

"Sounds good to me," said Vicky.

Jake set the overnight bag on the floor beside the couch. "Sure, I'll have some coffee," he said.

Beth gave each of them a cup then took one for herself. "How about you, Mama Cora? Would you like a cup?"

"No. I've done had all the coffee I can stand for one day. I've been up since four thirty."

Vicky smiled. "You sound like Jake. That's why we're so early. He even served me breakfast in bed this morning."

"Wow," said Kayleen. "Nobody ever brings me breakfast in bed."

"That's 'cause most weekends you sleep past noon," teased her mother.

The room became quiet. It was as though no one knew what to say next. Finally, Mama Cora broke the silence.

"Well, did ya find out anything or not?"

Jake looked at Vicky then reached for the bag. Carefully he opened it and took out the pictures first. He opened the envelope and placed the pictures of Dawson and Sudie on the table in front of him.

"As you all know, I took these pictures to my friend, Russell, who works as a sketch artist for the FBI. I had him do a composite drawing of what a child from these two people might look like at the age he or she would be now."

Slowly he pulled the sketch from the envelope and laid it beside the other pictures. Everyone leaned forward to get a closer look. Time seemed to stand still while Mama Cora, Beth, and Kayleen stared at the picture in disbelief. Finally, Mama Cora spoke first.

"Is it me, or does that picture look like the spitting image of Jake?"

No one answered. Beth's hands began to tremble. She set her cup of coffee on the end table beside her chair.

"Is this a joke, Jake?" she asked. "If it is, it's not funny."

Kayleen began shaking her head. "It is you, Jake. Isn't it?"

"I know it's a lot to comprehend," said Jake. "I was the same way when I first saw it. I didn't want to believe it either. I accused Russell of trying to pull a joke on me. He assured me he wasn't. Now you have to understand that this is simply a sketch of what Russell interprets the person would look like. It's not an exact science. It could be anyone with the same features. I decided to show the picture to my adopted mother. When I told her about all this, she told me a story I'd never heard before. It was a story about the night she first saw me."

Jake retold the same story his mother had told to him. When he was finished, he reached into the overnight bag and took out the ballerina.

"This figurine and the bloody coat I was wrapped in were the only two things that could tie me to where I came from. Do either of you know anything about this ballerina?"

No sooner than the question was asked, Dawson walked in the door. The first thing he saw was the lovely ballerina figurine sitting on the coffee table. He immediately walked over to the table and picked it up,

"Where did ya get this?" he asked somewhat angrily.

Jake looked at Dawson then stood to his feet. "My mother said my father brought it home with him the night I came to live with them. I was wrapped in a bloody coat, and the ballerina was in the coat beside me. Does it mean anything to you, Dawson?"

Dawson's eyes filled with tears. "I gave this to Sudie for our first anniversary. It sat on the table beside our bed. After she was killed, I looked for it. I wanted to keep it for Beth so she would have something that belonged to her mother. I couldn't find it. It was gone. I didn't know what had become of it. I decided one of the deputies must'a taken it."

Beth picked up the sketch and showed it to her father. "Look, Daddy. This is the picture the man at the FBI drew. Who does it look like to you?"

Dawson stared at the picture for several minutes. Tears ran down his cheeks and dropped on the paper. Slowly he raised his head. His eyes met Jake's eyes. In them, he could see something he had not noticed before. Jake had Sudie's eyes—the color, the depth of feelings. They stared at each other. Finally, Dawson spoke first.

"What do ya say, Jake? Are ya really...my son?"

Now it was Jake's turn to have tears in his eyes. "I know it's hard to believe but, yes, I think I am."

Dawson grabbed Jake in a bear hug and held him there for a long time. It was as though he thought if he let Jake go, he would disappear. Jake felt as though an empty spot in his heart was filling to the brim and running over. Everyone in the room was in tears. When Dawson eventually let go, his tears were tears of joy rather than tears of sadness. Soon, Beth took her turn hugging Jake. Next came Kayleen and then Mama Cora. Vicky was crying too. She knew how much Jake wanted to know his real parents. It was an unbelievable dream come true for the entire family.

The rest of the day was spent exchanging stories about their lives. Jake told them about his adoptive parents and the wonderful childhood he had growing up. He told them about his school days, of how he met Vicky, their courtship, and their eventual marriage. He talked about his job. Lastly he told them about Stella and how she had been the one who had instigated his search for the truth about Sudie's murder. Dawson drew in every word from his newly found son's mouth. Before him was the son he had always wanted.

The entire weekend was spent sharing their lives with one another. When Sunday afternoon arrived, neither Jake nor his newfound family was ready for it to end. However, Jake knew he had to get back to work. He also wanted the opportunity to talk to Stella. He wanted her to know what she had done for both him and his family. He knew he could never give her back all the wasted years she had spent in the mental hospital. His only hope was she would feel vindicated by everyone finally knowing she was not the person who had killed his mother.

At five o'clock that Sunday afternoon, Jake and Vicky said their good-byes to his family. Beth could see a light in her father's eyes she had never seen before. It was as though his step became lighter, his attitude brighter.

Vicky knew Jake would be preoccupied with his thoughts so she offered to drive home. For the first thirty miles of their trip, Jake spoke not a word. His thoughts whirled around in his head like a small bird in a windstorm. The whole situation was unbelievable. Finding his biological family was nothing short of a miracle. He went over the events in his head, which led up to his discovery: meeting Stella Hubert; his encounter at the restaurant with Sudie's brother, Ed; his adoptive mother telling him the true story about the night he was brought to her; and the ballerina. In his heart, Jake believed it was truly the hand of God that had caused everything to come together the way it did.

"Jake, are you all right?" Vicky asked.

He did not answer but continued to look out the window.

Vicky reached across the seat and touched his arm. "Jake, are you okay?" she asked again.

This time he turned to look at her. "What? I'm sorry. Did you say something?"

Vicky smiled. "I asked if you are all right?"

"Oh, sure," he answered. "I was just thinking about everything."

"I know. It's almost incomprehensible."

"I can hardly wait to tell Stella."

"You know it really is a shame she spent all those years in a mental hospital for something she didn't do."

"Well, Vicky, the truth is, Stella does have mental problems. As best I can tell from her records, she is a paranoid schizophrenic. She is also bipolar. So it is quite reasonable to say she would have wound up in a mental hospital anyway. But I agree; it is a shame she was dubbed a murderer."

"When are you going to tell her?"

"I'd like to tell her tonight, but she may be sleeping by the time we get back home."

Vicky looked at her watch. "It's only a quarter till six. We'll be home by seven. Do you know where she lives?"

"Yes. In fact, Ida's house is only a few blocks from where we live. I suppose we could drive by there. If the lights are still on, we could stop and see if she's still awake."

"Sounds like a plan to me."

It was a few minutes shy of seven o'clock when Vicky turned left onto Sycamore Drive.

"What is the house number, Jake?" she asked as she eased the car down the street.

"The house number is one eleven," he answered. "It's going to be on the left side of the street."

A few houses down was 111. It was an older, two-story house surrounded by several flower beds full of beautiful blooming daises, Black-eyed Susans, day lilies, and petunias. A wooden fence along the driveway was covered in an array of bright red, old-fashioned running roses. Lights were still on in the house. Vicky eased the car up the driveway. She turned off the ignition and turned toward Jake.

"Do you want me to wait here for you?" she asked.

"No. You can come in too. I'm sure Stella would enjoy meeting you."

Vicky and Jake opened the doors of the car and got out. Jake was nervous. His hands were trembling and his heart was racing. On the one hand, he was excited. On the other hand, he was leery of what Stella might say or do. He walked around to Vicky's side of the car, and together they walked up the sidewalk to the front porch. When they reached the porch, they could hear the television. Jake rang the doorbell. Several minutes later, the door opened, and there stood Jack.

Jake spoke first. "Hello, Jack. Remember me? I'm Jake Tillery, Stella's social worker. This is my wife, Vicky."

Jack stepped aside.

"Yeah, I remember ya. Y'all come on in. Ida's in the back bedroom with Stella. She ain't feeling none too good today. Just go on back. First door past the stairs on the left."

Jake thanked Jack, and then he and Vicky made their way down the darkened hallway. On the left of the hallway was a staircase leading to the second floor. To the right was the living room. Jake glanced at the television as they passed. Jack was watching an episode of *Bonanza*. The next room they passed was the dining room and then the kitchen. Just past the stairs was Stella's bedroom. Jake knocked softly on the door.

"Come in," a voice from within the room called out.

Jake opened the door. He and Vicky stepped inside.

"I hope we're not disturbing anyone," he said as politely as possible.

Stella raised her head from off the pillow. "Is that you, Jake?" she asked.

Jake walked closer to the bed. "Yes, it's me, Miss Stella. And this is my wife, Vicky."

"Come closer and let me get a look at ya," Stella said to Vicky.

Jake and Vicky walked over to the side of Stella's bed. Ida was sitting on the other side of the bed in a rocking chair with a Bible lying across her lap. She nodded at Jake and Vicky then went back to her reading.

Stella reached out and touched Vicky's extended hand. "She's a pretty thing, Jake. Ya done good for yourself."

Vicky smiled. "Thank you," she said.

"What are ya doing here, Jake?" Stella asked feebly.

Jake took Stella's hand. "I have something I want to tell you, Stella," said Jake.

"Well, pull ya up a chair and tell me 'bout it then," she replied.

Jake looked around the room. In one corner was a chair. He went over, picked it up, and placed it next to the bed. Ida stood up, laid the Bible on the side table, and offered the rocking chair to Vicky. At first Vicky declined until Ida explained she needed a break. Once both of them were seated, Jake once again took Stella's hand in his. He could tell she had made a turn for the worse. Her eyes were closed and her breathing shallow.

"Stella," he said, "I found Sudie's lost baby."

Stella opened her eyes and looked at Jake. "Did ya say ya found Sudie's baby?" she asked, almost in a whisper.

"Yes, Stella. I found the baby."

"Where? How?" she asked in disbelief.

"It took some doing, but once I started looking, it was as though everything just fell into place." He paused. "Stella, I am that lost baby."

Stella's eyes filled with tears. "Are ya sure, Jake?"

Jake explained all the research he had done and about the ballerina figurine.

Stella closed her eyes. Tears rolled down her temples and into her salt-and-pepper hair.

"I can hardly believe it. I knew ya looked familiar to me the first time I saw ya. I couldn't place who it was ya looked like. Now I know. Ya look like Dawson Hubert when he was young and you've got Sudie's eyes. Lord help me. I don't know what to say."

Jake kissed Stella's thin hand. "You don't have to say anything, my dear, sweet woman. Because of you, I found my real father. I have a sister, a niece, and a grandmother. I am so sorry you had to spend almost your entire life in that hospital and for something you didn't do. I can't give you back those years, but now at least, everyone will know you were innocent."

"Thank ya, Jake," Stella whispered. "I knew one day I would get to see my baby. Now here ya are."

Jake looked over at Vicky. She was weeping too. He looked back at Stella. "I know you're not feeling well, Stella. We will go now so you can get some rest."

Stella motioned him to come closer. Jake leaned in closer to her so he could hear what she wanted to say. She whispered something in his ear. A tear dropped from his eye and landed on the pillow beside her head. Gently he leaned in close to her ear and whispered something to her. Stella smiled. He kissed her on the forehead and stood up to leave.

"Good-bye, Jake," Stella said in an almost inaudible voice. She put her other hand out to Vicky. Vicky took her hand. "Take care of my boy," she said to Vicky.

"I will," Vicky promised.

Stella once again closed her eyes. Jake and Vicky headed for the door. Jake looked back one last time. There lay the woman who had helped him find the family he had never known. *How can I ever repay her?* he thought to himself.

On the way out, Jake and Vicky thanked Ida and Jack for taking care of Stella. They also explained to them about what they had learned. Ida cried. She said she had always believed in Stella's innocence. She was glad it could be confirmed.

When Jake and Vicky got back into their car, Vicky looked at Jake. "Jake, what did Stella whisper in your ear, and what did you whisper back to her?"

Jake looked at Vicky sadly. "She said, 'I love you, son. Will you call me "Mama" just one time?' I whispered to her, 'I love you too, Mama.'"

When Jake and Vicky got home, the phone was ringing. It was Ida. She wanted Jake to know that Stella passed away only minutes after they left. Jake's only comfort in her passing was that she died knowing for sure she was an innocent woman.